VEAL

MACKENZIE NOLAN

VEAL

a novel

Published by ECW Press
665 Gerrard Street East
Toronto, Ontario, Canada M4M 1Y2
416-694-3348 / info@ecwpress.com

Editor for the Press: Pia Singhal
Copy editor: Jen Albert
Cover design: Caroline Suzuki
Cover images: Photograph of doll parts by Luidmila Spot / Adobe Stock. Photograph of textured paper by Serhii Holdin / Adobe Stock

LIBRARY AND ARCHIVES CANADA CATALOGUING IN PUBLICATION

Title: Veal : a novel / Mackenzie Nolan.

Names: Nolan, Mackenzie, author.

Identifiers: Canadiana (print) 20250213265 | Canadiana (ebook) 20250217201

ISBN 9781770418066 (softcover)
ISBN 9781778524912 (PDF)
ISBN 9781778524905 (ePub)

Subjects: LCGFT: Novels.

Classification: LCC PS8627.O614 V43 2025 | DDC C813/.6—dc23

This book is funded in part by the Government of Canada. *Ce livre est financé en partie par le gouvernement du Canada.* We acknowledge the support of the Canada Council for the Arts. *Nous remercions le Conseil des arts du Canada de son soutien.* We would like to acknowledge the funding support of the Ontario Arts Council (OAC) and the Government of Ontario for their support. We also acknowledge the support of the Government of Ontario through the Ontario Book Publishing Tax Credit, and through Ontario Creates.

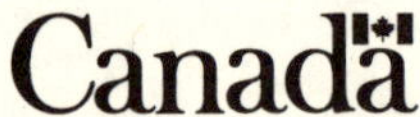

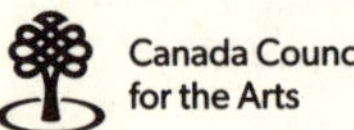

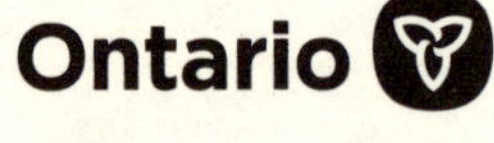

PRINTED AND BOUND IN CANADA

PRINTING: MARQUIS 5 4 3 2 1

For all women who are made to answer for the violence of men.

I will always be in your corner.

Give them hell.

VEAL

Mistaken Point sat at the edge of the earth, fog-filled and lined with lighthouses.

Gothic in winter and stifling in summer, trails weaved and bobbed throughout the trees, thick like maple syrup.

Frantic worship, frazzled disbelief, a population grown used to the grotesque will find unreality an inconvenience. Unanimously unruffled, it was the kind of place where a monster thrived; feasting on a diet of girls, forever twenty-three, stunted from growth like veal.

I'm told that scared meat tastes better.

I

Rain falling, fog thick like clothes, I chased Franky Delores through blood-soaked streets, desperate to make it out dead.

II

3 hours earlier

"You're going to get us killed."

"Not with that attitude."

III

3 months earlier

When Mom caught me kissing Anastasia Lanes in the schoolyard, she told me that queers will be ready for the apocalypse. Told me we've spent every day since Creation trying to make the world burn.

Dramatic prophecy to propel upon a child, but there might've been some truth to that; the skill to live as a hypothetical. To never feel robbed by childlessness, forever unmarried, comfortable with the art of dying young.

I was ten years old, and I still see the curl of her lips like a ghost in my peripheral. PTA president, Presbyterian princess, lesbian daughter. I was a rotten fruit in her garden of Eden; redesigning myself in her image left me botched. Frankenstein's sad attempt to play dutiful daughter.

It went like this: I had graduated university and was working a full-time job when it all fell apart. My Mondays in the break room, talks of intermittent fasting, keto diets, miserable marriages and flailing kids.

The pressure did not make a diamond of me, it simply transformed me into a strange, off-putting creature. I tried masking myself to fit into Corporate Culture, but not even a mask could fix the pieces of me that were fundamentally incompatible. I was too laid-back, too nihilistic, too gay. This wrongness grew larger, stronger, and I lost the ability or will to fix it. I spent the next month calling in sick, life spent in bed.

Half sober and sick on existentialism, I cut off my hair and moved to a small east coast town, Mistaken Point, bringing my first kiss and longest friend, Anatasia Lanes, along for the ride. Romantic inclinations abandoned in elementary school, we were both accepted into Mistaken Point University, finding a small apartment overlooking the cobblestone sidewalks.

It was idyllic, peaceful.

I'd be on the brink of death in three months.

ANOMALY

Anastasia Lanes was a bad kisser, and an even worse roommate. I told her as much over pad see ew, reminiscing on sandbox crushes and ultimatums.

"You were too aggressive," she shot back. "It's like you wanted to eat me raw."

"I did. That's my whole shtick."

"Consumption?" She wrinkled her nose, chewing thoughtfully. "I'm a gentle lover. We're fundamentally incompatible."

"She says after signing a year-long lease."

"Apparently I'm good at getting myself into stupid shit." She gestured widely around us. I dimly wondered if all stupid shit in Stasia's life could be traced back to me. She yelled at me to use a coaster, so I never got the chance to ask her.

Our apartment was right above a bakery, sweet-scented and sticky hot. I scored the bedroom facing the waterside, my window lined with hard-to-kill succulents and secondhand textbooks. We'd hardly been here a day, and I was only now feeling my blood pressure start to mellow. Mom hadn't stopped calling, but I hadn't stopped not answering her, so things were going relatively okay. Relatively. As in, compared to my mass breakdown about a month ago, I felt marginally less like killing myself.

The little life we built for ourselves held a feeling of peace unlike any other. We dragged a truck full of stuff across the country, filling small rooms to the brim. The fish tank in the corner, the ashtrays and knickknacks we sculpted. Haphazard blankets, pillows, floor full of rugs, fridge full of produce. Pictures and bills tacked on the fridge, walls like a scrapbook, stuff, stuff, stuff.

Anastasia Lanes stood amongst it all, gritting teeth through my maximalism and mania. Pretty, perky, type A in recovery. My getaway car.

"How do you feel?" I asked, wondering if she ever resented me.

She shrugged, tight ponytail bobbing. "Broad question. Make it more specific."

"Do you regret moving here with me?"

"Easy, tiger. It's been"—she checked the clock on the microwave—"five hours. Give me time to stew."

"Alright, stew away." I waited two minutes, watching our cat clock's tail flick back and forth. "So?" I asked.

She smiled. "I couldn't resent you if I tried, Del. And believe me, I've tried."

Delores "Lawrence" Franklin,

We are pleased to offer you conditional acceptance into MASTER OF LIBRARY & INFORMATION SCIENCE, Mistaken Point University, with admittance for the fall semester. You have three courses to complete prior to official admittance, which your file notes you have registered for, to be completed in the summer semester. Pending passing grades in these courses, you will receive an official offer letter.

I stared at it for hours, mindlessly bobbing a yo-yo up and down. Letting it clatter to the floor, reeling it back in like a fishing rod. Stasia always hated when I did this; I waited until she popped out to the grocery store before I started getting annoying.

She had a letter of her own, graduate school for chemical engineering, but I knew this wasn't her first choice. I was shocked she agreed to come here, a random town I sent her at three in the morning, on my thirtieth day calling in sick to work.

Stasia would kill me if she knew I found Mistaken Point because of the murders. A true crime fanatic to her core, she was on a conveniently timed media diet, missing the global phenomenon coined the Frankenstein Killer. A news article popped up on my social media feed, and the seaside town was so beautiful, I ended up in the wrong rabbit hole. Sure, the murders seemed grisly, but they had a great public transit system. Highly rated university. Cheap rent (likely due to the aforementioned murders, now that I think of it). In my defense, they caught the guy, so hoping it wasn't a "violence spreads a poisonous root through the town" situation, I chose Mistaken Point.

"Del?" Stasia called out, banging on our apartment door.

I sighed, watching my yo-yo spin away from me.

"Coming."

I dodged boxes and bags as I walked to the door, unhooking the latch and helping Stasia with the groceries. We piled them on the kitchen counter, picking through and putting them away.

"People here get really weird when they notice you're an out-of-towner," she commented, switching on the kettle. "Very suspicious."

I chewed my cheek, fighting to remain neutral. "That's like every small town."

"For sure." Stasia hummed, busying herself with organizing pasta boxes. "Especially ones with serial killers."

I froze, wincing as she shot me an exasperated expression I've seen countless times before. "The jig is up," I joked weakly.

"The jig never left the ground. You seriously thought I wouldn't research the place I was uprooting my entire life to move to?"

"I at least *hoped*—"

"Lawrence," she said sternly. "Don't be so stupid. You're terrible at it."

"So you're okay with it?"

"Well, they caught the guy, didn't they?" Stasia shrugged. "Apparently it was some local that went nuts after his divorce. Classic man."

Stasia wasn't usually such a misandrist. I enjoyed her rare moments of clarity. "Is it?"

"Classic of the media to blame his divorce," she amended. "Apparently, he was a well-loved guy, really respected in the community. Everyone was shocked, even the families of the victims could hardly believe it." She stirred sugar into her coffee, pausing to consider. "Funny that people always talk about how *nice* men are when they do something evil."

I hummed, wondering if Stasia herself might've been one of those people, considering our biggest fight in two decades of friendship was over her oldest brother. She didn't appreciate my belief that his shitty politics makes a shitty person. Maybe she'd be less forgiving if he were a murderer.

"He killed a bunch of girls, right?"

"*Women*," she corrected. "They were all of legal age."

"Huh." I whistled. "Strange choice."

"They were eighteen to twenty-five."

"Shot down in . . . what's the opposite of prime?"

"Shot down in the worst possible era of life?"

"Yeah," I agreed, shuddering. "As if being nineteen isn't bad enough."

We laughed because those girls weren't real, figments of a news story from some faraway town. Being in said town did not materialize them. If anything, it contributed to their fairytale glaze. An interesting part of being a woman: violence must never happen to you. It is always some other unlucky girl, easy to brush off and rationalize. Senseless violence must be escapable. It must be fluke.

"What happened to them was horrible," Stasia said, suddenly sober. "Unbelievably so."

I struggled to see what could shock her about this sleepy town's string of murders. I only knew surface-level details: young women butchered by angry man. It felt unfortunately run-of-the-mill.

"How bad was it?"

"You don't want to know," she shook her head. "Trust me, don't look into it."

I stared out the window, watching the people mill about, so normal and unaltered after unspeakable acts of horror. Violence must always be happening to someone else. Atrocities committed against you must be mere coincidence. It is always fluke.

"Do you think they caught the right guy?" I asked absently, a sea of umbrellas coloring the streets outside.

Stasia gave me a strange look. "They found body parts buried on his property. Apparently caught him in the middle of something crazy, too."

"Oh?"

"The police report was sealed from the public," she explained, pushing a mug of tea my way. "There's hardly any verified information out there, but I'd guess it was an almost-victim. Didn't want it to define her life."

I thought about that, the tragedy of being a victim, the horror of almost becoming one. That girl out there, finite and free. How must it have felt, to be the container for violence, and walk away from that with the knowledge of its presence. To become the anomaly, the statistic. To understand, finally understand, how hated you are in this world, how there is no such thing as fluke.

To know that violence does not happen to other people, it happens to *you*. Every single day. And to know you can never, ever, for as long as you live, find any anomaly or fluke that lets you breathe again. You will never be safe. Your loophole of safety has become a noose.

SPIDERWEB

Stasia and I settled well, following our strange first night discussing serial killers and failed romance.

Dissolving into a routine, we busied ourselves with the bustle of a new semester, determined to see less of each other to lessen the blow of starting fresh. Stasia was a constant reminder of what I left behind, and her contrarian nature was hardly comforting. At my lowest moments, she expressed concern through curt observations rather than gushy heart-to-hearts. The months I spent trying to fit into my old life, she called me Delores with a tongue-in-cheek irony. It pissed me off how astute Stasia could be with so few words. I *did* have to become Delores, a girl with long hair and skirts and makeup. I'd sit silent in break rooms full of boisterous men, being talked over and seen through. My mother's dream.

I thought back to the last time I saw Mom, her white knuckles gripping my corporate ladder, refusing to let me dismount.

She watched me drown for months in a life I hated. My post-holiday blues, my winter of woe. She watched me show up to family dinners curled in on myself, empty eyes and delayed laughter. She knew I was encroaching on a dangerous piece of misery, but it only became an issue for her when I started jeopardizing my career.

My success was once my compensation to her for being me; she could not tell her church friends and coworkers about my relationships, my hobbies, my interests. She *could*, however, tell them all about my fancy internships, the entry-level position at the Impressive Company. My path to success as plotted as the stars.

My mother's version of adulthood was reconstructive. She built a very tiny box for me and called it a life. I knew I'd have to kill Lawrence to make sense to her, to fit in this box, and I tried killing her every day for years to make my mother happy. She was proud of me for nine months, the nine months I successfully spent as someone else, but it was unsustainable. My fractured selves began to blur. I knew I had to kill either Lawrence or Delores.

I chose the latter for sacrifice in a fit of blind mania, running away with the only person I ever saw sticking. To ask that of Stasia was a tricky thing, I know, but it wasn't so simple. Stasia was just as miserable as I was, but too repressed to consider actually doing something about it. Spurred on through the necessity of saving me, she found her own escape as my getaway driver. I don't bring it up, because I know she'll never want to talk about it. We pretend she's only here as a favor to me, and we pretend that Stasia hasn't benefited just as much as I have, in distance from our families.

I spent the week leading up to summer semester marinating in bed, and before I knew it, it was the first day of school. While getting ready in the morning, I marveled at my shaking hands, ecstatic to have stress that felt familiar. Deadlines, papers, group projects. I've been dealing with them for as long as I can remember. In school, I could play a role of adulthood that felt safe. One with the illusion of consistency.

Syllabus day completed, I did some old breathing exercises and gathered my things, excited to go home and buy a fancy coffee for my troubles. I was striding across campus when a piece of paper fluttered to my feet, a gust of wind knocking an old advertisement off the post. I felt eyes follow me, strangers watching as the paper chased my trail across sun-hot pavement.

I buckled over to pick it up, intrigued by the colorful design.

FRANKLIN'S FUNHOUSE ARCADE

APPLY TODAY
BOOKKEEPING POSITION
FLEXIBLE HOURS
SEE FRANKY

Vague, nearly incomprehensible. No address, no phone number, no information. I pulled out my phone to research Franklin's Funhouse Arcade, finding it to be an apparent hub of activity and vibrant society in Mistaken Point. Go figure.

I tucked the advertisement into my back pocket, thinking I should probably figure out a way to make money. I was receiving crumbs of cash from my scholarship, and had a nest egg saved up from my six months working an Adult Job, but it wouldn't last forever. Especially with Rent and Cost of Living raining down on me.

I rewound my cassette to replay a favorite song, wondering if I should invest in a motorcycle for my daily commute. I watched the stream of students pass me by, college brochure picturesque, summer sun, muggy day, a sea of sunburnt shoulders. White People Island, Stasia joked, jostled by the lack of diversity in the small town. I parted the crowds, tote bag heavy on my shoulder as I turned down a cobblestone street, tunneled by trees.

My first day went well. A classmate said something spectacularly stupid, and I smiled into my fist. Wondered about the allegedly prestigious program admission requirements. Bought a sandwich at the student cafe. Texted Stasia about the sandwich.

I was so busy with the delusion that I might just be okay, I hardly noticed the decaying missing posters, tacked on top of each other like stacked plates.

The cutthroat competition of grief. Which one of us will outlive the others, who will become the face of this tragedy? It was always the youngest, the prettiest, the whitest. There was no tragedy in being plain, no attention spared to girls who had it coming.

I avoided eye contact with them, desperate to remake myself in this town. Desperate to build something on top of bones. I watched the missing posters peel away at the edges. Sun-damaged and waterlogged, letters bleeding together. All that was left of those girls, those *women*. A few measly posters scattered across the town that killed them, blowing through the road like leaves. A sea of women remembered as victims. A legacy of guts and gore.

I shook a loose missing poster off my foot, sparing time to read the name. Penelope Hawk. A woman with a life, a family, hopes for the future, reduced to an ashy piece of paper clinging to the bottom of my shoe.

Oh, how terrible, the stupid shit we leave behind.

TEETH

The arcade was a quick bus ride from campus. I met Francesca Delores there, buckled over a chai latte.

She glanced up at me for seven seconds before losing interest, turning back to scribbling in her notebook. She was as handsome as she was beautiful, backwards baseball cap, tight muscle tee, sea of shaggy brown hair.

I wanted to wrap her up and bring her to the past. Show her to a younger, more terrified Lawrence, one who didn't think anyone on earth could possibly encapsulate my "type." I could hardly remember the first girl I fell in love with, twelve years old and scared as an infant, but I illogically wished it was this girl in front of me. I looked at her and felt like a kid again. A pigtailed child with a slushy heart, silly over a schoolyard crush.

I traced her figure to find her left arm stopped just below the elbow, reconnected tissue tapering to a stump. She caught me staring and glared back, kohl eyes and sour scowl.

"Hey," I greeted, sauntering up to the desk. "I'm, um, I'm here about the job application?"

She tapped her pen against the paper, studying me. Window shopping. "Name?"

"Delores Franklin."

"No shit." Her grim mouth broke into a tiny smile. "I'm Franky Delores."

"No shit." I grinned, biting my tongue. "What are the odds of that?"

Uninteresting question, apparently. Franky went back to her notebook.

"Um." I tried to recapture her attention. "The job—?"

She kept writing, expression blank. "Resume?"

"I'm in grad school."

She barely blinked. "Resume?"

I laughed, couldn't help myself. "Alright, um." I dug through my fanny pack, unearthing a folded-up list of scholarships.

Franky made a big show of flattening the wrinkles, squinting down at my biography.

"Twenty-four."

"Yep."

"New in town?"

"Yep."

"Alright." Franky rubbed her brow. "You ever work in an arcade before?"

"Did you miss the grad student part?"

She stared at me.

"No. Never."

She studied me: green fleece, baggy gym shorts, fuzzy Crocs. The picture of professionalism. I tried to hide my recent instability, the post-apocalyptic haze.

In a low voice that sizzled like butter, she uttered, "You'll do."

Pen tucked behind her ear, Franky gave me a tour of the arcade. It was a man-made labyrinth, Theseus and the minotaur walking circles around pinball machines. I watched the back of her head, the gentle slope of her neck. There was a delicate chain of jewelry, an artifact tucked beneath her tank top. Maybe a cross, a heart-shaped locket? I ached to ask her.

She was speaking about power grids, bookkeeping, profit margins. I hummed, cheek resting in my palm. Her fringe curtained honey-brown eyes, deer-like in their attempt to be daunting. My admiration had to be aloof. She was flighty.

"And here's the break room." She swept a hand into a small green space, hosting two overstuffed couches, a kitchen table, and a makeshift kitchenette. "And down here would be our office," we walked across the hallway into a small room with two desks, chairs back-to-back.

"*Our* office?" I clarified. "Does that mean I officially got the job?"

She caught me staring for the thirty-seventh time, taken aback by the version of herself reflected in my eyes. I watched a seismic shift, a barely perceptible change of manner. Her shoulders straightened, eyebrow quirked.

"Yeah, sure." She paused to consider me, my open-mouthed desperation. "Funhouse could use more eye candy."

She said it so matter-of-factly, it made my jaw ache. It was not flirtatious, it was hardly a come-on; she just stated my supposed beauty like the weather. I was as perplexed as I was awestruck.

"A-are you fucking with me?" I stuttered.

"I don't say things that I don't mean."

"So we . . . You think I'm pretty?"

"Sure."

Sure. She gave me a look, one that seemed to say, *What do you want me to do about it?* Nothing, was evidently my answer. I blinked a few times, trying to think up something clever to say. Maybe a monologue of gratitude, a marriage proposal, an attempt to correct her unfathomable belief that *I* was the eye candy here.

Franky tired quickly of my trepidation, glancing down at her watch. "You got any questions?"

I recovered quickly. "Do you make a habit of flirting with new employees, or am I just the exception?"

A reaction. Franky laughed, despite herself. "Flirting?" She grinned. "It was an observation, Delores."

"Lawrence," I corrected. "I go by Lawrence."

"Alright," she smiled to herself. "It was an observation, *Lawrence.*"

"Do you make a habit of *observing* new employees?"

"Sure," she said. "If they give me something to look at."

"And I—you like what you see?"

"Can't say." She shrugged, shark smile. "I don't make a habit of flirting with my employees."

I felt a warm heat, a forgotten one. I cursed under my breath, rendered speechless for the second time in ten minutes.

Franky laughed to herself, pressing her necklace to her lips. A bird talon. I reached forward to wrap my finger around the chain, gently tugging it from her mouth.

"What does it mean?" I asked.

Something complicated crossed her face, staring up at me as I curled my finger, knuckle brushing her collarbone. Her playfulness dissipated, taking a strange new shape.

"Helps keep me focused." She stepped back, studying me suspiciously. "We can start your training tomorrow morning."

"Oh—?"

"I'll see you then?"

Disappointed by her inexplicable change in manner, I nodded, lips tight.

"Bring your class schedule." She tossed over her shoulder, all but running away, platform boots stomping down the hall.

I made to follow her out but got distracted by the open office door. A bulletin board hung on an angle, every inch of it pinned down with missing posters. Young women, victims of that serial killer. I bit the inside of my cheek, wondering why Franky would have some weird collage of dead girls. They caught the guy, didn't they? What's left to figure out about the murders, and why was Franky the one attempting to?

I stared down the empty hallway, wondering how long I could realistically loiter here before looking suspicious. Figuring I could investigate tomorrow, I took one last glance at the murder board before walking away, tracing the arcade noise to find my way out.

I stopped at the front desk, surveying the scene. A group of teen boys yelling over pinball, a family playing pool. Not a sign of Franky Delores. She was gone without a trace.

I got home late to the smell of roasted vegetables, toeing off my shoes and hanging my keys on the hook. The kitchen window was open, sweet breeze cooling my damp forehead.

"Hey," Stasia greeted, pulling out her headphones. "You hungry?"

"Extremely," I said, throwing myself and my book bag on the couch in a big lump. "How was your day?"

"Not terrible. My supervisor seems fine."

"Really?"

"No, he's an asshole. But I can handle it."

I hummed, dreading the moodiness sure to arise from Stasia being stuck in yet another shitty lab environment. "I got a job today."

"Oh?"

"Yeah, the arcade on Main Street."

Stasia hummed, flipping the chicken. "Random."

"Yeah." I sat up, gesturing to the stovetop. "Need help?"

She asked me to grab the cutlery as she started plating our supper. Roast chicken and vegetables, small glass of white wine. We balanced plates on our laps and sat in front of the television, arguing over what to watch before settling on an old sitcom. It was just like we used to do in grade school, eating in front of the television, hours of silence.

After we ate, Stasia instructed me to load the dishwasher, burrowing into her room to call her two older brothers. I tidied the kitchen and made two cups of coffee, scrolling through my phone until Stasia reappeared, throwing herself onto the couch beside me. She looked bothered, shame ridden. It was her resting state.

"They still don't like me?" I asked.

"It's not you."

"The idea of me," I half joked. "And the big gay stain I represent on your life."

"They're protective."

"They're oppressive."

Stasia conceded, kind enough to avoid the obvious rebuttal: that my older sister doesn't care enough to check in on me, doesn't care enough to have misguided hate for random friends. I don't envy her; I couldn't envy something I can't even fathom.

"You're almost twenty-four," I reminded her, birthday at the tail end of August. "They can't fuss over you forever."

"You're so resentful of love."

"That's not love, that's control."

Stasia conceded, cruel enough to avoid the obvious rebuttal: that with my mother, the two are intertwined to the point of consumption. A snake eating its own tail.

"They don't care enough to hate you," Stasia said finally. "They just don't agree with the choices I've made. You're collateral for that."

Collateral. I took a long sip of coffee.

"Don't look so crestfallen, Lawrence." She sighed. "You're my mother's worst nightmare. Let that be enough."

"I thought Christians weren't supposed to feel hate."

"Her distaste for you transcends religion."

I couldn't help but laugh, pulling myself out of the tangly complications that came from being Stasia's best friend. "What an honor."

"Add it to your resume," Stasia said dryly. "It's not like your mom is my biggest fan, either."

"O sweet Juliet . . ."

Stasia threw a pillow at me, pointing threateningly in warning. I was kind enough to drop it, knowing that Stasia took my mother's hatred to heart. Mom had a lot of pull back home, with her empire of neoliberal moms and church-regulars. Stasia worshipped pull, reveled in social capital. She wasn't a loving person, but I never doubted her friendship. Ruining herself to run away with me was a herculean display of our love.

"I don't mind it, you know," she said, as if reading my mind. "It used to really upset me, but . . ."

I watched her deliberate.

"I think there's been some freedom in proving her worst fears right."

"Meaning?"

"She was always terrified I would ruin your life."

"I ruined my own."

"But I'm here, aren't I?"

I conceded.

"It's funny that our moms don't like each other when they have so much in common."

I snorted. "They could've made a real powerful duo, if they could see past their own noses."

Stasia's mom was all sharp edges and Pentecostal sensibilities. She was widowed young and remarried immediately, groomed for a life within four walls, stay-at-home mom extraordinaire. She clashed with my mother, who existed as her carnival mirror image. Mom was uptight, obsessed with social rules, but too stubborn to submit to my father in a way Mrs. Lanes could approve of. Her ideas of right and wrong came from societal scripts, while Mrs. Lanes came from religious scripture itself.

"God help us if they ever team up." Stasia laughed.

I grabbed our now empty glasses of wine and went to the kitchen, refilling both. Placing it in front of her as an offering, I sat back down and turned on the television. Put on her favorite show.

"Have you heard from your dad?" she asked.

I shook my head.

"I'm surprised he hasn't reached out."

"I'm surprised you're surprised." I forced a smile. "Mom hasn't stopped texting. Dad's politely giving me space, to the point of forgetting that I exist. Not much has changed since I left."

Nothing at all, in fact.

Stasia took a long sip of wine, expression tight. "You don't give her much leeway."

I controlled my temper, sitting peacefully as it thrashed. In lieu of response, I nodded and turned up the television, effectively ending the conversation. Stasia had trouble wrapping her head around my mother's passive aggression. When Mrs. Lanes found out Stasia was gay, she attempted an exorcism. I think she still asks when she'll get a boyfriend. Mom told me I would start an apocalypse, then never uttered another word about it. Stasia laughed whenever I complained about Mom ignoring my sexuality, incapable of taking what she perceived to be a blessing as something so insidious.

It was ironic, to have our uniting source of trauma be an uninhabitable space for us to coexist. Stasia couldn't take my pain seriously and felt that I took her pain *too* seriously. We never met in the middle, rarely met at all. I've gotten better at dodging her.

"It's an observation, Lawrence," Stasia prodded.

"I acknowledge it."

Stasia stared at me, expression stony. She softened under my downcast eyes, sighing in resignation. "You need to rewind," she said. "I missed the last ten minutes."

"Not my fault." I grinned, victorious.

"Orphan by choice, dickhead by nature," Stasia observed, shaking her head.

I let it slide, too indebted to her to bother shaking our life raft. I threw her the remote, sinking deeper into our inherited couch. She jabbed at the buttons, muttering about batteries as I stared at flickering streetlights. The candle she lit earlier crackled away, some cookie flavor or other filling the room. I finished my wine, then hers. Browsed some online stores, asked Stasia's opinion on a pair of loafers during commercial break.

We went to bed early, scrolling our phones in separate rooms until sundown. I set my alarm for work tomorrow, shivering at the memory that the action elicited. The emails each morning to my old boss, the responses. *Call me when you can, we need to figure out a plan forward.* My plan forward was as murky as the gray summer skies. It made me feel sick to try to conceptualize a life for myself in Mistaken Point, to try and think of anything but the bleary relief of being free. I don't know where I fit into adult life; I chose this university program on a whim, and I can't bear the thought that I might crash and burn in every avenue. I try to go with the flow, the only thing I've ever been good at, but sometimes I get stuck on the leftover shame of failing my family. If I had only been born different, born better. Work addicted as my sister, uptight as my mother. If only I could stomach being what she wanted. If only she could stomach me not being what she wanted.

I listened to Stasia's feet pad around the apartment, slippers soft against scattered rugs. I wasn't good enough for my old life, but that doesn't matter anymore. Lazarus rises from the dead, Lazarus attempts to find some new semblance of normalcy. A path away from the rubble that finally makes sense.

I let out a shaky breath, dry swallowing sleeping medication.

Lazarus goes to bed.

PREY

Coffee thermos in hand, I pushed into Franklin's Funhouse, sighing in relief as the crisp conditioned air hit my skin. It was muggy warm today, air thick with smoke. Tall trees offered shade on my walk over, but there was little reprieve from the ever-present heat. I wiped away sweat and makeup, regretting my attempt to appear presentable.

"Morning," Franky greeted, sitting behind the front desk.

Her shaggy hair was held back by two miniature space buns, fringe and stray strands framing her face. She tucked her notebook away as I walked over, standing to meet me.

"Morning." I yawned. "Did you notice the smoke?"

Franky blinked, eyes darting to the front window.

"I'm not sure where it's coming from. Anyone I tried to talk to about it on the walk over just ignored me." I forced a laugh, hoping I didn't sound like the Village Fool. "Antisocial spot, hey?"

Franky quirked a brow, but didn't answer. With one avenue of conversation failing, I tried another.

"So how are you?"

Franky nodded, gesturing for me to follow her. She led the way through the maze of games, pointing out several glitches or fun facts about each.

"Franklin's Funhouse," I remarked. "Do you have any relation to the owner?"

Franky gave me a look but didn't answer. She was far away, closed like a clam shell, and I couldn't figure out what caused that shift. Had I scared her off? Pushed things too far? Or had she undergone some major life event, preoccupying her from paying attention to me?

We ended up back in her office, *our* office, and it was the exact same as it was last time, same disarray and disorder, except for one crucial detail: the murder board was missing. I subtly searched for it, checking behind the desks and mini fridge, but it was no use. It was nowhere to be found, and it felt too personal to inquire about. The only remaining souvenir was a sticky note sitting in a pile of dust, yellow eyes sketched menacingly onto faded pink paper. Strange. Franky caught me staring and swept the note under her desk, clearing her throat to catch my attention.

"Here's your computer, your desk, the filing cabinet, which has everything you'll need. Part of your job would be digitizing that, of course. Um . . ." Franky paused, licking her lips. "Mostly you'll be handling payroll and bookkeeping. I can go through that process now."

"Were you doing all of this before?"

Franky nodded, pulling up her chair and gesturing to mine.

"Was that difficult?"

"Yep," Franky said, rolling her chair over to the filing cabinet, pulling out books and binders. "Alright, let's get started."

The next few hours went about the same; Franky skirted around my attempts at conversation, while I tried my best to stay engaged in her dry explanation of my duties. She had a distinct way of speaking: slow, soft, almost lazy at times. There was a pleasant rasp to her voice, ember-warm. Though bored out of my tree, I sat by every word she said, toasty like a campfire. We wrapped up around noon, both yawning into our fists.

"Wanna grab coffee?" I asked, checking my watch. It was quarter to one.

"Can't," she said.

I stared, waiting for an explanation that never came. Begrudgingly impressed by her complete lack of social niceties, I laughed, standing to stretch.

"Want me to bring you back anything?"

Franky looked genuinely confused by the offer, frozen in place for a moment before unsticking herself, waving me off. "You're done for the day. I'll email your schedule later tonight."

"Alright." I nodded. "See you later, then?"

Franky nodded, already absorbed back in her notebook. "Yep. Have a good one."

It was hot and rainy, thundershowers falling like slate. Stasia was at class when I got home, the apartment dark and dreary in its emptiness. The walk back was strange; the smoke from earlier had disappeared, and people kept crossing the street to avoid me. I tried smiling hello to a random old man, tried sparking a conversation with the coffee shop barista, but they glared at me with such venomous hatred it took my breath away. Small town synocracy, maybe, but I was happy to be back home.

I fanned my face, emptying the dehumidifier and turning it back on. The posters in my room were beginning to curl, coiling in on themselves. I threw myself on the bed, pulling up my phone to scour social media. Stasia sent a text a few minutes ago saying she'd be home late, something about a local softball league. I sent back a thumbs up and switched back to social media, trying to find evidence of Francesca Delores.

She was an anomaly, a ghost in a sea of online avatars. I considered googling her, losing interest in the idea once Stasia texted back.

STAS

Want me to bring home pizza?

ME

always

I let my phone drop onto the bed beside me, bouncing away dejectedly. I stared at my book bag in the corner, stared at my charging laptop, stared out the window, into the sea, foaming and angry like shaken pop.

Mistaken Point was beautiful, living up to every tourist brochure and online review. I thought briefly of the murders, the swirl of half-hearted research I did on the subject. Girls. Legal age, but isn't that the flimsiest argument of all time. They were all under twenty-five, hardly established and barely alive. I watched the lighthouse, catty-corner from my apartment window. The beam of light circled like prey, illuminating my bedroom in bursts of light. I wondered if Franky knew any of the girls, if she grew up with them. Her rolling accent felt local, vowels loose and hearty on her tongue. I wondered if she knew the man who did it.

I wandered over to the window, pressing a hand against the glass. It felt cool to the touch, the coldness of passing rain. Another flash of light, too quick to discern if it was the lighthouse or lightning. I grabbed a sticky note off my bureau, absently writing *everything looks like something else*. I pressed the paper to the glass, inhaling deeply. The rain kept falling, and Stasia kept being gone, and for a second, I could imagine what this might have been like without her.

Lonely, I decided. Melancholic. Dangerous.

Temporarily satiating my guilt complex, I went back to staring out at the rain, transfixed by the rotating light. One big yellow eye, winking at me forever.

I winked back, silent solitude broken by a loud crash of thunder. The sticky note fluttered to the floor, landing by my feet. With shaking hands, I snapped the curtains shut and gathered the fallen note, crumpling it in my palm.

I threw myself back on the bed, flicking on my cassette player. The staticky music mixed with the rain, wailing thundershowers and soft strumming. I uncrumpled the note, pen still tucked behind my ear. In neat writing beneath the previous message, I considered my new viewpoint carefully, wary of the universe pushing back against me.

Everything looks like something else if you believe it does.

Satisfied, I stuck the note to the wall beside my bed, letting it shadow over me. Another clap of lightning. Stasia came home before I could bother changing my mind again.

HUNGER

As attractive as she was, Franky turned out to be crabby. And standoffish. And, at times, on straight up another planet. Always doodling in her little notebook, muttering to herself, having conversations with thin air.

I started cataloging each version of her to keep myself busy, coining Bravado Franky and Far-Away Franky to make sense of the shift. The former hadn't reappeared, and the latter was here, but only physically.

As far as bosses go, I've had worse. School was picking up, and Franky didn't seem to mind when I picked away at classwork during slow shifts. During admin hours, we sat back-to-back, poring over paperwork and prehistoric filings. Sometimes I'd spin my chair around and stare at her back, trying to make sense of the nonsense. Other times, I'd sit forward and listen, the scrape of pen against paper, shuffling documents, manic typing.

I wasn't sure how this place stayed afloat, with her whole-hearted dedication to whatever this side quest was. I assumed that's why she hired me. I took care of the bookkeeping; she took care of the All-Consuming Fixation. Sometimes we met in the middle, to discuss budgeting and profit margins. Oftentimes we didn't.

She didn't ask me much about myself; we hardly spoke at all. I spent hours in that place, willing her to make some sort of move. Not even necessarily romantic, just a shift in any direction. But she remained stagnant, and I watched her inaction like a hawk, desperate for subtext.

At the end of my first week working at Funhouse, I finally met another employee: Pippa Peterson. Allegedly in charge of the ticket booth and shopkeeping, Pippa sauntered into the break room hours late, iced coffee in hand. She took a moment to notice me, pushing her sunglasses into her braided hair.

"You're new." She pointed at me. "Delores?"

"Lawrence."

"Pippa." She pointed at herself. "You're the bookkeeper?"

"Allegedly."

She grinned at this. "Have you seen Franky around?"

"Not today. Usually she leaves for lunch."

"That's new." Pippa clicked her tongue, pulling up a chair to sit across from me. "So where'd you come from?"

I froze, delighted to meet someone friendly, or at least someone besides Stasia who was willing to talk to me.

"Like, generally, or—?"

She waved a hand around.

"Kilmore University. I lived close by, did my undergrad there. I'm here for grad school, um, moved here with my friend—"

"Is she cute?"

I laughed. "You'd like her."

"This is a random place to choose for school," she remarked, sizing me up. Suspicious and silly, two incompatible traits she balanced perfectly.

I forced a neutral expression, not in the mood to tell a coworker about my untimely demise in the corporate world. "I liked the sailboats," I answered honestly, which seemed enough for Pippa.

She nodded sagely. "They do rock."

We were interrupted by a loud crash at the front of shop, coins rolling, glass door slammed.

"That silly motherfucker." Pippa sighed.

The breakroom was nestled away in a back corner, down a dimly lit hallway. Franklin's Funhouse was a labyrinth, as windy and inaccessible as its namesake. Sack of coins in tow like a cartoon burglar, Franky appeared in the break room moments later, cursing to herself.

"Hey," I said, overshadowed by Pippa's louder "Sup?"

"We need to fix that loose board," she announced in lieu of greeting, dumping the coins on the table. Several dislodged themselves and rolled to freedom, landing in front of my trail mix.

"How are you?" I asked.

Franky gave me a strange look, causing an eruption of laughter from Pippa.

"You're usually never this mean to pretty girls, Frank," Pippa chided, tutting disapprovingly. "I taught you better than that."

"Don't flirt with my staff, Pippa," Franky snapped.

"It's more of a brotherly rapport myself and Lawrence are developing. No need to be jealous."

"She's not my type," I confirmed.

"What is your type?" Pippa asked.

I shot her a conspiratory smile, leaning my chin in my palms to give Franky a wolfish grin. "Mean."

Pippa whooped and cheered. "Well have I got the woman for you, Lawrence!"

"The *disrespect*," Franky muttered to herself, grumbling that the last thing Pippa needed was encouragement.

"Sit down, will you?" Pippa kicked out a chair. "Join in on the fun."

"How was your morning?" I tried again, softer this time.

Franky studied me, surprised to find genuine interest. She narrowed her eyes, sitting next to me.

"It was okay," she answered finally. "I just ran some errands."

"Did those errands include pillaging a nearby town?" Pippa gestured to the sack of coins.

"I pillaged your mother," Franky snapped, shocked to see me laugh.

"She's got jokes!"

"Nothing funny about it," she continued timidly. "Me and Mrs. Peterson are *quite* serious."

I cackled, watching Franky warm up to me. "Is it a monogamous situation, or can I cut in?"

"I don't know." Franky rubbed her chin thoughtfully. "Hey, Pip, think your mom would like Lawrence?"

"She hardly likes *me*."

"That makes two of us."

"I could never compete with you, anyway," I told Franky, attraction oozing from every pore.

"Jeez!" Pippa cackled. "Low standards, Lawrence?"

"Impossibly high ones, actually."

Franky tilted her head to the side, leaning forward to steal a handful of my trail mix. She was hot in a way that required self-awareness, but seemed utterly detatched from the matter. Like an old jacket she hadn't worn in a while.

"Don't give me that look," I simpered. "Pretty thing like you must have girls lined up for miles."

She choked on a piece of granola, looking incredulously to me, then Pippa, then back to me. I was worried I pushed things too far, but the moment broke, crumbling like candy. "*Pretty?*" she parroted, torn between shock and self-satisfaction. "You think I'm *pretty*?"

"Mean, too." Pippa sipped her coffee with a smirk. "Let's not forget mean."

"And that's my type," I bantered with Pippa. "Mean, pretty, clumsy—"

"*Clumsy*?"

"A walking calamity." Pippa nodded thoughtfully. "Though, we shouldn't be too hasty, Lawrence. Maybe the lineup of girls is what tripped Franky up on her way in."

Muttering to herself, Franky gathered the coins, stole Pippa's iced coffee, and stormed off.

"You know." Pippa stole a handful of my trail mix, chewing thoughtfully. "I think she really likes you."

I didn't see Franky for the rest of my shift, bouncing back and forth between the back office and front desk, hoping she'd reappear. Pippa kept me entertained, prattling on about local gossip and folklore and her plans for lunch tomorrow. I liked being around her, playing along like little kids.

Pippa was munching on the trail mix I surrendered to her hours ago, bartering with a bunch of tweens at the ticket booth. I sat behind her, spinning slow circles in my desk chair, wondering if I had fucked things up with Franky by being too forward twice now. Wondered if Franklin's Funhouse had HR, which would inevitably take me down for being too desperate for my boss. Wondered if Pippa would ever want to hang out outside of work. She seemed fun.

"Best I can do is a million tickets," Pippa said, expression serious.

"For a bouncy ball?" a kid exclaimed, voice hitting a desperate edge.

"You make a good point." Pippa rubbed her chin. "Two million tickets. Best offer I got."

With a laugh, I read the sign behind the counter. Five tickets for a bouncy ball. I grabbed a bright blue one and held it out for the kid. He watched me warily.

"Five tickets," I told him. "Limited time offer."

"Thanks, Miss." The kid gave me the tickets and hurriedly took the ball, sticking his tongue out at Pippa. Pippa stuck her tongue out right back, the two clearly familiar and friendly with each other.

"Another hard day's work." She yawned, stretching arms behind her head.

"How long have you been working here?"

"Long as Franky."

I stared, waiting for her to elaborate. When she didn't, I tried again. "How long has Franky been working here?"

"Long as me."

I clicked my tongue. With a shit-eating grin, Pippa offered me a handful of my own trail mix. Overcome with laughter, I accepted, turning back to the books. Though bogging me down with details, Franky gave me the most general overview of day-to-day management. I took a liberal estimate of what my job was supposed to be, figuring I could keep things afloat, impress Franky, and maybe find a way to coax out that barely suppressed smile.

Pippa threw a nut at me. "No daydreaming on the clock," she joked, mock serious.

I held up my hands in surrender, checking the time on the work computer. Ten minutes until the end of my shift.

"What time are you off?"

Pippa shrugged. "Until Franky comes back, I guess."

"Does she wander off like that often?"

"If she gets a new lead, yeah."

"Is that related to the murder board?"

Pippa choked on a piece of granola, pounding her own back. "Murder *what*?"

"There was this bulletin board," I explained. "Full of missing posters from that serial killer they caught? I noticed it on my first day here, but it disappeared from the office."

Pippa stared at me, clearly assessing something. "Do you know much about the murders?"

I shook my head.

"Keep it that way. Seriously."

I thought back to Stasia giving me the same advice. "But what about—"

"But nothing," Pippa interrupted, forcing a laugh. "Just promise you'll never ask Franky about it. Seriously dude. *Never.*"

I was torn, chronically curious about all things Franky. I thought of what I did know; nine young women, brutally butchered. Middle-aged man in jail, arrested for some other crime when police found evidence of the murders on his property. I assumed Pippa was so uptight about it because Franky was some true crime conspiracy theorist. Must get annoying. I remember when Stasia had a podcasting phase, I also had to warn people.

"Alright," I conceded, hands up in surrender. "I'll never ask her about the murder board. I'll live my life, endlessly wondering why my boss is trying to solve a solved case. Happy?"

"Almost always." Pippa grinned, giving me a wink.

Resigned, I sat silently beside Pippa as she worked on beaded earrings. We were comfortably quiet for the next few minutes, and when the clock finally hit five, I stood and stretched, yawning as I gathered my things.

"You're off?" Pippa asked.

"Yep." I shrugged on my jacket. "I guess I'll see you around?"

"You certainly will." She pointed a finger at me. "And that's a threat."

I laughed, waving goodbye as I pushed open the double glass doors. It was chillier today, a rare drop in temperature that warranted a coat. Bundling into my sweater, I checked my phone before heading off, loading directions on Franklin's wifi. Headphones in, I began the thirteen-minute trek home, wishing it was autumn and wishing I had something better to do than sit at home, waiting for Stasia to show up.

I opened my messages, staring at the recent one between me and Franky. She had sent a curt paragraph explaining the auditing process. She had also ignored the flirty joke I sent back. Asking her to hang out seemed unfathomable, out of the question, but I still ached to defrost her. I take one step forward, and she takes two steps away from me, but maybe one day, she'll stop running so far. Maybe she'd let me in, inch by inch, into whatever was going on in her secret land. Resigned to my temporary loneliness, I turned off my phone and focused on the music.

Her suppressed smile stayed on my mind the entire walk home.

Every Friday night, Stasia and I had Debriefings, catching each other up on the events of the past week. It started as a joke, when I was in misery and just listed all the reasons I wanted to kill myself, then it became a running gag. We'd boil a pot of tea, scrounge up snacks, and sit on either end of the sofa with jot notes of the Happenings.

"My supervisor liked my thesis idea," Stasia said, reading from her notepad, "but he almost killed me when I suggested a better way of running his experiment."

"What'd he say?"

"Nothing noteworthy," she brushed me off. "I shouldn't have said anything."

"But he doesn't have to be rude."

Stasia glanced up from her notes, surprised by my indignation. "I shouldn't have said anything. *I* was being rude."

"But you—"

"I was being a know-it-all."

"But . . ."

Stasia arched a brow, effectively silencing my protest. She continued. "Tried the Thai place on Meteor Street, not that great."

"No?"

"Eh, it was fine." She paused, finding her spot. "Almost got in a fight with someone in my lab group."

"Your supervisor?"

"No." Her brow furrowed. "Why would I fight him?"

"Because he—" I gave up early. "What was the fight?"

"Someone was being stupid."

I made the "continue on" gesture, pulling the plate of fries towards me.

"Our supervisor was being a dick, and this girl made a big fuss of it," Stasia said, rolling her eyes at my expression. "And don't start Lawrence, it wasn't a misogyny thing, I swear. But even if it was, we're hardly going to dismantle the patriarchy by making the entire lab uncomfortable. She just made us look bad."

I shoved a few fries in my mouth, expression pinched.

"What?" she demanded sharply.

"Why are you on his side?"

"I—Lawrence, don't be stupid. I'm not on his *side*, there are no sides. We're *adults*. I'm just saying—"

"Of course there's sides. By being a dick he's created sides."

"There's no sides!" Stasia's voice bordered on shrill. "He's just . . . I need to earn his respect. We all do. She seems to think she's entitled to it, when—"

"How does he treat the men in your lab?" I interrupted. "Assuming they're the majority. Is there any difference in how he treats them?"

Stasia swallowed, eyes focused on her notepad. She worried at a tiny tear in the paper. "They've been there longer," she said at last. "Of course they would have a stronger rapport."

"Hm."

"That's—that's not even the point, anyway."

"What is the point?"

"That this girl doesn't get it. She's doing all this, causing such a shitstorm, but it just seems like a self-fulfilling prophecy, to assume they hate her because she's a woman. They don't give me trouble. There's a reason for that, I . . ." Her voice cracked. "I keep my head down."

She thought they didn't give her any trouble because they respected her. But the thing is they *did* give her trouble. I remember her undergraduate degree, how she came home each day sliced into smaller and smaller pieces, desperate to take up less space. I noticed every day since we moved here, how she stressed herself into ribbons trying to justify her place in her male-dominated lab. They stole her ideas, ignored her, spoke over any thought she dared share. But she was quiet, polite, did everything right. She couldn't stomach being punished for nothing, so in her world, she wasn't. Stasia always hated irrationality, hated illogical hatred. To be a woman was nothing but.

"You know I disagree," I said simply.

"I know."

"And you know I think that it's always stupid to align yourself with men."

"Yes, you've always made that quite clear."

I nodded, satisfied. We sat in silence for a few moments, chewing thoughtfully.

"I joined a softball league," Stasia said.

"Gay?"

"Hardly." She laughed. "Hmm . . . I think that's it."

"Solid round up."

"I pass the floor." Stasia bowed, passing an imaginary talking stick.

"I think I have a thing for my boss." I started strong, blunt, the only thing on my mind. "She's so . . ."

"So what?"

"I don't know." I sighed. "She can be so *charming*, but then she'll switch up out of nowhere and turn all brooding and distant. It's like she's suspicious of me or something—"

"Smart girl."

I smacked her arm. "Don't patronize me, I'm suffering."

Stasia hummed thoughtfully. "Is her name Franky?"

"How'd you know that?"

"Someone in my lab group was talking about her today. I figured there can't be more than one hot lesbian who runs an arcade."

"You'd be surprised," I joked. "So what'd they say about her?"

"Not much. Just that they missed having her around. Apparently she used to be really cool."

"Past tense?"

"Indeed," Stasia confirmed. "It was a weird conversation, seemed like they were avoiding something."

"Like what?"

"Whatever happened to make Franky go off the deep end."

I furrowed my brows, considering this new intel. "She seems sane enough to me."

"If I had a dollar."

I threw a fry at her. "What else did they say?"

"I dunno." She plucked the fry from her sweater, placing it back on the plate. "To be honest, I wasn't really listening."

"You're a terrible wingman."

"Hardly knew I had to be one."

I sighed dramatically, staring out the window at the bobbing boats in the harbor. Hitting a brick wall with my unfortunate pursuit, I considered other, more fruitful ways to spend the evening.

"Wanna smoke and grab coffee?"

Stasia agreed, grabbing a joint and rushing out the door in a flash, leaving it open behind her. I grabbed my loafers and fanny pack, padding along in her shadow. We walked through the cobblestone streets in single file, the night painted orange hues, muggy air oppressive. Neon street signs reflected in puddles, condensation dripping down closed store window fronts. Summer hours, everything eternally closed. I wasn't sure if it was superstition or suspicion, but the energy felt *odd*, tonight. Almost unsafe. I didn't ask Stasia about it because I knew she'd make fun of me, but I kept checking over my shoulder, feeling dark eyes heavy on mine. Something horrible happened here, and the ghost of it catches me off guard, sometimes. I wondered if anyone else felt it, too. I wondered if that's why the residents of Mistaken Point seemed to hate me. Did I reflect something back to them, something better left unacknowledged?

We passed a rundown bar on our journey across town, and I dragged Stasia to the other side of the street without explanation, warily eying the men smoking outside. They shouted something incomprehensible to us as I pulled Stasia along, eyes straight and shoulders high. The men kept monologuing about exposed summer skin, begging us to cross the road again and join their night of fun.

I picked up the pace, breaths coming slower the farther we walked. I slowly unstuck myself from Stasia's side as we turned a corner, adrenaline spike simmering.

"We didn't have to run away like that," Stasia muttered, checking over her shoulder. "It probably just spurred them on."

"Right." I sighed, knowing better than to fight her on it. "Next time, *we'll* kick *them* to the other side of the road. Really stake our claim."

She rolled her eyes, checking over her shoulder again. We kept walking through town, and I didn't mention that her hands were shaking.

We grabbed iced coffee and wandered around until we found a secluded park bench, pitching camp to pass the joint back and forth. I was still a bit jumpy, but Stasia was stubborn in her right to freedom, insistent that to return home would be to surrender. To what, exactly, I wasn't sure, but I figured those men were tethered enough to the bar for us to be safe.

We didn't talk much, in one of our melancholic moods where we walked wide circles around each other. It was my most cherished part of our friendship: the breathing room. If we had a shot in hell at being romantically compatible, I always thought that Stasia would make an excellent wife.

I traced the tree line, sitting on the brink of a tunnel of wildlife. Everything green. Baby hairs stuck to the back of my neck, my chop job of a shag cut fuzzy in the late night mist. I watched smoke rise from the tip of the joint, hopping up and down on the wind. The wooden bench was damp against the back of my thighs, hitching skin whenever I shifted. I let my eyes flutter shut, feeling the effects of the weed wash over slow. I offered Stasia the last hit, stubbing it out on the stone pathway when she declined. We stood and stretched, tossing the roach in a nearby trash can before making our slow, meandering journey back home.

Home. I shook my head incredulously.

Stasia was chatting about deadlines when I heard something, a suspicious rustle in the trees. I froze, doubling back.

"Did you hear that?" I asked, grabbing the back of her sweater to stop her.

"Ow, Lawrence, this is vintage cashmere—"

"Shh!"

We stood in silence, my fist of fabric tightening. Moments passed without another sound, Stasia's thin patience wearing thinner. She muttered to herself about sending me a cleaning bill, complaining about my ash-covered fingers and death grip.

I followed behind her, slower now, convinced there had been something watching us from the trees. Something . . . *off.* I couldn't place my finger on the feeling, it felt too static to pin down. Just an eerie emptiness, an esoteric moment. I stared into the dark forest for a long moment, squinting at the outline of shapes and trees, anxious brain making fictional connections.

"Did you seriously not hear anything?" I asked, turning back to find Stasia long gone.

I turned tepid with terror, wondering how long I had been standing here, staring into space. The rustling started again, then a slow, scraping sound, the bending and buckling of branches. Something massive pushing its way through the trees. Something . . . *hungry.*

I caught a shadow far off, wiry in frame, repelling light like a black hole. Had a random man followed us out here? Had he been watching us sit and smoke? Scrambling for my phone with shaking fingers, I debated using the flashlight, hesitant to draw attention to myself. I stood still as death, scared as the day I was born. A silly, simple thing, thrust into something too big to handle. The . . . the thing, the shadow, the whatever I was looking at, it stared right back at me, misshapen head turning my way. Far enough away to be a trick of the eye, close enough to be real. The longer I stared, the stranger it looked, a mosaic of wrongness that I couldn't place. It took a step forward, low growling vibrating the trees.

A snap of a nearby branch unfroze me, Stasia doubling back. "Lawrence!" she called, her form materializing through far-off fog. "Lawrence?"

I whipped my head in her direction, losing sight of the figure for just a moment. When I glanced back, mobilized by the frantic crunching of forest leaves, all I saw was yellow eyes, an inch from mine. Frozen with terror, I screamed, falling back as I frantically shone my flashlight around like a madman.

"LAWRENCE!" Stasia rushed to my side, crouching on the ground as she shook me. "Dude, are you okay? Are you hurt?"

"The—the—the—" I stammered, shell-shocked. "It—we—"

"You're high," she explained calmly, holding me down with a firm grip on my shoulders. "You're high. It's okay. We smoked too much after such a long tolerance break."

"But—it—"

"Lawrence, it's okay. C'mon, let's go home."

"But—" I pointed to the forest, the space where the two eyes had been. Nothing. Not even a footprint. Shaky and desolate, I allowed Stasia to pull me to my feet, reluctantly dragging myself home, checking over my shoulder at every passing second. She kept murmuring that everything was okay, that we were alone out there, that she only left my side for three seconds, assuming I followed behind her.

"But . . ." I gulped, seeing yellow every time I closed my eyes. "It felt real."

"These things always do," she said soothingly, side-eyeing me. "Feeling real and being real are two very different things, though."

Chewing my cheek, it took every ounce of willpower to bite back a curious *Is it, though?* Something out there hated me, it wanted to consume me, and isn't that real enough? But I was too scared to debate metaphysics, too tired to terrify myself.

Limp and shaky, I let Stasia drag me home.

CANNIBAL

Still shaken, I spent the weekend in bed, skipping class and rolling into work Monday afternoon with a stack of overdue readings. Glasses sliding down the tip of my nose, I unlocked the office door to find a Frankyless room, her desk chair still spinning. She must've just left.

I dumped my stack of notes on the desk, pushing paperwork aside to gain some semblance of organization. I grabbed a pen from my bag, running it back and forth a few times to find it dry. I turned, digging through Franky's hurricane space to find something to write with. I carefully plucked through a minefield of mess, pushing aside sticky notes with doodles of creatures, doll parts, and cartoon question marks.

I unearthed a pen just as Pippa pushed open the office door.

"Lawrence." She bowed in greeting. "Find anything juicy in there?"

"A pen." I held it up in explanation. "I don't know how she gets any work done."

Pippa shrugged, tossing herself into Franky's office chair to poke through the debris. "Who says she does?"

"Our lights still being on."

"Franky could never mess up business here, even if she tried. Everyone loves this place."

"It's hers, right?"

Pippa stared at me, face blank.

"What?" I asked, met with silence. "Did she buy it herself? Is she the titular Franklin? Or did she inherit it? Win it? Wander in here and take over?"

Pippa shrugged, voice thin. "You'd have to ask her."

I tapped my pen against the page, tiny dots covering the margins. "She'd never tell me."

"Which is exactly why you'd have to ask her." Pippa looked away, digging through Franky's desk. "Aha!" She unearthed a slinky. "Thought I lost this. Hey, you free this weekend?"

I raised a brow, allowing her to take me off topic. "Sure."

"My friend Gummy is throwing a party. She's a grad student at MPU, too, so I'm sure you'll know a few faces. You could even bring your roommate if you want. Meant to be a big shindig."

"I'd love to come," I said, shooting Stasia a text. "I'm sure Stas would, too, she's been working too hard. Needs a break."

Pippa cheered, tilting her head towards the door at the sound of the front bell. "Oops, gotta run." She rolled the chair away, riding it like a horse.

"Godspeed," I called after her, shaking my head incredulously.

I pulled out my class notes, scribbling an essay outline and a list of readings to complete before class tomorrow. I picked through a few menial tasks for work, considering I was getting paid to be here, before circling back to start on my paper. I managed to make a dent in the general skeleton before checking the clock, figuring I should go find Pippa to take our lunch break together.

Standing to stretch, I grabbed my phone and water bottle, wandering through windy hallways to the front. Pippa sat cross-legged on the main desk, playing with a piece of string she made into a cat's cradle. Funhouse was sparsely furnished with dawdling tourists and teenagers.

"Pip," I greeted, rapping my knuckles on the desk. "Wanna grab lunch?"

"Always." She unsnarled her fingers to check the time on her phone. "Got any trail mix?"

"Yeah." I packed an extra bag just for her. "I'll give you some if you're nice."

"That doesn't sound like something I'd do." Pippa hopped off the desk, throwing an arm around my neck.

"Should we . . ." I gestured to the customers. "Close up or something?"

Pippa waved off my concern. "No one really comes in this time of day. These guys can take care of themselves."

Generally uninvested, I let Pippa lead me to the break room, chattering mindlessly about the last hour she spent perfecting her cat's cradle technique. She offered to show me, blind to my flimsy interest. We sat at the dining room table, spreading our lunch out, buffet style. I gave Pippa my trail mix, and she gave me half her sandwich. We grabbed two forks to share my leftover pasta, and I flicked on the coffee machine, grabbing two mugs and sugar.

"Do you think I'd make a good marine biologist?" Pippa asked, standing to grab the now brewed coffee.

"Sure," I said. "Is that what you did in school?"

"Nope."

"What did you—"

"Nothing. I dropped out after a few semesters. Kept floating around and eventually floated right out."

"Did you have any idea what you wanted to do?"

"Never in my life."

I laughed, stirring sugar into my coffee. "Me either. My mom just told me what to do."

"Classic upper-middle-class dilemma." Pippa shook her head sadly. "Too rich to have grit for the soul-sucking nine to five, too poor to live off of a trust fund."

"Not a bad analysis, Peterson." I hummed, smiling playfully. "Are you saying I don't have grit?"

"Oh, don't mistake me, Franklin. You've got nothing but."

I snorted into my coffee, wanting to give her the finger but unsure if we were close enough for that kind of camaraderie.

"So what did your mom tell you to do?" At my confused look, Pippa elaborated. "In university. What program did she force you into?"

"Oh. Um, business degree," I stammered. "Said it would be a stable job, that I'd always be employed."

"Employed and miserable."

"Precisely." I grinned. "Mom wanted me to do one thing she could be proud of, so I let her plot out my career."

"That's dark."

Was it? "Just the truth." I forced a laugh. Pippa was right, I was getting too dark. I added a lilt of humor to my voice, a dry irony. "She didn't really factor personal fulfillment or mental health into the equation, though."

"Mothers never do," Pippa observed. "Is that why you're here? Running away from home?"

Close to the bone. I forced a smile, tried to keep it casual. "I wanted to start fresh. To figure out what I wanted."

My voice cracked, floaty and far away. The sounds of the arcade echoed our conversation. Far-off music, mumbling, animated cries of victory. I stared down at my pasta, feeling Pippa's eyes on mine. I suspected that she might be more perceptive than people gave her credit for. With a thoughtful hum, she refilled my coffee mug and grabbed a cheese string from the work fridge, splitting it in two.

"Sometimes you've got to cannibalize yourself to figure out what you taste like."

It was nonsensical, macabre, saintly. It was like she read my mind.

I grinned, refilling her coffee mug. "I couldn't agree more."

She met my silly smile with a sillier one, and in that moment, Pippa Peterson traversed the impossible territory from coworker to friend.

Anastasia Lanes was a composed, careful creature. Graceful and poised, forever finicky and hyperaware of every unwritten rule. All tact flew out the window, however, when it came to couponing. Neurotic to her core, she spent hours poring over fliers and virtual deals, dragging me along to the grocery store every second Sunday to browse produce, heckle half-off selections, and talk me into sharing a jug of near-expired kombucha.

It was pouring rain yesterday, so Stasia dragged me to the store today, drowning out my grumbling complaints with a cheery monologue about the sale on papaya.

"I don't even know what a papaya looks like."

Stasia showed me the coupon clipping with a picture of a papaya, penciled heart around it like a teenager defacing a yearbook.

"Learn something new every day," I said.

"Speaking of." She wiped her Birkenstocks on the welcome mat, grabbing a shopping cart to lay her sensible purse in. "Am I to understand that we're attending a party this weekend?"

"If you want to." I shrugged, dragging behind her like a child. "Pippa invited me today at work. She's really cool, I think you'd like her."

"Does she go to MPU as well?"

"Nah, she's just a free floater."

Stasia checked her grocery list, steering us towards the produce section. I dodged an old couple that gave us a strange stare, eyes caught on my short hair, Stasia's fingers full of rings. The old man muttered something I didn't catch, but Stasia paled, pulling us away.

"What'd he say?" I whispered.

"What were you saying about Pippa?" Stasia's voice cracked, waving me off. "She's not the one you have a thing for, is she?"

"No." I gave her a suspicious look, watching her dive into the fruit display. "That's Franky."

"Franky . . ." Stasia hummed absently, squeezing and smelling random fruit. "Hmm . . ."

"Yes, Franky. Do you want me to give you two some privacy?" I gestured to her and the orange, peering over her shoulder at the list. "I can grab rice and eggs?"

"Not eggs." She refocused. "I meant to scratch that out. My lab partner has chickens."

"Alright, just rice then."

Stasia threw a bag of discounted oranges in the cart, processing my plan. "No, no, stay with me! I want to hear about your week. We've been so busy."

"Alright," I grumbled, pretending not to be pleased. "Nothing even happened. I just went to work and school."

Stasia gave me a turn pushing the cart, careful brown eyes analyzing mine. "Have you heard from your mom lately?"

Innocent seeming question, but in reality, layered thick like sandstone. I faltered, pushing the cart into a cracker display, laughing weakly as I scrambled to clean it up.

"N-no," I said, straightening up. "I haven't."

Stasia stared at me, waiting for more.

"I still haven't answered her." I picked up a fancy cheese, examining the cartoon logo.

"Since when?"

"Since we left."

Stasia was a tricky thing; she could be unbearably cruel without saying a word. Her furrowed brows, the pursed lips. Maybe I'm projecting too much on her, pushing my own fears onto a silent companion. I'm always worried that she thinks I'm not justified in my severance.

"I'm not wrong for that."

Tell me I'm not wrong for that.

"I never said you were."

I gestured to her entire demeanor.

"Don't think so little of me," she scolded. "I can have an opinion on something and still support what you do. They don't cancel each other out."

"Don't they?"

Stasia gave me a look. "I support whatever choice you feel like you had to make, but I'm a very different person, Del. I'm not going to immediately subscribe to whatever set of reasoning you used."

I bit back a snide remark, figuring we were too old to be throwing jabs about our mothers.

"I'm serious, I support you," Stasia said. "I always will."

I let myself be pulled into purposeful eye contact, giving her a small nod of acknowledgment. I couldn't help but understand where she was coming from, too close to resent her for stuff like this. She's always had more roots than me, roots like a straitjacket. As evil as Mrs. Lanes was, she had to be a fixture in Stasia's life. If she cut off her mother, she would bleed out.

"Always?" I confirmed.

"Always."

"What if I murder someone?"

Stasia sighed, rubbing the space between her brows. "Can you not threaten homicide in the bakery section?"

"I can wait until the frozen section?"

"Fair compromise." She gave me a crooked smile from childhood. Silly and uncomplicated. "C'mon, big shot, we're burning daylight. Go get the rice."

So I went and got the rice. I thought about the years Stasia and I drifted, her spurt of popularity in middle school, my debate club phase in junior high, her softball fame in high school. The figure eights we looped around each other, best friends to first kiss to acquaintances to enemies to best friends to friends to best friends, the years we spent orbiting. Complicated and neurotic as she was, I couldn't have asked for a better person to come home to.

Grocery list completed, we met up again by the cash, looping together like we always did. She scanned, I bagged, and we bickered and bantered and then gathered our things and went home. Home together, home to each other.

I let her pick tonight's movie.

The next day was pouring rain.

Bored to tears, I spent the morning color coding my filing cabinet, singing to myself and debating supper plans. Franky found me sprawled out on the floor hours later, scrolling through social media looking at motorcycles for sale.

"Hey, Lawrence," she greeted softly, smiling as I hid my phone to appear productive. "We just got a new shipment in, and it's looking like a two-person job. Could you help me out?"

We had hardly spoken since last week. I would've unpacked every shipment in this city for a chance to know her better.

"Of course!" I jumped to my feet, paper scattering around me.

Franky looked reluctantly charmed by my eagerness, shaking her head incredulously. She led the way out front, humming the same song I was singing earlier. We stopped in front of a box the size of me, wrapped in a layer of tape like a winter coat.

I leaned closer to examine the order slip, unable to stop myself from laughing.

"Jesus." I giggled, poking the box with my foot. "This is full of *bouncy balls?*"

"Yes." Franky let out a long-suffering sigh, her cranky demeanor hilarious, considering the circumstances. "I must've fucked up the order."

I dug through my cargo pants for a box cutter, the weapon I kept on hand in case of emergencies.

"Prepared," Franky noted.

"Scared," I corrected, half joking.

She nodded sagely, studying me for a moment. "That's smart."

"My roommate calls me paranoid."

"People say the same about me."

I thought back to the murder board, ached to ask her about it. "You, um—"

"You were probably safer in your big city," Franky interrupted. "I doubt you missed the news about what's happened here."

"I missed most of it."

Franky stopped, suspicious and shocked. "Really?"

"Yeah, I'm not into that sort of thing. I only saw the gist of it on social media. Fucked up, hey? I can't imagine living through that."

She hummed, watching me with new eyes.

I couldn't figure out what made her so strange, rerunning what she said. "Hey, how'd you know I came from the city?"

Franky took the blade from my hand, kneeling by the box. "Your resume," she said, struggling to cut it. "Can you—"

I knelt beside her, holding the box steady as she used her one hand to make a clean cut along the seam. I pried the box open to find about a million bouncy balls, multicolored and big as tangerines.

"Certainly not the most suspicious delivery Funhouse has ever gotten," Franky observed. "But maybe one of the strangest."

I laughed, grabbing a mint green ball to bounce once, twice. I missed the third bounce, watching it roll away into a sea of arcade games.

"We'll never see that again," Franky said mournfully.

I passed her a pink bouncy ball, her fingers warm against mine. She shifted closer, rolling the ball around in her palm.

"I used to play baseball," she murmured. "Third base. Was never really good at it."

"Really?" I asked. "You don't strike me as sporty."

"And why not?"

"You seem like more of an academic." At her amused look, I elaborated. "The whole research thing you're always doing, with the notebook and file folders."

Her eyes flashed. "You're paying close attention to me, Lawrence."

"You're my boss!" I squeaked. "And, um, it's hard not to notice that you're working on something."

"I'm just trying to keep track of your findings," she said. "So far I'm an academic, pretty, and, what else was it, *mean*?"

"Y-you certainly could be nicer," I bantered weakly.

"My social skills are a bit out of practice," she admitted, shifting closer. "But you don't seem to mind."

It was a question, a statement, soft and shockingly hesitant. Franky surprised me by reaching out and brushing a thumb along my blushing cheek. Collecting evidence. She looked like she wanted to say something, something important, but she never got the chance. The door crashed open, and a group of teens flooded the arcade entrance, bubbling and loud as a babbling brook. Franky stiffened, subtly shifting to tuck her left side against mine. I felt her amputated arm press into my stomach, and I billowed my jacket, offering as much coverage as possible.

The teenagers quieted when they noticed Franky, giggling to themselves and muttering under their breath. I thought I heard one of the girls say *Franky-Stein*, showing off to a pimply boy who snickered with laughter. I watched the girls of the group sadly, watched their peacocking, their open and cruel disdain of Franky. I wasn't sure what their problem was, but I wanted to pull them aside and warn them. Those boys would never choose them, never value them. They haven't realized it yet, maybe never would, but if their friends find humor in the suffering of other women, what makes them think that they won't be the target the second they stop performing the right way?

Franky's right hand clasped the ball so tight, it split like old leather. She inhaled sharply, seemingly reluctant to pick a fight with paying customers. The teens moved on, distracted by the new pinball machine, and I was left glaring after them, pressing closer against Franky's side.

Her jaw clenched, twitching as she chewed her inner cheek.

"Hey," I whispered, placing a gentle hand on her back. "Hey, Franky, what other sports did you play as a kid?"

She peered over at me, looking small.

"My mom wouldn't let me join any." I forced a lightness, a casual tone. "I begged her to put me in hockey, but she forced me into ballet. It was a *nightmare*. My ballet teacher called my limbs 'grotesquely tangled' once. Said I looked like a tree."

Franky considered me, staring into the box of bouncy balls. She seemed surprised by my continued attention, as if a group of dickhead kids could make me change my mind about her.

"Hockey," she answered, voice raspy. "I was the hockey captain." She licked her lips, checking over her shoulder. The teens had disappeared into the arcade, and I watched her shoulders melt with a shame-ridden relief.

I wanted to comfort her, pull her close, tell her that fifteen-year-olds are the worst people on the planet and I'd happily chew them out if she wanted me to. But I didn't have the words. I just nudged my knee against hers, hoping it would be enough.

"I would've loved to have you on my team," she said, former intensity melting into Far-Away Franky. I liked them both, I just wondered which one was more authentic.

"Now would be a good time to tell you that I can't skate."

A small giggle broke out. A warm, bubbling laugh slipping through her sheet of ice. She shook her head, shaking away the whimsy.

"Grab that end of the box, would you?" she asked, climbing to her feet. "We need to bring this to the storage room."

I balanced the back end as Franky led us through the twisting games, dropping her end of the box to open the storage room. We tucked the box in a back corner and turned to each other, struck by the smallness of the space.

"Thank you," Franky mumbled, embarrassed in a way that made me think she was thanking me for more than just helping out with a delivery. And thus a new Franky had been unlocked, Vulnerable Franky. She stared up at me, warm and waterlogged, exposed as an open wound.

"Anytime, sweetheart." I poked her belly, for some reason. Wondering when I lost all my game and became a fumbling fool.

Silly as it was, she seemed to like it. Franky blushed, delicious crimson red, sweet as cherries. I thought I finally understood vampires, their ferocity for fresh blood. I wanted to drink her up like a juice box.

Starving off further incident, she waved me off, letting me leave work early.

I smiled the entire walk home.

SEVERED

Work was dry today. Pippa and I had the morning shift, yawning over each other as we scanned the room with bleary eyes. Pippa perched on the desk beading earrings, while I sat behind her working on a paper. I doodled eyes in the corner of my notebook, crooked and lined with malice. A group of teen boys came in and started causing a ruckus, but Pippa hardly seemed to notice. She continued beading away, blind to their yelled slurs and yawning destruction.

"Want me to kick them out?" I muttered under my breath, gesturing to the teen boys currently assaulting a cardboard cutout of Lara Croft. One had ripped off her arm and started hitting the others with it.

"What?" Pippa glanced up. "No, no, who cares?" She brushed me off. "Hey, are you going to the party tonight?"

I raised a brow, trying to ignore the pandemonium in front of us. "Yeah, I think so."

She nodded happily, and I turned back to my drawing.

"Franky was asking after you."

"She—" My hand slipped, notebook and pen clattering to the floor. "What?"

Pippa laughed at my floundering. "She asked if you'd be attending tonight. Seemed invested in the answer." She reconsidered. "As invested as Franks can be, in something that's not her—" she stopped herself, frozen.

I let it slide, too ecstatic over the previous news. Pippa looked relieved, which I filed away for later use. "She really asked about me?" I had to reconfirm, stroking my ego.

"Calm down, Lawrence, the steam emitting off your body is making it hard for patrons to see."

I shoved her dangling legs, grinning despite myself. She could tease me all she wanted. I was making progress. Passably pretty caught Franky's eye. What a victory. I plotted my plan forward, already wondering which strand of hair I could cut off to gift her inside a locket.

"Hey, Lawrence." Pippa tapped my knee with her foot, catching my attention. "Don't get too excited. Seriously. Franky's got a lot going on. Don't be shocked if you don't get anywhere."

"It's okay." I smiled. "Seriously, don't worry about me. I'm rarely invested enough in anything to get my feelings hurt."

Pippa was satisfied, but I had just lied through my teeth. My mission was as stupid as it was simple, spurred on by Pippa's backhanded encouragement. I wondered who Franky loved before me, which girls in town caught her eye. The good-weather women, if they were pretty, smart, butch, femme. I considered my appearance, considered sharp edges and hard head. Fluffy chopped hair, dark brows, spindly legs and silly smile. I was okay. I got by on charm, determination, and the inclination to give up. I didn't want to give up this time. Pippa strolled away from me and the day soldiered on, but I stayed stuck on the thought of being thought of, sought after. Stuck on the flimsiest hope of taking up space in Franky's meandering mind.

Lazarus deletes dating apps, committing her heart to one woman. Lazarus on fire, trying to measure up to a ghost.

Stasia and I showed up late to the party, bungalow overflowing with grad students. We dodged conga lines and smoke circles, seeking out a familiar face.

"Lawrence!" Pippa yelled, emerging from a sea of people.

Her outfit was heinous, checked green men's shorts, bright orange tank top, and tie-dye overshirt. I shielded my eyes, smiling. She danced over to me, Crocs squeaking.

"You look epic." I let her pull me into a bro hug, nearly dropping my case of cider as she jostled me. "This is my roommate, Stasia."

Stasia stood off to the side with a tight smile. Pippa bowed low, head knocking against her stomach.

"Charmed, m'lady." She tipped an invisible hat. "I'm Pippa."

"Oh, um. I'm Stasia. The roommate. Lawrence already said that, but . . ."

We stood in silence for a moment.

"Is that a joint behind your ear?" Stasia blurted out uncharacteristically.

"Sure is, darling." Pippa grinned. "I'm sober tonight, but Franks gave it to me to hold."

"Is she here?" I asked.

"Somewhere." Pippa plucked the joint and passed it to me. "Go find her, tell her I said to share."

I grinned, nodding at Stasia. "I'm gonna find the fridge, I'll be back in a sec."

As I pushed my way through the smog, I heard Pippa asking Stasia if she had ever tried pickling strawberries. I debated finding Franky, spurred on by Pippa's suggestion, but thought it would be unfair to Stasia. Give her time to warm up, get accustomed to the crowd, before I dive into the real mission.

Pushing my case of cider into the overflowing fridge, I nodded politely to anyone who caught my eye. I walked past my classmate, Deidre Valentine, chewing out some random man she deemed to be acting suspicious around the communal drink table.

She was nice, one of the only acquaintances I've made. We usually sat by each other every Tuesday and Thursday, friendship stopping and starting on campus grounds. I watched the creep worm away, muttering profanities under his breath as Deidre threatened his back. I took his space beside her, smiling warmly.

"Hey," I greeted, nodding after the man. "What happened there?"

"Some weirdo tried to mess with my friend's drink," she said. "He claimed that he thought it was his own. Refused to drink it when I all but forced him to, though. Isn't that funny?"

I hummed, shaking my head. I admired Deidre's fire, but it worried me, sometimes. Her social media rants, the constant protests, her angry monologues against male classmates and professors. She was as angry as I used to be before I realized the futility of it. I guess I have privilege in never having to gain the respect and love of a man. I see them a bit more clearly than she can and can walk away without driving myself crazy.

"What brings you here?" she asked. "I didn't realize you knew Gummy."

"I don't. Pippa invited me."

"Peterson? That's interesting." Deidre hummed. "Then you must know Franky too, right?"

"Sure."

"I always felt so bad for her." Deidre shook her head sadly. "Such a sad case."

"What?"

Deidre was distracted by a nearby shout, some man messing with a keg stand. She giggled when she caught his eye, pretending not to watch him.

"What were you saying about Franky?" I prompted, trying to recapture her attention. "You knew her?"

"Oh, sure," she answered distractedly. "I was in her seventh-grade class."

"And she's . . ." I juggled words. "The sad case thing?"

Deidre studied me, and I wondered if she saw my open-mouthed desperation. She seemed to take my curiosity as something else, though, chugging her drink and fluffing her hair, as if preparing for a television interview.

"I guess she was always a little sad," Deidre started. "Clearly had some shit going on at home, always pulled out to the guidance office, that type of thing. Everyone always assumed it was her mother causing trouble, 'cause she was such a nasty woman. But I guess now it's—" She laughed awkwardly, hiccupping. "Now it seems like *Franklin* was the problem, but it was just so"—she hiccupped—"random! He always seemed so chill."

"Her dad—?"

"Franky used to be so cool," Deidre interrupted, floaty and far away. I was still competing with the keg stand man for her attention. "She only ever complained about her mom. Isn't that funny?"

My head was spinning trying to keep up. I thought of Stasia's labmates, how she mentioned them having the exact same perspective. "Franky used to be cool?"

I tried to hide my affection, my belief that she was *still* cool, but I had no point of comparison like the rest of them.

"The *coolest*. She was such a firecracker, man. Didn't take anything seriously, and was so *funny*, too."

"She's not like that anymore?"

She shook her head. "It's like a switch flipped when her mom left, a few years back. She shot into the stratosphere." Deidre took a long pull from her cooler. "Then the killings started, and that godawful arrest . . ." She shuddered. "I always felt bad for her, but she just got so *intense*. It makes people uncomfortable."

"How?"

Deidre played with the hem of her tank top, avoiding my eye. "We're all trying to move forward, obviously, but *all* she wants to talk about is the murders. She'll go up to people asking the *weirdest* questions, then get super worked up if you try to brush it off as a joke. I mean, at first, we all thought she was joking, cause she was always talking about aliens and monsters and shit. Even had this cute Mulder thing going on back in high school. But it's gotten a lot darker, since, um—" Deidre stumbled, clearing her throat. "Well. You know."

I didn't, but she was moving too quickly for me to fill in the blanks.

"Pippa might be the only person on earth chill enough to put up with it," Deidre continued. "Everyone else just avoids her, now. I think she's hiding out somewhere here, but no one is brave enough to look for her."

Brave. I thought of Deidre's fury. Her protective instincts and open heart. What made Franky beyond saving? What about her made everyone so uncomfortable?

"Did you know any of the victims?" I asked, sheer curiosity.

Deidre sobered up at this question. She was sent into orbit, pensive and far away.

"Yeah," she murmured. "Yeah, it's a small town. I didn't know them all personally, but . . . yeah. I knew a few."

"Were they—" I cleared my throat, lost on how I could possibly ask for more information.

"My childhood best friend, Tiffany Summers." Her voice was barely above a whisper. I had to lean closer to hear her. "We hadn't spoken in years, she was a nasty piece of work. But I didn't realize how comforting it was, to know someone like her existed in the world. She's someone I shared a decade of my life growing up with." Deidre chugged the rest of her drink, crushing the can. "They never found her head. The forums call her one of the 'incomplete victims.' How fucked up is that?"

Forums? *Incomplete* victim? I shivered, jostled by a group of girls rushing by us.

"I'm sorry," I whispered, watching the girls recognize Deidre.

"Dee!" one of them announced, nearly trampling me. She noticed me slowly, head tilting to the side. "And, um, who is she? Or, sorry, he?"

I stiffened, pulling on my shaggy hair, touching my makeup-free face. "She," I corrected with an awkward smile. Christ.

"This is my classmate, Delores," Deidre introduced me awkwardly. "She's friends with Pippa."

The girls turned to me, mouths forming identical O's. The neon sign on my forehead spelling *lesbian* grew a bit brighter in my association with Pippa. Ah, well. There are worse ways to be profiled.

"Franky, too?" a blonde asked, voice dropping low.

I turned to Deidre, but she was avoiding my eye. "Yep," I answered simply, cataloging the shifts of discomfort.

"She punched my brother last month." Girl Two sniffed disdainfully. "Almost broke his nose."

"Your brother is a dick, Gracie." Deidre laughed awkwardly, solidarity in strange places. "He had it coming."

"He was just *joking*—"

"He asked Franky if she needed a man to look after her, since she lost her arm and—"

"Alright!" Gracie waved her off, forcing a smile. "He just has a dark sense of humor."

I studied them, fascinated by the dynamic. Girls like this were once the source of my internalized misogyny, then later became the cure. They would ostracize me, treat me like an outsider, then marry high school boyfriends who provided two children, a house by twenty-six, and endless affairs. I used to scoff at them, but they'll have all their life goals accomplished by thirty, whilst I flounder forever searching for something *more*, so aren't I the fool here? No wonder Mom was desperate for me to follow their trajectory; their box seems comfortable.

"Dark humor is such a cop out," Deidre muttered.

The other girls exchanged a look, evidently exhausted by Deidre's contrarian bite. I didn't like these girls, but I felt an ache of empathy for the three of them, sharpest when I considered Deidre's predicament. She was like my fun house mirror; I could be laid-back in places where Deidre had to make space. I reflected on my journey of unpacking internalized misogyny, remembered how being "one of the boys" lost its appeal once me and the boys realized I didn't want to sleep with them. My Cool Girl attitude at once turned dismissive and frosty. It was interesting that Deidre seemed to have a similar journey to me, seemed to understand the stupidity of centering men, but she was stuck. I felt her frustration with her friends, but at the same time understood her occasional appeasement of their ideals. They just wanted companionship. Loving, equal, attentive companionship. I couldn't begrudge any of them for approaching this quest with a vaguely delusional state of mind.

I *could* poke a bit of fun, though. That seems fair.

"I'm sorry Franky beat up your brother," I offered.

Deidre snorted into her fist.

"She didn't *win*—" the girl squawked.

"I hope he considers picking on people his own size, though." I bulldozed on. "Because if he considers Franky an equal opponent, the guy must be a real shrimp."

"N-no, he's—Devon's, like, over six feet tall!"

"With or without heels?" I asked, condescendingly sincere.

"Obviously he—"

"Well, it's been charming to meet you all," I interrupted, forcing a smile. "But I should go find my friends."

Girl Two was still muttering about heels while the others nodded, dismissing me with poorly concealed relief.

"Ah, okay!" Deidre waved me off, smile stopping at her cheeks. "It was nice seeing you!" she called out, letting herself get pulled back by the tide. Her group of friends migrated towards the keg stand, cheering on the boys.

I smiled stiffly, waving back. "Take it easy, Valentine."

She held her hand over her heart, tapping it twice as she disappeared into the crowd. I watched the space where she was and thought about Tiffany Summers. I wondered if she would've been here; if in another life, she might've trampled me on the way to the bathroom. I wondered how hard it could be to find a missing head.

Numbly pushing my way through the party, I grabbed a few drinks and a handful of chips from a random bowl, circling back to Stasia and Pippa to find them discussing the process of pickling. They took a moment to notice my return, with Stasia's eyes narrowing in on my harrowed expression. I waved her off, passing Stasia a cider and Pippa a bottle of water.

"You were gone a while," Pippa observed, stealing a chip from my palm.

"Ran into a classmate." I tried to appear normal. "Did I miss anything?"

"Nothing," Stasia answered at the same time Pippa said, "Loads."

We settled into a corner of the party, studying the crowd.

"Do you know many people here?" I asked.

"Most." Pippa skimmed the room. "A lot went to high school with me."

"You grew up here?"

"Me and Franks did."

"You guys have been friends that long?"

"Kind of." Pippa was briefly side-tracked, stealing Funyuns from a random girl passing by. "We were friends as kids, then drifted apart for a while—"

"Why?" I interrupted, ignoring the disapproving look from Stasia.

"Um." Pippa blinked. "I'm a year older than her, so we weren't in the same grade or anything, and she, um—" She paused, picking lint off her shirt. "She used to be closer to my cousin."

I furrowed my brows, logging my memory for mention of this rogue cousin, when Stasia interjected.

"Do you like working at Funhouse?"

Relieved with the change in topic, Pippa gave her a long-winded answer, half sincere in her moody praise of the arcade. Distracted, I glanced out the window, watching a group of girls share a cigarette. I let my eyes wander the backyard, curiously tracing a line of red liquid across the patio. Red wine, I assumed. With a loud creek from the forest, the three girls turned to the trees, searching alongside me. I heard their muffled conversation, watched them stub out the cigarette at the request of a clearly terrified blonde. I kept scanning the tree line, straining my eyes to see a rustle of low branches. I saw a glimpse of yellow, a trick of light that was just a cell phone flashlight. I gulped back cold fear, remembering that night in the park.

"You're fogging up the glass," Pippa said, pushing her face next to mine to look out the window. "Whatcha looking at?"

"N-nothing." I stepped back, wiping condensation off the glass. "Hold on, I'll be right back."

They waved me off, discussing a winery nearby that they wanted to check out. Stasia gave me a quick look before I departed, and I sent her back what I hoped was a convincing thumbs up. She turned back to Pippa, and I disappeared into the party, making my way to the back porch. The sliding glass door was cracked open, letting cool night air breeze through the kitchen. The group of girls were long gone. I glanced around the kitchen, finding an uninteresting room of uninterested drunk people. I didn't bother to be mysterious, just slipped out the glass door and made my way along the wooden patio, placing my almost empty cider bottle on the railing.

I stood on my tiptoes, glancing over the edge. The patio dropped about six feet down, the sloping hill leading to a haze of black trees. I scanned the area, finding nothing but cigarette butts and beer cans in the grass. No cracking tree branches, no rustling movements, no . . . no yellow-eyed monster.

I shook myself, rolling my eyes at my own superstition. The girls from earlier probably just saw a deer or something. I forced myself to laugh it off but couldn't shake the hair-prickling fear of being out here alone. The party continued on mere inches away, an open glass door separating me from about fifty other people, but in that moment, I felt like the only person on Earth.

I stayed, staring at the tree line for far too long. I kept squinting, daring the forest to show me something worth coming out here for, but the forest would not relent.

"Whatever," I mumbled, turning to leave.

As my back faced the trees, a loud *crack* echoed the air. I spun so fast I crashed into a patio chair, frantically scrambling away from the edge of the deck. I heard something like footsteps beneath me, a low scraping nose on the wooden parameter. I searched the tiny gaps between the panels of wood, desperate to catch sight of something, *anything*, that made sense. Cold terror washed through my body, sensing that whatever was beneath me, it was growing closer, rustling under the patio. I held my breath, paralyzed with fear. Ancient patio wood was the only thing protecting me from whatever was down there. I felt a squeeze in my chest, anxiety tightening its cold hand around my larynx.

"Lawrence!"

I turned so fast I gave myself whiplash, finding Pippa and Stasia staring down at me from the doorway.

"You're doing a terrible job of smoking a joint," Pippa observed, raising a brow at my defensive position.

I stilled, quiet as death, waiting for the next noise to come. It never did. On shaky feet, I pulled myself up and brushed off my pants, forcing a laugh.

"Didn't want to start without you guys," I said.

"If you're done doing yoga out here, I can show you guys somewhere *really* cool." Pippa grinned.

Creature of mischief, I shrugged off the gloom and followed her meandering trail. I was too old to play make believe with made-up ghosts, anyway.

Stas, Pippa, and I ended up lying near a koi pond, secluded by thick trees tracing a cobblestone path. Our heads huddled together, bodies spread out like a ninja star. Pippa and Stasia were debating the ethics of wasteland, while I sipped a cider and stared up at the stars.

The forest on this side of the house was quiet, unintimidating. I periodically scanned the trees, searching for a sight of something sinister, but it was too well lit out here to commit to the terror, fairy lights and lanterns hardly creating a compelling horror scene. I tried not to think about my made-up monster. Franky was allegedly here, somewhere. I tried not to think about that, either.

"Franky says the exact same thing." Pippa sighed, peeling the label off her kombucha.

Damn.

"Says what?" I intervened, ears perking up like a dog.

"A lot of dumb shit."

"She seems half smart," I said. "Or maybe I'm just misaligning intelligence to her being hard to read."

"Always confused me when people said that." Pippa laughed. "She wears her heart on her sleeve."

"Home team advantage."

"Or *disadvantage*," Stasia suggested. "Maybe you're too close to her and are taking your assumptions as fact."

"Maybe." Pippa waved us off, surrendering with an easy smile. She was too mellow to feed into my and Stasia's addiction to back and forth.

"I just want to get to know her," I admitted, achingly sincere. "I'm trying my best, but she doesn't make it easy."

Pippa's expression was complicated, turning to study me. I thought of what Deidre said, wondering why Pippa was the only friend who stuck around. What could she stomach in Franky that no one else could?

"She seems to like you," Pippa started cautiously. "It's been a while since Franky's liked anyone, but you make her laugh. A lot of people forgot that she could do that."

"Unsurprising." Stasia snorted, "Lawrence is so ridiculous, one can't help but laugh."

"Seems like Franky has met her ridiculous match, then."

"Match made in ridiculous heaven."

Pippa laughed, bantering with Stasia on strange tangents. I sat up, staring at the house looming over us. Nearby conversations trickled over, smoke circles, beer pong tournaments. I thought about Pippa's assessment, remembered her claim that Franky was asking after me.

I clamored to my feet, telling the two I was going to the bathroom before heading into the simmering house. Drunk and high and dancing across rocks, I sought her out, desperate to break through the ice, keep her smiling for longer this time. I thought of my long list of ex-girlfriends, all as anxiously attached as my mother. Franky dangled in front of me like the ultimate test, my boss battle. Her ebbing avoidance was gasoline to my fire, but she liked me, I could feel it.

I pushed my way into the house and wandered through the hallways, wishing I brought a red string to find my way back. Peeking into half-open doorways, I froze when I saw Franky behind lucky door number three, recognizing her cloud of hair anywhere.

I shyly poked my head in, ecstatic to find her alone. She was sprawled across the carpet, unlit joint dangling from her lips. Skater jeans and combat boots, electric green eyeliner and tighter than skin sports bra.

"Hey," I greeted, closing the door behind me.

Franky lifted her head from the carpet, cataloging me. "Lawrence."

"What are you doing in here?" I asked, tiptoeing across the floor to sit beside her. My crossed knees touched her bare stomach.

"Hiding," Franky said, plucking the joint from her lips to lie on her stomach. "Got tired of the crowd."

I thought of what Deidre said, wondering if the crowd got tired of Franky first.

"You're so antisocial."

"And here I thought I was a flourishing social butterfly," she deadpanned, lolling her head to look at me. "How tragic, to be so misunderstood. I thought you knew me better than that, Lawrence."

She was poking fun, mocking my incessant attention, but I couldn't tell if it was indulgent or dismissive.

"Should I leave you to your brooding?" I forced a joke, hoping I didn't sound too heartbroken that she might not want me around.

"Not brooding," Franky said. "I'm theorizing."

"Care to share?"

Franky met my eye, dark brown eyes nearly black, pinpoints of focus. She seemed to be looking for sincerity. I did my best to scrape some together.

"Do you really care?"

"I tracked you down, didn't I?" I joked. "Surely you're not shocked that I'd take an interest in whatever you're so busy with."

"Hmm." She picked up the joint, twirling it between her fingers. "Got a light?"

Mercifully, for the first time in my life, something went right for me. I scrambled to look cool, pulling the tiny barbecue lighter from one of the countless pockets in my pants. Franky hummed a thanks, pushing herself to her feet to amble over to the window. Rather than light the joint, she just tucked it behind her ear and started playing with the lighter, flicking it on and letting it die out with detached focus. She seemed to be considering something.

The room had shaggy blue carpet, band posters curling off the wall in the oppressive summer heat. The ceiling was lined with fairy lights, blinking different colors with each passing moment. Lavender. Blue. White. Pink. The windowsill fit two people perfectly, lined with plants Franky carefully moved to the floor.

"Grab a drink," she instructed, "and I'll give you the rundown."

I tried not to look crazy, rushing from the room to track down my abandoned drinks. I pushed through the fridge, almost causing an avalanche of produce in my quest to grab the bottles of cider. With a tight smile to the person waiting behind me, I forced myself to slowly amble back to the bedroom and closed the door behind me.

"Okay," I announced, using a bottle opener from my carabiner to open two bottles. "Shoot."

Franky grabbed the offered bottle with a grin, pointing to the matching joint behind my ear. Bright blue rolling paper. "Is that mine?"

"Pippa gave it to me." I grinned, wiggling up onto the windowsill beside her. "Now shoot."

"Okay, okay." She took a long sip of cider, leaning her head back against the wall. Her legs pulled tight against her chest, skin warm like a space heater. "How much do you know about me?"

I chewed on this, remembering the breadcrumbs Deidre gave me.

"Not much."

"Do you know what I'm researching?"

"The murder board?" I guessed. "With the missing posters?"

Her smile struck like lightning. "Attentive girl."

"So you're . . . the research is about the serial killer, right? But, um . . ." I scratched my chin, remembering Pippa's warning. "They caught him, didn't they?"

Franky studied me. Quiet, contemplative. "What if I told you there's more?"

"More victims?"

"No. Well, yes, but—" She gathered courage, grabbing the notebook from her pocket. "More violence. More horror. More . . . What if I told you there's a monster?"

I stared at her, waiting for the punchline. She just stared back, once far away eyes now bright fluorescent.

"I'm sorry, *what*?"

"The—have you noticed, like, the—" She cut herself off, frustrated. Flipped through a few pages of her notebook, retracing her steps. "What do you know about the murders?"

"Not much. Bunch of young women torn to shreds, right?"

"Right. Do you . . ." She chewed her cheek. "Do you know much about the killer?"

I shook my head. "You said there's *more*. Has anything else happened since they arrested that guy?"

"Nothing *substantial*. But it's not so simple. It's an energy, a feeling. Women are still unsafe. They're being watched, hunted, they—" She stared down at her notebook.

"I've been tracking things, connecting the murders. The way they show up, the gruesomeness, the patterns. I've noticed—do you have a weak stomach?"

I shook my head. I did.

"I noticed the bodies are always covered in claw marks. Covered in bites."

"Bites?"

"Pieces are missing. Never found. *Consumed*, I suspect."

I cringed.

"And, and, they're always in pieces. The same pieces. Legs, torso, arms, head, all severed. Like a kid cutting up dolls."

Her full lips formed the most unhinged sentences I'd ever had the pleasure of hearing. I leaned forward, trying to frame my interest as intrigue, trying to stay on task.

"And?"

"And there's always one limb missing! All the victims, all missing one limb! Victim One lost an arm, Victim Two lost a right leg. Victim—" She cut herself off, expression complicated. My eyes flickered down to her prosthetic arm, the awkward way she held it. She must've put it on for the party. New, I suspected. Related?

"So . . ." I racked my brain to bring back her fire. "Frankenstein?"

She took the bait. "Possibly? The pieces, they all . . . the themes are fascinating. Consumption, severance, robbery. These women, they're—it's like this monster is dissecting them, devouring them, to put something together . . ."

"What makes you think it's a creature?" I asked. "And not just that sick weirdo they arrested playing doctor?"

It was at this that Franky paused, chewing her bottom lip. She reached forward, and for one stupid moment, I thought she was going to grab my cheek. She remained ever impassive to her charm, missed my blushing, stumbling, stammering, instead gently plucking the joint from behind my ear. I watched her light it, watched her hold the smoke for a long moment, passing it back to me through the fog. I waited for her to circle back to me, waited for the big blowout. She met my eye and gave me the world's saddest smile.

"I've seen it."

Jesus.

"You—?"

"I—hear me out—I was there, one of the nights."

"Jesus."

"No, it's not bad."

"Not *bad*?"

"I didn't *really* see anything. I was just there, with one of the girls. We were at my house, it was late at night, and I saw . . . I saw something. A fucking . . . a *creature*. With yellow eyes. It was outside my window."

My eyes lit up with recognition, leaning forward.

"It was like . . . I don't know what it was. It was a monster, and it felt . . ."

"Hungry?"

"Insatiable," she confirmed. "I'm not sure. It had this clear aura around it."

"W-what happened to the girl?"

"She went home. I begged her to stay, but she called me crazy." Franky's jaw clenched. "They found her in pieces, days later."

"Jesus."

I leaned forward, passing back the joint. Franky was untethered, unstable, but her conviction felt as real as skin. She was magnetic. I could've eaten her alive.

It was when our fingers touched, smoke passing between them, that the door was pushed open. Pippa and Stasia poked their heads into the room like children, one stacked on top of the other.

"May we come in, sir?" Pippa asked in a silly accent, eyes surveying the scene.

Franky jerked her chin in approval, pulling her hand back from mine. I clenched my fist to stop myself from chasing her.

Pippa and Stasia ducked into the room, leaving the door open a crack.

"You two are so antisocial," Stasia joked, catching my eye to give me an appraising look.

I felt guilty for abandoning her with Pippa, hoping she felt guilty for interrupting my modicum of progress.

"I was getting a rundown on the town creatures," I joked, carefully watching Franky's reaction. I didn't notice Pippa's panic.

Franky didn't seem put off by my sarcasm, smiling around the joint. "I'm going to trap it," she whispered conspiratorially, eyes alive with determination.

"*What*?" I exclaimed, head thrown back in laughter. "You should get proof it even exists before you start planning a heist."

"I have proof," she insisted. "I've been building a case—"

"Okay, let's confiscate that." Pippa grabbed Franky's joint and tossed it out the window. "Sorry guys, she loves to break out the bulletin board when she's high."

"I was enjoying myself," I protested, caught between flirting and genuine interest. "Besides, I didn't even get to share my info."

Franky leaned forward, eyes electric. "You have—"

"Enough!" Pippa snapped. "No more monster talk."

Stasia jolted, taken aback by the uncharacteristic intensity. She opened her mouth to question us but was cut off by Franky.

"Alright." Franky shrugged, a wild animal retreating into the shadows. I tried to catch her eye, tried to prolong our momentary connection. No luck. She was out of orbit. "Ready to go?" she asked Pippa, checking her watch.

Pippa looked to Stasia, debating something. Whatever it was settled away when Stasia wouldn't meet her eye, too busy studying me. "Yeah, sure."

Franky nodded, plucking the joint from behind her ear to place between her teeth. Kicking the window open wider, she crawled through the gap, landing on the damp grass outside. She turned back, catching my eye with the ghost of a smile. Leaning back in the window, she dug her hand into my pants pocket, unearthing my lighter. With a grim salute, she backed into the darkness. I watched a tiny flame flicker in the fog, my lighter guiding her way.

Speechless, I turned back to the girls. Pippa looked exhausted. Stasia seemed mystified.

"Well," Stasia announced. "I guess you need a new lighter."

We walked Pippa to the door and went our separate ways. Stasia and I stumbled home, arms linked against the warm wind. I dodged her questions on Franky, distracting her with chatter about Pippa. We went about our nightly routines, taking turns in the small bathroom, brushing teeth side by side. I retired to bed as Stasia hopped in the shower, neurotic in her need to always "wash the outside off of her." I lay beneath blankets and stared up at the ceiling, listening to the soft wind, the rain of Stasia's shower. Thought about Franky's monster, her mischievous smile, the trickle of fire chasing her across town. It was magical, the time-share I purchased in her little oasis.

Room spinning around me, I fell asleep smiling.

DEATH ROW

Loose limbed in rubber heat, Pippa and I spent the afternoon sitting in front of a rotating fan, awkwardly avoiding monster talk and taking turns complaining about the humidity. We would've continued doing so indefinitely, I imagine, if Franky hadn't stormed into the break room.

"Why is Sherry alone out there?"

Pippa and I stared at each other, mirrored confusion.

"Sherry?" Pippa asked, mouth hanging open to catch the breeze.

"The new employee. The *teenager*. She's flailing like a fish out of water while you two are in here, making moves on an electric fan."

"Easy, Franks. We've hardly gotten to second base."

"Sorry," I interjected, blushing under the heat of Franky's eyes. "It's just really hot out."

She shook her head, stomping over to sit between us on the couch. It was the first time I had seen her since the party three days ago, and I felt like she was avoiding me. Lost on how I could possibly bring this up, I simply watched her. She was a sight to behold, an iceberg drifting by. I watched her basketball shorts rise up, toned thigh pressing against mine. Skin sticking together, leg hair soft and staticky. She leaned forward to catch a breeze, beads of sweat running down her long neck, dipping into the valley of collarbones. Her cropped band tee hung on an angle, exposed shoulder sun-kissed and sticky. Franky took off her backwards baseball hat and ruffled her hair, fluffy fringe falling into her eyes.

I looked away, catching Pippa's eyes to find a picture of amusement.

"I, um, I'll help Sherry with cash?" I jumped up, dabbing the sweat off my forehead.

Franky gave me a strange look, while Pippa burst into laughter, waving off my fury and Franky's confusion. "Just laughing at how dedicated Lawrence is," Pippa explained weakly, still giggling.

Franky stood to join me in the doorway, hand reaching up to my waist, steadying me. I hadn't realized that I was swaying.

"Thanks, kid." She gave me a small smile, fingers brushing back and forth along my sliver of exposed skin. "Try not to melt out there."

I was trying not to melt in *here*. Her hand must've been a million degrees, it was unbearable. I could've stayed there forever, warm in her sun.

"If you do," she continued, amused by the clear effect she had on me, "I'll send Pippa out to mop you up."

"That's not in my job description," Pippa retorted, a million miles away.

"Why can't you?" It came out under my breath, desperate and whiny.

"Hardly in my job description either, honey." Franky smiled. "But alright. If you turn into a puddle, let me know." She shifted closer, leaning into me. Her voice dropped on the next bit, too quiet for Pippa to hear, almost too quiet for me. "I'll bring a straw."

Unfortunate creature that I am, I wheezed and coughed like a drowning fool, choking to the point of feeling that my safety was compromised. Franky watched me struggle for a moment, eyebrow raised and deliciously unruffled. I barely pulled myself together when she pulled away, giving me one last scorching look. It was over too soon. I sunk in on myself as I watched her slink away.

"Jesus, Lawrence," Pippa exclaimed from behind me. "Way to be subtle."

I flipped her off, mouth flat. Pippa's laughter followed me from the room, and I couldn't help but smile. My attempts to break through to Franky akin to defrosting an iceberg with a hair dryer, but I was getting somewhere. My skin was still warm from the places she touched me.

Francesca Delores was a wonder of limbs, hair, and men's apparel.

I could've killed myself, I wanted her that bad. I kept asking around town about her, an investigative journalist chasing smoke. I struck gold with Sherry, Franky's new hire and a nosey local. Also, loose-lipped and easily bought.

"Her father's on death row," Sherry said, staring down at a finger trap I gifted her.

"No shit." I whistled. "I thought that was illegal."

"Made a special exemption for him. That's how grisly it was."

I hummed thoughtfully, letting a moment of silence pass. "So, is she single?"

"Christ, Lawrence," Pippa let out a quick snort of laughter, appearing behind me. Sherry peeled off, abandoning her chair, finger trap, and the conversation, for Pippa to take over. "You're so tactful. Anyone ever tell you that?"

I snorted at her sarcasm, the attempt to push me off base. "You've hid a lot from me."

"I told you Franky had a lot going on."

"You didn't say it was *this much.*"

"Not my information to share."

I hummed, annoyed to admit that she was right. "So is she single?" I tried again, insistent that Franky's dating status was surely in the public domain.

Pippa considered me for a long moment, considering her options. "Yeah," she said finally, laughing despite herself. "Yeah, I guess she is."

"But the death row thing?"

"Don't bring it up," she warned. "It was—Jesus. Do I seriously have to tell you this?"

"If you don't, someone else will."

Pippa scrubbed a hand over her face, resigned. "Fine. Fine! Just don't tell her I told you." She searched for words, finding the investigation fruitless. "He . . . Okay. The murders. I'm sure you know about the murders."

"What about—" It clicked slowly, terribly. My chest hurt. "Her *dad*—?"

We held horrible eye contact, the reality of this revelation heavy in the air between us.

"Yeah," she answered, giving me a moment to marinate in shock. "I still don't know how they connected it to him, but I'm sure you know how word travels in small towns." She jammed her fingers into the finger trap, breathing heavier. "Apparently they found pieces of the victims buried on his property. Connect the dot puzzle sprawled across the abandoned lot at the other end of town."

I thought of the space in question: the shell of unfinished buildings, nothing but concrete walls, graffiti, and vines. I walked past it every day. A graveyard on Franky's property. "*Christ*," I muttered.

"Yeah." Pippa grimaced. "So, give Franky some wiggle room. She's a bit . . . neurotic."

I reconsidered Franky's monster, with the context of her father being the killer. It was a big puzzle piece. The entire picture shifted around it.

"The murders . . ." I trailed off, unsure how to get into this without institutionalizing Franky. "She thinks a monster did it?"

Pippa looked like she wanted to rub her temples, but she was still stuck in the finger trap. "She's always been into this kind of stuff. She's been dragging me along on cryptid hunts for as long as I can remember." Pippa smiled faintly. "This is an unfortunate place to end up, but it's not as insane as it looks."

"I don't think it's insane, it's just . . ." I struggled to put my thoughts into words. "Did you know him?"

"Her dad?" A strange expression crossed Pippa's face, something guarded and faraway. "I didn't know him that well."

"But you and Franky grew up together?"

Pippa stared at me, mouth flat.

"Was he around much?"

She kept staring.

"Do you guys talk about it?"

"Never." She gave me a meaningful look. "Franky doesn't mention her father, and I've made it clear that I'm not interested in being involved in a monster hunt."

I thought of my strange moments in Mistaken Point, moments I still struggled to wrap my head around. I wanted to ask more, but Pippa seemed to be nearing the end of her willingness to indulge me.

"I still really like her," I said.

"You don't know her."

"I'm trying to."

"Trying indeed." She met my eye for a long moment. It was gory, whatever she was looking for. "Tread carefully, Lawrence," she said at last. "I know you have good intentions, but you don't know what you're getting into. This monster, it's . . . it's more than you might think. It's *intense.*"

"I'm a lesbian," I joked. "I can do intense."

"No, more than that. She's . . ."

"Traumatized?"

"More than that."

"That's okay. I'm not going to run off screaming—"

"It's not just the murders, he . . ."

"—because she's processing the most insane—"

"Her *hand*," Pippa interrupted, voice low with impatience. "Her dad ripped off her fucking hand, Lawrence."

"Wha—" I choked on my own spit, nearly falling to the ground. "No . . ."

"That's what everyone thinks." Pippa's eyes hardened. "Franks had a left hand before all this went down. Now she doesn't. I dunno. Maybe people aren't so crazy for connecting those dots."

"He—o-or the thing, it—"

Pippa shut me down quickly. "I don't know, Lawrence. I truly don't know."

I held my hands up in surrender.

"She never told me a thing," Pippa muttered. "Never uttered a damn word about it, no matter how hard I tried. So if you—" She paused to think. "If *you* can somehow manage to get something out of her, be my guest. But hear this"—she freed one hand, pointing the finger trap at my face in warning—"do not fuck around with her. If you're serious, if you're really, *really* serious, tread carefully. But if you're not? Back away. I'm not kidding."

I opened my mouth to agree, pushing the finger trap away from my nose.

"Seriously, Lawrence. This isn't a challenge or exaggeration. Franky is my best friend, I've known her for years. There's . . ." She cut herself off with a sigh. "Just be careful with her."

I wanted to ask Pippa who she was so worried about, Franky or *me*. I never got the chance, a group of preteen boys pushed into Funhouse, demanding Pippa's assistance at the front desk. But her expression haunted me for the rest of the day, the shadow of fear darkening every attempt at lightness.

It's me, I thought distantly, watching her count out tickets. *She's worried about me.*

And to be concerned about a new coworker over a longtime friend, well. There's something to that.

Stasia and I didn't get a chance to chat until Debriefing Friday, both busy with coursework and jobs and Stasia casually seeing a girl that could've passed for her sister.

"So," Stasia greeted, throwing herself onto the opposite end of the couch. "I met Franky."

I waited for her to get settled, blanket draped across her legs despite the oppressive heat. We smiled at each other, amused with the chaos since our last touchdown. I couldn't help but feel nervous, anxiously awaiting her review.

"You met Franky."

"She's insane."

I sighed dreamily, chin resting in my palm. "I know."

"Pippa is very protective over her."

"*You're* very protective over *me*."

She conceded, however insisted the two were vastly different. "You're not chasing smoke."

"I've certainly attempted to."

"Your metaphors are so trite. Running away from home is incomparable to chasing a made-up monster."

"Who . . ." I took a long sip of my coffee, working up the nerve to step into a bear trap. "Who says it's made up?"

"*Delores Franklin*."

"What! I'm just saying—"

"I know you're not being sucked into—"

"There's a *possibility*—"

"—a literal *conspiracy* because you think this girl is—is—"

"I'm open-minded!"

"—is *hot*."

"But she is hot!" I whined.

"You need to get laid."

I conceded that both were true, stuck on the subject. "I'm monopolizing Debriefing Night, I know. She's just . . ."

"Yeah." Stasia sighed, picking at the order label on her coffee. "I saw."

"And I discovered some new information about her the other day, that, um . . . it adds a bit of context."

Stasia waved me on.

"You're gonna get mad at me."

"Why would I possibly—" Stasia stared at me, eyebrows shooting up at my expression. "Oh my God, what?"

"Her . . ." I sighed, collecting courage. "Herdadwasthekiller," I spewed out in one breath, hands held up as I prepared for the blow.

"*LAWRENCE!*"

"I knew you'd get mad!"

"Mad? This is *insane*. She's the Frankenstein Killer's daughter? I didn't even know he *had* a daughter, how did they—" Stasia's mouth dropped, connecting dots at the speed of light. "Oh, God, her hand . . . oh, God, do you think—wait, wait, wait . . . the monster . . . does she really—?"

I grimaced, shrugging.

"*Lawrence.*"

"I know it's—I know how it looks, but—"

"*Lawrence!*"

"But why would she lie?"

"Her dad—"

"Okay, okay, just—she says there's something strange out there, right? I've seen strange things!"

"And?"

"And . . . maybe it's just that simple?"

"A *monster* is that simple? Think about what you're saying, Lawrence. A *monster*. A *creature*. A big, spooky, woman-eating *beast*."

I thought back to that night in the park, the strange thing hunting me down. I was high, sure I was high, but I've been high lots of times without seeing spooky visions. Was that *thing* Franky's monster? Or am I going too far, with my attraction to Franky and general absurdism?

"Alright, alright, maybe not a monster," I surrendered. "Maybe just . . . leftovers? Strange energy left behind from the murders. Don't you feel how weird this place is?"

Stasia narrowed her eyes. "Elaborate."

"People are watching us, and they're being weird about it, remember? The—the grocery store man, the guys at the bar, it seems more extreme than your typical small-town attitude. It freaks me out, Stas, seriously, and Franky's the first person I've found who's willing to talk about it. She's the first person who . . ." I trailed off, staring out the window. "Fuck it, maybe it *is* a monster. Why not? Why not hear her out when she's probably the closest person on earth to all of this?"

Stasia's eye twitched, trying to reason with me. "Don't you think her being so close to it discredits her?"

"Maybe." I shrugged. "Or maybe it gives her the clearest perspective."

"*Lawrence.*"

"*Stasia.*"

"A monster," she repeated. "C'mon, Del. I know Franky's hot, but she's not *that* hot."

"What would she gain by lying?"

"Her father's freedom?"

"Come on, man. If he's *really* the serial killer, if her own *father* hates women enough to butcher them, then why would she want him free? Why would she go through so much work to invent a creature when no one even believes her anyway?"

Stasia grumbled to herself, annoyed that I piqued her interest. "Monster aside," she relented, "you have to admit that her dad being the killer adds an insane layer."

I conceded.

"And what if serial killing is genetic, and you're waltzing right into a bear trap?"

"Hottest bear trap I've ever seen."

"You—" Stasia laughed despite herself, shaking her head incredulously. "You're ridiculous."

"I just like her." I shrugged. "And it's not as bad as it sounds. She's just . . . traumatized."

"And you can fix her?"

"I can at least *try*."

"Lawrence . . ." She shook her head. "Would you just . . . God, just be careful, would you?"

"Alright." I held my hands up in surrender. "I won't do anything stupid."

"That'll be a first."

I checked the time. "Anything else to yell at me for?"

Stasia considered. "No, I think I've emptied the tank."

"Awesome. Wanna do sides and apps?"

Broke students, Stasia and I started a tradition in first-year university where we'd order only cheap side dishes and appetizers from a restaurant, sharing the loot. Stasia agreed, pulling up her phone to research local restaurant menus. We put in a delivery order of mozzarella sticks, truffle fries, and chicken wings, with Stasia setting the cutlery while putting me on Track the Delivery duty.

"She's here!" I announced excitedly, slipping on my clogs to meet the driver at the door.

Stasia mumbled something in reply, too far away for me to hear.

I left the door unlocked behind me, racing down the staircase to watch a young woman with a paper bag walking towards the door. I waved through the glass, but she didn't notice me. She was frozen, staring to the right of the apartment. I tried to map out what she might be looking at, wondering if I was right in thinking there was a parking lot in that direction.

I reached out to open the door, but the woman let out a bloodcurdling scream, scrambling away to her car. I heard muffled pleading, her voice thick with tears as she backed away.

Confusion turned to terror as I noticed a dark figure cross the window, chasing the woman with a horrifying slowness, as if it had all the time in the world. The shadow stopped in front of the doorway, as if sensing my presence, and I jumped back before I could get a clear picture, knocking into the staircase banister and falling hard on my side.

Everything was still for a moment, still and silent. I heard the delivery woman slam her car door shut behind her, standing to see her speeding off down the street, bag abandoned near frantic tire tracks. The figure following her had disappeared into the darkness. I waited for a painstaking moment, frozen in fear. Nothing happened.

Inching towards the door, I pressed my nose flat against the frosted glass window, trying to spot something that would make a grown woman fall over herself in terror. Nothing. The tree line was silent, streets empty. Slowly, carefully, I inched the door open, cautiously sneaking out to grab the food. Nothing bit my arm off, nothing jumped out at me. Quick as lightning, I shot back inside and locked the door. Still, nothing happened. I scanned the area for whatever was chasing her, trying to process the snapshot I saw. Tall, dark, scary. Was it a man? Or that . . . that Franky-monster that kept popping up?

I heard a car engine start, and I pressed my nose against the glass to see a man drive past the apartment, following the direction of the driver. Was he the threat? Or just a coincidence? I stepped away slowly, letting out a shaky breath. The food was warm, pressed against my stomach.

With shaking hands and an ache from where I fell, I walked back upstairs, clutching tight to the paper bag.

"What took you so long?" Stasia asked, meeting me at the door to help with the bags.

"I—she—" I stumbled over words, waving her off. "Nothing."

Stasia nodded, bringing the food to the counter to unpack and divide it out. She paused, leaning closer to inspect the brown paper bag. "Huh," she said, holding it against the light. "Why's our order all crumpled up?" She traced the dirt, the rips and tears. "Was it a hit-and-run kind of drop off or something?"

"I . . ." I chewed my cheek. "I didn't get a good glimpse of the driver."

"She must've been in a rush." Stasia pulled a smushed take-out container out of the bag. "Our mozzarella sticks have been compromised."

I forced a laugh, breathing deep. I fought off the urge to confess, to tell her what I saw, because in all honesty, I couldn't even be sure. What did I see? A woman frightened by a trick of light, or a victim of something bad?

"That's weird," I announced finally. A full truth and half lie. "Can I see the order for a second?"

Stasia passed me her phone, opened to the delivery app. She was still speaking to me, sputtering about service these days, encouraging me to request a refund. I wasn't listening. A message popped up, prompting me to rate my experience with the driver. Maxine. I stared at her smiling icon, wondering how concerned I could logically be about a stranger who seemed to get away. And get away from *what*, exactly? I hadn't even seen anything. Not really.

I resolved to keep an eye on it, maybe ask around about local Maxines if I got the chance. Stasia took back her phone and passed me a plate, gently hurdling my attention away from mountains of anxiety and doom. We spent the night sitting side by side on the couch, picking away at supper before picking away at coursework. The night passed slow, and my mind wandered on. By the time midnight rolled around, I stood with shaky feet, pushing away a perpetual paper.

"Are you okay?" Stasia asked.

I turned to see her watching me warily. "Sure," I said. "Why?"

"You've been acting strange all night."

I nodded, too tired to argue. "Feeling weird."

Stasia nodded. "Go to bed."

I obliged, calling out a tired *goodnight* as I finished getting ready and closed my bedroom door behind me. I stared at the wall, stared out the window, considered the strange, unforgiving sea that bordered our town. The only way off this island was by boat, or the small bridge connecting us to the mainland. Lobster pots lined the coast, bobbing like apples.

Sleep came slow. I tossed and turned and thought of a million different things, but mostly my cowardice. Instead of helping Maxine, I kept the door locked. Propelled backwards and away from the mysterious threat. I could've made a noise, could've scared off whatever scared her, but I just jumped back. And now what do I have? A snapshot of somethings: a woman terrified, something following her, a car chasing hers. What is that? What could I possibly do except marinate in the discomfort of being an unwilling witness?

I felt guilt flare in my chest, warm as winter embers; someone else was on fire, but I still tuck-and-rolled.

YELLOW

I strolled into class with two minutes to spare, iced matcha dripping condensation onto my desk. I wiped the puddle with the sleeve of my fleece, too hot for this type of weather, but my class today was in a notoriously cold building, crisp air making me excited for fall.

I pulled out my laptop, opening a word document to take notes. A text from Stasia loudly chimed in, and I scrambled to turn my ringer off, sending a bashful smile across the room. A crowd of classmates glared at me, their grumbling complaints barely placated by Deidre, who hadn't sat next to me since the party.

STAS
Do you have work tonight?

ME
yep
5-9

STAS

Okay. I'll save you some leftovers.

I sent back a string of heart and kissing emojis, tuning back into the lecture. The professor trailed off, instructing us to spend today's class time obtaining research for our upcoming literature review. My phone vibrated again.

DAD

Hi Delores just checking in I hope ur doing well. U should check in with ur mother she's worried about you

I stared down at the message, curl of anxiety in my chest. With a spark of guilt, I heart-reacted to his message, leaving it sitting open on my phone.

Contemplating why I went easier on my father, why I could respond to him and not my mom, I opened my text chain with her. The last message was easy enough to respond to.

MOM

Hello?? Are you alive???

ME

i'm doing well, hope you are too

She answered immediately.

MOM

Is that all I get after weeks of you ignoring me??

I scrolled up. She was right. Four weeks since I last touched base.

MOM

What are you doing with your life??

Excellent question. I turned my phone on Do Not Disturb, then turned it completely off for good measure.

Before I could focus back on my schoolwork, I caught whispers of a nearby conversation, classmates circling over a recent news story. Something about a missing woman.

I tucked my hair behind my ear, turning my head their way to catch something to work with. A few girls were giggling at this guy for mentioning an online board, apparently rife with conspiracy. They seemed amused, charmed, even, by his reverent defense of the site, but my stomach churned, recalling what Deidre told me at the party. As the girls poked fun at the guy, I dimmed the brightness of my laptop and tracked down the forum, horrified to find hundreds upon hundreds of posts defending Franky's father.

I clicked through a few threads, cold wet fear slithering through my stomach like a snake. While the majority of commenters seemed to be anonymous internet trolls, there were a significant amount who claimed to be from Mistaken Point, sprinkling "insider info" throughout each post. Those commenters always seemed to blame Franky's mother, Catherine Delores. They claimed that Franklin was a stand-up guy, a real pillar of the community. Some even went so far as to claim that Franky's mother abused Franklin, noting instances of bruising and scratches on the man. Stellar logic these guys have, to trace the natural progression from domestic abuse victim to serial killer madman.

The worst of it all appeared in a thread dedicated to "local anecdotes," encouraging those formerly or presently residing in Mistaken Point to share their perspective.

dirtpirate: I was born and raised in MP and Franklin was always a great guy . . . Everyone is too poisoned against men to see the real danger here.

---

reasonable-dagger: his wife cunt-tharine is definitely behind it all. she's been MIA for ages, has she even checked on her daughter? Maybe because they committed the crime together and knew a low profile would be necessary

user109: its all performative "feminism" mumbo. they don't have the critical thinking skills to see that franklin was the victim.

---

creeppatrol: I'm around his daughters age and she seemed fine growing up but shes a real weirdo now. Wouldn't be shocked if its because of some kind of involvement.

---

dirtpirate: Funny how cuntharine was always town villain until the unjustful arrest, now everyone is too afraid to question these lies! How would franklin even be the bad guy? Cuntharine is the one who up and left, meanwhile Franklin stuck around for his daughter!

It was a community of freaks; excitable women-haters getting together to discuss the victims like cattle. I shuddered, clicking into the "current happenings" thread to read into the recent disappearance. Excluding the small but passionate faction convinced it was Franky or her mother committing the murders, the forum seemed almost *excited* at the prospect of a copycat killer, begging the newbie to come forward and reveal the inner details of the crime.

Closing the tab with the forum and pulling up the local news site, I browsed the top stories, landing on the results immediately.

LOCAL WOMAN MISSING, CALL WITH ANY RELEVANT INFORMATION

Beneath the headline was a picture of a young woman, a little older than me. The delivery driver.

I jumped up from my seat, slamming the laptop screen shut. Classmates sent a few curious glances my way, watching me blaze from the room with my laptop and matcha barely balanced against my chest. I ran to the nearest empty room, opening my computer and scrolling through the details. Young woman, missing since last night. Suspicion of foul play. Police are currently following, looking for any information to help further the investigation.

I thought back to her bloodcurdling scream, the face of pure terror.

But she had gotten away, hadn't she? I struggled to remember, certain I had seen her pickup truck peel off down the street.

My mouse hovered over the anonymous tip hotline and email inbox, guilt chewing through my intestines. Opening my email, I typed a quick summary of my exchange with the woman last night, describing her expression of terror, the speed with which she escaped. I gave my number and address, said I could answer any questions they might have.

I refreshed my email tirelessly all day. I never heard back.

Franklin's Funhouse lived in eternal darkness. Blackout glass, windowless rooms. The neon lights and blinking games served as the only solace, a synthetic sun in a sea of machinery.

Franky showed up an hour after me, arms loaded with documents, papers floating behind her. She muttered a greeting, staring blankly at the coffee I laid amongst the chaos on her desk.

"It's for you," I explained. "You'll have to heat it up."

Franky let the papers drop to her chair, shrugging out of her brown corduroy jacket. "Um. Thank you."

I waved her off. "I was going anyway."

"I . . ." Franky grabbed the coffee, expression puzzled. I turned from my computer, waiting for her to say something, just to be met with silence. She turned and left the room.

I shrugged, clicking through emails, responding to some, deleting others, organizing the rest into folders. It was boring, menial work. I adored it.

Franky returned a few minutes later, reheated coffee in hand. "I, um." She cleared her throat to get my attention. Foolish move, she already had it. "I have some documents, if you wanna check them out?"

"Oh?" I twirled my chair around, rolling over to her desk. "These here?"

"Yeah, it's . . ." Franky laid her coffee on her closed laptop, digging into the pile of papers she just dropped in her chair. "Photographs. Monster photographs."

I nodded, rolling closer. It was a large stack of papers, doodled jot notes, theories, and a manila envelope.

"Do you want to see them?"

I glanced up, taken aback by her shy sincerity. I couldn't place this version of her, confused by how it contradicted every other Franky. Bravado-slick, unhinged-obsessive, faraway floater. I've seen her vulnerable, sure, but never in relation to her monster. It felt like a direct opposition to how manic she was at the party. It was like she was shocked at being listened to for once, and afraid of being shut down. Precious girl, she misunderstands me. I'd stop the world before I'd stop that slow, sweet-like-cinnamon stutter.

"Yeah," I spoke softly, wary of startling her. "Yeah, I'd love to."

Franky nodded, audibly swallowing. Her blunt nails cut into the envelope, tearing it open. The tension was bubbly thick, her standing close between my spread legs. I looked up at her, trying not to roll my chair closer.

"Miss Delores?"

We jumped apart, heads snapping towards the door. A teenage employee shyly poked her head in, apologetic smile.

"S-sorry, there's an issue with the cash?"

Franky gave me a look, stepping away to lay the manila envelope on her desk. I forced a polite smile at the employee as Franky followed her out, drumming my fingers against my thigh as I stared at the envelope. Fuck it. I rolled forward and grabbed it, glancing guiltily at the open door. I know Franky was about to show me, but I couldn't wait however long for her to return and recycle her preamble, if she even brought it up again at all. Better scope through the "evidence" myself and scramble into another chance at intimacy.

I pulled out a stack of photographs, developed in a dark room. The first one was a tree with a long scratch mark through it, probably a bear or something. I kept flicking through the pictures, finding scratch marks, suspicious-looking footprints, signs of struggle against a latched door. It was all excusable, all explainable. I was hoping my moments of terror might align with Franky's quest, but it seemed I was out of luck. I sighed, flicking past yet another scratch mark when my blood ran cold.

I stared down at the photograph in my hand, fingers shaking.

Eyes, the yellow eyes. Empty and hungry and hateful.

It was a picture of a backyard, with two yellow dots peering out from the trees. It could've been headlights, flashlights, an animal, but the hunger felt familiar to me. I squinted, barely anything else was visible, no shape or form or figure, but those *eyes*. I'd recognize them anywhere. The feeling of being watched. The sensation of being hated. My mouth ran dry.

"Lawrence." Franky knocked on the door, leaning against the doorframe. "You looked through them."

I was too shaken to apologize, holding up the picture. "I—I . . ."

"What?" Franky recognized my panic immediately, ducking into the office and shutting the door behind her. "What is it?"

"I—I've *seen* this," I rasped, voice raw. "In the park, one night, it—it . . . I was *terrified*—"

"YOU—" She took a deep breath, steadied herself. Tried again, quieter this time. "You've seen this?"

"The eyes," I explained. "I thought I was—um . . . I was smoking weed in the park with Stasia a few weeks ago, and on the walk home, she went ahead without me. I—I heard this rustling in the trees, went for a closer look and saw this—this—" I gestured around, lost for words. "This thing? I guess you could call it? I don't know, I just remember the yellow eyes staring back at me, and they were *terrifying*. I don't know what would've happened if Stas hadn't come back. She convinced me I was just high and seeing shit."

Franky pushed a fistful of hair away from her face, mouth soft with disbelief. "You saw it . . ." she marveled, almost smiling. It was the closest I had ever seen her look to something like happy.

I tried to calm my manic excitement, laying the picture face down on her desk. "If that's your monster, then yeah, I've seen it."

Franky reached out to me, stopping herself midway. With a disbelieving sigh, she grabbed her notebook, jumble of papers, and manila envelope, shoving them back into her backpack.

"Are you going somewhere?"

Franky waved me off, searching the rubble of her desk for her phone. "Can you text me a shorthand account of what you just said? I need to go."

"You're leaving?"

Franky found her phone beneath a slinky, muttering something about Pippa. She shot me a grateful smile, regarding me with a shy sort of disbelief, like I was some sort of deity gracing the earth.

"I'll see you later." She shrugged on her backpack. "Don't forget about the text."

I watched her tear out of the room, Hurricane Franky off to strike another coast. I shuddered at the memory of the photograph, pulling out my cell phone to text her the requested account of what I had seen. She responded with a simple *thanks*, typing bubble ebbing and flowing before flatlining. I stared at it for a minute, in case she circled back. Fruitless. She was out of orbit again.

Franky chased the monster, and I chased Franky.

I thought about making myself a monster, hoping she'd chase me.

I drowned myself in schoolwork, desperate to keep my mind off of Franky's photographs and the woman's scream of terror. It worked until it didn't; I hit a wall around eight, willing away the last hour of my shift.

Pippa knocked on my office door after what felt like years of staring at the wall, recycling what I'd seen. She gave me an appraising look, eyebrow quirked in question. Dark hair pulled back into two French braids, she traced a finger up and down the straight line tattooed on her chin, thoughtful and curious.

"You alright?" She asked.

I shook myself, crawling out of my hole. "Yeah." I rubbed my eyes. "How's it going?"

"Slow as hell out there." Pippa sat in Franky's chair, rolling back and forth along the length of the tiny room. "You got any plans tonight?"

"Nope." I checked the time. "Just planned to go home, probably hang out with Stasia." I considered Pippa's fidgety attempts to bond, remembered how much Stasia seemed to like her. "Do you wanna come?"

"Really?" Pippa's eyes lit up, excited smile instantly upping my mood. "I'd love to. We could get high?"

"Sure," I agreed. "You can come over around ten? I'm off soon."

"I'll bring the weed." Pippa saluted, happily wandering back to the front once again, leaving me alone with my thoughts.

I debated heading home early, gathering my things when my phone started ringing. Private number. I answered warily, gently shutting the office door.

"Hello, Mrs. Franklin?" A deep voice connected. I confirmed. "I was calling about the tip you submitted, regarding the missing persons report. Would you be able to provide a brief summary of what you saw?"

"Oh, yeah, um. Okay." I paused. "Now? I guess I'll just . . . well, it was last night, she delivered my food. Seemed scared by something she saw, I think a man was chasing her? I'm not sure, I didn't get a good look at it."

"*It?*"

"I'm just assuming it was a man, I really don't know. It had a weird shadow."

"Then what happened?"

"Oh, then she, um . . . I think she drove off."

"Did you see any identifying features of the man that scared her? Or, *heh*, sorry, the *thing*."

I didn't like the officer's tone. So condescending, like I was wasting his time.

"No," I snapped. "I didn't. But she seemed terrified, so—"

"Thank you for the information, Mrs. Franklin."

"Miss."

"Right. *Miss* Franklin."

"Is that it?" I asked, trying not to grow shrill.

"Yes, Mrs. Franklin. That's it."

"Has there been any sign of her?"

I heard a barely suppressed sigh. "It's looking like she just skipped town, wanted a fresh start from an ex-boyfriend. That's not a crime to follow up on."

"But . . . she—"

"Do you have any other relevant information?"

I bit my tongue, angered by the emphasis on *relevant*. I closed my eyes to count to ten. "No."

"Thank you for your time," he said curtly. "Have a nice day, now."

"You, too," I forced out, knuckles white.

I stared down at my phone, blood pressure brimming with annoyance. I took several deep breaths, considering their theory. Hoped beyond a shadow of a doubt that it was true.

Maxine. Maybe she saw this alleged ex-boyfriend following her, maybe he roughed her up a bit when he reached her vehicle. Maybe then she got scared and skipped town. It was plausible. Would explain everything and would sure as hell exonerate me from tossing and turning over her well-being.

I shelved my concerns and gathered my things, replaying my conversation with the police for the entire walk home. I tried to absolve myself, but the sticky anxiety kept getting tangled up in how unfinished it felt. She was gone, the police didn't care, and all I had to soothe myself with was the hope that maybe she had gotten away from whatever scared her so much.

It hung over my head like an anvil. I tried desperately to distract myself yet couldn't help but see her around every corner.

It angered me, to have been made a witness. I didn't know what to do with the guilt that accompanied that, omnipresent as a shadow, heavy as skin. I wanted to put it down, but no one would let me, no resolution arrived. She was just gone, and I couldn't help her. Nothing or no one on earth could let me rewind the clock to help her.

For one shining moment, I thought I might finally understand a little better just how Franky might feel.

RAPTURE

Pippa came over at ten on the dot, surprisingly punctual for a girl one expected to be anything but. She pulled three joints out of her dungaree pockets, bright blue rolling paper.

"Rolled by the best." She winked, amused by my recognition.

"Where is Franky?" Stasia asked, because she knew I wanted to. God love her.

"Lead on her monster." Pippa shrugged. "I don't ask much."

"Ever?"

Pippa shook her head. "I'm too old for Franky's ghost hunts."

I understood Pippa's refusal to feed into the delusion, but I wondered if Franky wanted her to ask. Wanted *anyone* to ask. I recalled the lightness in her eyes, the *relief*. Drunk on validation, town crazy listened to for once. I wondered if she was warm beneath my rapture.

With a smile, I led Pippa to the couch and cracked open a window. I think I found my in.

We all sat balanced on the decrepit fire escape, hands stained with rust. The joint passed between us, sticky summer air. I barely registered Pippa and Stasia's conversation, they were debating the logistics and legalities of running the North Pole. Stasia was reluctant to agree with Pippa's assertion that Santa was a capitalist. I started down at my phone, waving the offered joint away. I was trying to man up and text Franky.

ME
hey

She took thirteen minutes to respond. I sipped a cider, watching the black phone screen.

FRANKY
?

Chronically to the point, the woman was incapable of small talk. I cut to the chase.

ME
do you want help with the monster hunt?

Fifteen minutes without an answer. I circled back and tried again.

ME
i can shoot a gun

FRANKY
calm down rambo

ME
i know you're intrigued by what i saw
let me join

FRANKY
why?

Why, why, why. Christ, she's so suspicious. Why? Could I tell her the truth, in all its raw, gooey details? Because I want her in some sick, immature way I haven't felt since grade school. Primal, poiseless, post-apocalyptic. Because I feel my heart beating inside my body when she walks through the door, old aches returning like a phantom limb. Because I love this game we play, the dizzying circles, the way she tries to ignore the world, but can never seem to ignore me. Because it's been too long, and I've never had to chase something before. Because I miss. I simply *miss*. I'll chase a monster for months if that's what catches her attention, I'd do a lot of things to catch her attention. Because I'm curious.

ME
because im curious

I wasn't sure if it was sufficient, but it was the only truth I could tell her. The night paddled on. Pippa managed to ensnare my attention, Stasia lit up another joint.

"So, you two cowboys skipped town," Pippa commented, blowing a smoke ring Stasia studied like an acolyte. "The locals must've had a lot to say."

"Never gave them a chance to," I responded. "We made out like bandits."

"We basically snuck away," Stasia clarified, trying to replicate the smoke ring. "I told Mom that I was moving in with Lawrence. Didn't mention it was across the country."

Pippa looked to me, but I didn't explain. Couldn't. I gave her a wry smile, thinking back on the night I spent loading a rental car, leaving nothing but a letter. "Did you know that Stasia was my first kiss?"

Pippa threw her head back in laughter, allowing me to gently herd her off my scent. "That's insane," she laughed. "Frank's like my brother. I can't even imagine puckering up to smooch *that*."

My mouth went dry. I almost wished Pippa and Franky had been more than close friends. I wanted reviews, testimonials. I wanted no one on earth to touch her but me.

"Lawrence is like my brother, too." Stasia lightly smacked Pippa, trying to calm her down. "We were, like, ten years old. Hardly the love affair of the century or anything."

"Mom certainly thought it was," I joked, letting Stasia explain that my mom caught us playing house, let her leave out that quote about gays starting the apocalypse. I was a kid. I probably misremembered.

"You guys have such rich lore," Pippa joked. "Any other tales you'd like to tell me?"

My phone buzzed.

FRANKY

are you with the girls?

ME

yea

Back to radio silence. I tuned in to hear Stasia telling Pippa a truly horrendous story about me, embarrassing as all hell. I yelled aimlessly to drown out her voice, stealing the joint in retribution.

"Thief!"

"Traitor!"

"Hey, come on!" Pippa held back our play fighting, stealing back the joint. "She might as well finish the story now, we already passed the mortifying part."

"No . . ." I grimaced. "She hasn't."

"There's *more*?"

My phone buzzed as Pippa shook Stasia's arm, begging her to finish the tale.

FRANKY

ok

invite them over to mine tomorrow afternoon

She sent the address.

FRANKY

i'll see you guys then

Half irritated that I managed to unwittingly invite my friend and coworker along on my seduction mission, I once again grabbed the joint to grab their attention.

"Girls," I said, taking a hit. "How would you feel about chasing a monster?"

I was met with a chorus of booing.

ME

they're down

i'll see you then :)

We ended up on Stasia's carpet, heads mashed together, red eyes looking up at her popcorn ceiling. Stasia shyly traced Pippa's tattoos, asking her questions about each one.

"Importance of the animal," she explained as Stasia circled animal tracks. "Water," she explained a circle. "Just looked cool," she laughed when Stasia's walking fingers reached a fish bone. "One of the victims," she said quietly, referring to a small tattoo of a hawk.

"Did you know any of them?" I asked, high enough to be tactless.

I turned my head to the side, catching a complicated expression of grief.

"Yeah," she answered softly, fingers falling from Stasia's. "I grew up with most of them. One—" She cut herself off, voice thick with emotion. "One was my cousin. Penelope."

Stasia and I sat in silence, slow like peanut butter. It was so horrible, to know something like this about such a casual friend. I felt like an asshole for pulling her into Franky's monster hunt. I stammered, stared, lost on how to respond.

"What was she like?" Stasia asked, gentle in a way she never was.

"Oh, she was a bastard." Pippa smiled. "Smartest person I've ever met, but never smart enough to keep her mouth shut. Mom used to call her a firecracker; she was always causing trouble, getting in fights . . ." Pippa trailed off, trying to compose herself. "I used to get picked on a lot when I was a kid, but she kept me safe. She must've chased a million boys away from me, once threw worms at this guy who was giving me trouble. I don't know who I'd be without her." She forced a laugh. "Except I guess I do." She gestured sadly to herself. "I'd be this."

I shivered, pulling my knees against my chest. We were all frozen in place, staring up at the spinning ceiling.

"Jesus, Pippa," I mumbled, breathless. "That's really fucked up. I'm sorry."

She shrugged. "These things never happen to you until they happen to you. It's almost been a year now. I'm doing better."

I did some quick math. Franky's dad was arrested in February, Pippa's cousin must've been one of the first victims, late last summer. He had a good run, evidently. I hated to think of Franky's dad as the killer, but it was hard to think of a monster when faced with Pippa's agonizing reality.

"How do you . . ." I stopped myself, staring up at the ceiling. "How do you stomach her?"

I didn't have to elaborate. She knew what I meant.

"I . . ." Pippa chewed her cheek, staring up at the ceiling. "I understand her." Pippa said, voice tinny and soft. "It's hard to resent someone you understand."

I tried not to be offended by Stasia's mumbles of assent.

"I know why she can't face reality, and I know why she's been so different since the murders. She's fractured herself." Pippa mimed an explosion. A supernova. A million pieces scattering in a million different directions. "She can't handle being whole, anymore, so she's built this Franky-world where nothing can touch her. Nothing except little monster theories. Everything else gets discarded."

"Like you?" Stasia asked bluntly.

"It's not . . ." Pippa bristled. "I'm making it sound too dramatic. She's not fully gone; I can still see the old Franky in her. She's just not fully there, either."

I thought of the glimpses. The momentary flashes from the past, lightning-hot moments when Franky felt like the sun. I liked her multitudes, enjoyed the cranky intensity and slip-ups of shimmer, but I understood Pippa missing the person she used to be. That was the friend she loved, these new Frankys must've felt like body snatchers.

"You deserve a better friend, Pippa," Stasia said.

"She was the best." Pippa rubbed her eyes, angrily pushing away trailing tears. "You didn't know her, but . . . but she was the best."

I watched her face harden, tear-filled eyes fluttering shut. Her grief was a complicated thing. She was too close to it, I understood that now. She could never be impartial.

Franky's devotion to this monster felt at once immature, insensitive. She was trampling over her best friend's pain, desperate to make sense of her own. I liked the complications of it, the sticky sweetness of crossed wires. Their frayed string of fate was something I could work with. Stasia had been my best friend for years, I could handle juggling some delicate temperaments.

"I'm sorry, Pippa." I gently placed my hand over hers. "I won't let Franky get too carried away with the whole . . ."

I couldn't finish. It felt like a slap in the face to mention something so silly as a monster hunt, when Pippa was in tears over her lost family. And what could I do to rein Franky in, anyway? I'd have better luck controlling a snowstorm.

"That train has left the station, Lawrence." Pippa snorted, expression morphing into something easygoing and amused. A flawless mask. "And I hope you're ready for whatever's coming. Because if she's willing to make up a monster to avoid processing her father's crimes?" Pippa let out a low whistle. "Then she's willing to do *anything* to avoid facing reality."

Reality. I considered that, remembering the note I wrote myself, staring at the lighthouse. The night in the park, the difference between perception and belief. Franky believed in the monster; like me, she saw something that wanted to hurt her, and doesn't that make it real? A layer of reality, at least. One Pippa seemed uninterested in unpacking.

I let the moment pass. Pippa left soon after that, but long after we said our goodbyes, I couldn't help but repeat what she said, bouncing around my brain all night. Her voice so careful, so certain. Franky was not to be trifled with, she was hardly to be tolerated. I watched the lighthouse beam bounce across my room, wondering if in Franky's quest to find a monster, she was running from the real one: her father.

GRIEF

My hair grew dense and coily in this weather, thick as wool. I tangled and untangled my fingers in it—spin, twist, release. Used nonexistent nails to scratch a weather-dry scalp. I stared at my phone, lips pressed together.

MOM

You can't ignore me forever

Rash with indecision, I felt like messaging back *that was my plan, actually*, which in turn would sabotage my plan. I tried to feel above this kind of thing, aged beyond my years. Silly as it was, at twenty-four I felt thick with layers like an onion. Every single Lawrence lined up inside me on death row, each choosing insolence as a last meal. Each Lawrence mad at her mother, incapable of closing the gap.

I remember the first sign of the cracks, the shaky footing. When she realized that I was skipping work, falling into a depressive state, unable to start myself back up again. Reboots failed, pit in stomach, brink of oblivion. She was furious, spoke of my reputation and work ethic the way one might speak of a person's soul and brain: essential to survival, indicative of character. It grossed me out. I told her I'm just a kid, I hated living like this. She told me I was twenty-four years old and didn't get to decide how to live anymore. I asked her if I ever did; she just stared at me.

I told her I cannot fit into modern society. She looked at me like I was stupid, said that everyone feels that way, they just deal with it. I asked her if she ever considered doing something about that. She looked at me in abject horror. We didn't talk about it again. I quit my job and moved across the country a week later.

I wondered what Franky's mom was like, reflecting on her alleged reign of terror. I wondered if Franky would ever like me enough to actually tell me.

MOM

I know you're reading this. I'm still paying your phone bill, you know...

I let my head drop into my hands, watching her typing bubble rise and fall like the tide. I wasn't sure what else to say. She thought that families were a matter of control, I felt like they were a choice. Fundamentally incompatible, I missed her like a childhood Sunday.

My mother's pain was my own. She resented me for being unable to stomach it. I resented her for making me heir to a kingdom of grief. I resented her for—

"Del?"

Stasia at my bedroom door. Impeccable timing. I resented my mother for *me*.

"You okay?"

I forced a grim smile, pointing to my phone. She nodded, walking across the room to gently ruffle my hair.

"Terri-Lynn giving you trouble?" she asked, reading the texts over my shoulder.

"Nothing but."

Stasia was quiet behind me, but I could hear her think. "Do you . . ."

"I don't know," I answered her millions of questions all at once. "I know she's . . . she was never a *bad* mother. Maybe that's exactly my problem."

Stasia was too pragmatic for this to make sense, but she knew me too well for it not to. "It's never easy."

I smiled, breaking into a little laugh. We giggled together, basking in the hilarity of being daughters and having mothers and all the stupid shit that comes along with that. We kept laughing until Pippa's old beater pulled up to our street, honking three times in greeting. It was time to go.

The drive to Franky's house was strange.

Sitting in the mid-afternoon sun, we stared out the windshield in silence; the deafening mix of music and air-conditioning blasted away any attempts at conversation. Stasia kept trying to gauge Pippa's feelings on the excursion, but she kept tight-lipped and synthetically silly. Turning up the music or fiddling with the temperature controls to drown her out. Pippa insisted that she was coming along out of boredom, joking that she didn't want to be left out, but I knew there was something stranger beneath her insistence that nothing was strange. Her shift from vulnerable exhaustion to easygoing cynic felt jarring.

"I'm sorry I've got you involved," I lamented. "I really am."

Pippa waved me off with a tight smile, turning up the radio.

"We don't have to talk about it," I offered, reaching forward to shut off the music. "I told Franky I was interested in the monster hunt, and she assumed you both would be, too. We can just shut her down and play a board game or something."

"You've opened the can of worms." Pippa forced a laugh. "Can't close it now. We need to see this thing through."

"Pippa," Stasia said, sitting shotgun. "No we don't."

"Let's just hear her out," Pippa said. "She'll be heartbroken if we don't. Lawrence has got her all worked up to talk about her monster."

Her monster. I considered that, leaning forward as Pippa pulled into a cul-de-sac. Franky sat spread eagle on her front porch steps, guarding a blue bungalow with grim determination. She stood up as Pippa pulled into her stone driveway, walking a cobblestone path to meet us at the gate.

"Ladies," she greeted, brushing off plaid trousers and a massive black T-shirt. The sleeves had been sliced off, armholes down to her belly button. I watched the sliver of skin beneath flowy fabric, watched her pull Pippa into a side hug, baby hairs sticking to the small of her neck.

"Lawrence," she greeted. "Stasia. Welcome to my home."

"Yours?" Stasia asked.

Franky opened her mouth to respond, but Pippa beat her to the chase. "Intergenerational wealth," Pippa said, shaking her head sagely. "Franky might be the only homeowner in the country under thirty."

"Only homeowner under *seventy*," Stasia responded wryly, turning back to Franky. "You bought it yourself?"

"I came into a sum of money, recently," Franky explained stiffly. "And needed new accommodations. For, um . . ."

We stared at her, jointly understanding why Franky wouldn't want to live in the old murder house she grew up in. I wondered what her childhood was like, with a man like that.

"Right." Stasia nodded, easing up on the line of questioning and letting Franky lead the way inside.

The living room was small, all windows and light. Overgrown plants lined green walls, television stand hosting the murder board from my first day at Funhouse, alive with red string and Post-it notes. A whiteboard covered in half-finished thoughts stood beside it. It was sticky warm, dehumidifier humming in the kitchen, open windows blowing sweet air. There was a wind chime in the corner, throwing slivers of rainbow light across the room. A shard caught Franky's smile, and for a moment she was beautiful and uncomplicated.

"So you guys want to help me catch a monster?"

She shifted, and the light was lost. Back to complicated.

"Is that what we're doing?" Pippa joked. "I'm here because Lawrence said there'd be snacks."

Stasia dug around her purse, unearthing a small pack of candies. "My contribution."

Franky rolled her eyes, wandering into the small kitchen to collect a bowl of chips and four drinks. Three goblets of strawberry liquor, and a bottle of apple juice for our chauffeur, Pippa.

Stasia and Pippa crashed on the love seat, with Franky staking claim to the lawn chair beside the bulletin board. I curled up in the recliner, gently rocking back and forth.

"Here's my evidence," she said in lieu of explanation, gesturing to the board.

She looked like a little kid, shy in front of the grown-ups. It seemed to be too intense for her, too much. Her cheeks were apple red, chest rising and falling rapidly. I wanted to pull her aside and ask if she was okay, but Stasia beat me to the punch, brittle as always.

"You don't have a pitch?"

Franky stared at Stasia, too astonished to be anxious anymore. "Am I meant to give a sales pitch for a monster hunt?"

"A general outline would be helpful," she said. "Like, maybe convince us why we should risk our lives for this."

"Risk your lives?" Franky parroted, incredulous little smile. "Does that mean you believe me?"

Stasia tightened her ponytail, squinting at the bulletin board. "Maybe if you had a solid pitch."

Franky sighed, catching my eye. I gave her what I hoped was an encouraging smile, but I probably just looked unhinged. I was positive she caught me committing the lines of her face to memory.

"Lawrence and I have seen a monster," she said matter-of-factly, fingers fidgeting with the edge of her shirt. "That's what killed those girls."

"Lawrence, you—"

"That night we smoked, remember?" I sipped the wine. Sweet. "I, um, saw something. I told Franky, and it turns out she saw the same thing. Didn't feel like a coincidence."

Stasia chewed her inner cheek, thoughtful. Pippa looked less impressed, picking the label off her apple juice.

"It's—I can't describe it. That's what drives me crazy," Franky said. "There've been little moments, too. Little connections. Once you see it, you keep seeing it. It's like being haunted."

"Great," Pippa muttered jokingly. "More ghosts."

"It's not like that," Franky snapped. "We're not kids playing pretend anymore. I'm serious this time."

Pippa looked like she wanted to say more, eyes stuck on Franky's desperation. I studied them like an anthropologist.

"Have you seen it since?" Franky asked me, almost pleading.

I paused, debating lying to preserve her attention and sanity. "I have seen, like, *weird* things. Just not the actual . . . *thing*."

Franky looked crushed. I scrambled to rectify.

"I thought I saw something at that party, a few weeks ago."

"That time you were on the patio ground?" Stasia asked, eyes lighting up with recognition.

"Yeah, I was—it's stupid."

Franky waved me on, at the edge of her seat.

I explained what happened, dismissive to satisfy Pippa and Stasia, indulgent to keep Franky hooked. I threw in the story of the delivery driver as well, surprised when Franky jumped to her feet.

"Maxine Teller!" she exclaimed, writing the name among many others on the board, scribbling down my testimony. "She was my old babysitter."

"And first crush," Pippa said snidely.

Franky ignored her. "She's older than the others . . ." She had a list of each victim and their age: twenty-two, twenty-five, eighteen, nineteen, twenty-four, twenty-three, nineteen, twenty, twenty-four. Then Maxine: thirty-one.

"Breaking the pattern," Stasia observed, intrigued despite herself. "That's strange. Maybe a copycat killer who didn't do their research?"

Franky tapped her chin, deep in thought. "It's never deviated from the pattern before. How long has Maxine been missing?"

Stasia pulled up the news article on her phone. "Three days."

"Still no sign of her?"

I shook my head. "The police spoke to me yesterday about what I saw, but they seem to think she just took off. Something about a shitty ex-boyfriend? I dunno."

"So her leg hasn't appeared outside of the grocery store. That's a positive," Pippa joked. At my confused look, she explained. "That's how they found lucky victim number one. She was left in pieces along Allister Street, body parts like a trail of breadcrumbs to her heart."

"Fuck," I swore. "Colorful crimes you guys have here."

I felt a wave of nausea, wondering what happened to Pippa's cousin. I could never ask her.

"Nothing but the best," Franky joked weakly. Morbid, considering the millions of circumstances. "So should we make a group chat?"

I couldn't help but notice how quickly she moved on from the gore, how focused she was on the fictional pieces of the story. No wonder she was so excited about Maxine going missing. It was the first disappearance since her father's arrest.

"Who said that I wanted to be a part of this?" Stasia asked, cold in a way that made me think she was still holding Pippa's feelings from last night.

Franky met her energy and matched it tenfold. "You just said it was strange."

"*Strange*, not—"

"And you came to my house, asking for a pitch."

"I've yet to hear one."

"Women are in danger. I want to find what's hurting them. Is that a good enough pitch for you?"

"Would be. Except haven't the police beat you to it?"

"Stas . . ." I mumbled. "Come on."

"No, it's alright," Franky said, holding her hand up to me. "You're not from here, Stasia. I wouldn't expect you to get it. But there are things about this case that don't make sense, things that the police refuse to explain. Have you researched it?" Stasia shifted, nodding awkwardly. "Then you know exactly what I'm talking about. The police dropped the ball. They didn't interview key witnesses, they fumbled the evidence. Hell, they only made an arrest because it was served to them on a silver platter."

I remembered the news articles; killer caught doing something crazy, something redacted, and got linked to the murders because of it. What on earth did he do?

"Okay," Stasia responded at last, reluctant to concede. "Okay, sure. Police incompetence is hardly a revolutionary take. But that doesn't mean—"

"It's not just that," Franky interrupted, hooking into Stasia's inch, desperate to make it a mile. "Everyone's so desperate to tuck this away, they're willing to ignore that things are still happening. It's been snowballing for so long, and now the danger is back, just like I've been saying, I—" She paused, letting her mania simmer. When she spoke again, it was quieter. More conformed. "I know something else is out there. It feels like I'm the only one on the planet who wants to talk about it."

"Why?"

Franky bit her thumb, turning away from us to trace her board of twine. Every connection, every coincidence.

"Because it makes people uncomfortable," Franky announced, walking closer to the board. "They want one person to pin the violence on. They want it neat and resolved, and they've found him. But that didn't magically make it stop. It's . . . it's still out there, and it's getting worse." Her voice broke. "Can't you feel it?"

Stasia looked out the living room window, considering the world around us under Franky's frantic fear.

"Can't you see it?" she pressed, desperate.

Her vulnerability bordered on tragic. Precious, pedantic girl. I wanted to swallow her.

"*Please*, I—" She begged. "Do you understand what I'm saying?"

Stasia broke, just a little, under the earnest heat of Franky's eyes. "You're not entirely full of shit," she said at last, moving to stand beside Franky at the bulletin board.

She analyzed the evidence, lingering longest at my account of Maxine.

"There are countless cases just like that," Franky said. "This is just the first time it's amounted to something more."

Stasia followed Franky to the section of the board labeled *TESTIMONIALS*.

"You compiled all of this?"

"Interviews, eavesdropping, local gossip." Franky nodded. "Look, Maxine told me she felt someone watching her back in March, then again in May. She said she couldn't pick out what it was, but the eyes . . ."

"The eyes line up," Stasia finished, skimming through every account. "The common thread is intriguing, Franky, I won't lie. All of these women are pointing out the same pattern, without presumably ever talking to each other about it."

"You see the theme!" Franky bounced on her heels, gesturing for Stasia to follow her to the part of the board labeled *DETAIL*. "Notice how all their descriptions focus on a *feeling*, rather than tangible, physical presence? It's like they can't pin it down, they just know something is out there. Not some*one*, some*thing*."

Stasia rubbed her chin, lips moving as she mouthed direct quotes.

"Am I onto something?" Franky asked, manic excitement seeming to snap Stasia out of it. "Isn't it . . . isn't there something here?"

Stasia stepped away from the board like a deep-sea diver coming up for air. She seemed to remember that she lived in a world without monsters, chewing on her cheek as she looked to me, then Pippa. "What do you make of all of this?" she asked Pippa, voice soft.

Pippa inhaled, closed her eyes, exhaled. She opened them to watch Franky, studying the precarious light in her eyes, the small fire she nurtured through the storm.

"I don't believe in monsters," she said at last.

Her voice was slow, careful, and I wondered how long these two have been dodging each other. Franky's face fell at the words, surprised despite herself. It broke my heart.

"But don't you think this place is weird?" I interjected.

"Out of towners." Pippa rolled her eyes, tension buried beneath a playful panache. "You're five feet from a strip mall and start getting the shakes."

"No, it's—c'mon, it's more than that." I turned to Stasia. "We were talking about this the other night, remember? People are weird, here. I always feel watched, and everyone seems to hate me. Don't give me that look, Stas, I haven't been here nearly long enough to justify it."

"You underestimate how irritating you are," Stasia muttered.

"People are scared," Franky cut in, shoulders straight to hide her shaking hand. "They're scared, and they don't trust each other. You don't have to believe in my monster, Pippa, but you have to believe that."

We were quiet for a long time, tension mounting.

"This town always was a shithole," Pippa relented. "But that doesn't mean I want to spend all my time thinking about it."

"You could check out the evidence—"

Pippa gave her a brutal look, withering with heat. I scanned the board, mouth dry as I landed on Penelope's name.

"Or you could . . ."

"Could what, Franky?"

Stasia and I were out of our depth. We exchanged an awkward glance, watching what seemed like months of resentment come to a boil.

"You could join for fun," Franky broke. "You could come over and hang out and dunk on my theories and just . . . just be around me again, man. I feel like I hardly see you outside of work anymore and I—I miss you. I know it's . . ." Franky gestured awkwardly. "I know it's been hard and weird since we lost her. I know this is all . . . I just *know*, okay? But I want you around, if you wanna be around." She took a deep breath, gathering courage. "I'd like for you to be here."

Pippa seemed beaten down, crushed under the weight of Franky's heavy heart.

"Okay," she broke softly. The moment shattered around us. "Okay."

"Okay?"

"Yeah. Fuck it, let's investigate."

Stasia's brows shot up. "You really want to be a part of this?"

"You guys clearly need me. No way Frank here has the grit to pull this off."

"Detective Pippa," Franky joked softly. "You always got to the bottom of my mysteries, remember?"

Pippa smiled, resigned into a recycled sort of fondness. "I guess I can be persuaded out of retirement."

Franky bit back a smile, ruffling Pippa's hair. "Stasia?"

Stasia studied Franky, reluctantly softened by her stumbling sincerity.

"Sure." She cracked a smile, squinting at the board. "I suppose I'll join your little monster hunt."

"You sound excited," Franky observed dryly.

"Ecstatic," Stasia quipped, laughing at the absurdity. "Whatever. I needed more after school extracurriculars, anyway."

Stasia and I walked home arm in arm, shivering against the late evening chill. The Atlantic wind picked up, salty sweet and fresh off the ocean. Capelin season.

"So what do you think?" I asked.

"Of which part?"

"All of it."

Stasia reflected for a moment, rubbing her chin. "It's fucked." She announced.

"You've got a keen eye."

"Not much else to say," she said, almost mournfully. "My classmate said that Maxine's ex-boyfriend was really scary. Why . . . why didn't you tell me what you saw?"

I shrugged, uncomfortable. "I wasn't sure *what* I saw."

"I'm sure it was nothing." Stasia squeezed my arm, eyes far away in thought. "I just hope she's okay."

"Are *you* okay?"

Stasia considered me, watching my movements. I knew she was primed to hate the paranormal, the illogical. Her mother wouldn't let her look up her birth chart in fear of witchcraft, consulted a priest when she discovered Stasia's affinity for true crime podcasts. I can't imagine Mrs. Lanes would approve of a monster hunt; surely it would be ungodly.

"Yeah," she answered at last. "Are you?"

I considered her. She knew I barely scraped my way out of the darkness, knew I still spent some nights arguing myself into moving forward. She disapproved of my infatuation with Franky, disapproved of every stupid place it led me. She's not wrong, but it's not that simple, either. They don't understand her like I do. Franky needs kindness, attention, and this is the only way she'll openly accept it. I recognize her monster, I've seen something strange. But above all else, I want her warm and smiling. I want her whole again.

"Yeah," I said. "I'm okay."

And I was. Not consistently, and by no means dazzlingly so, but I did feel okay. We got home and made two cups of tea, arguing over which show to watch. As the night melted by, I felt a small fire in the palm of my hand. New text from Franky.

> **GORE GIRLS**
> **FRANKY**
> stay vigilant girls
> to hunt a monster is to be hunted.

Stasia muttered something about the dramatics, but I couldn't help but nod somberly. Truth be told, there's something to some of the insane shit she says. There just is.

GROTESQUE

Pippa and I spent the afternoon making earrings, sitting on top of and behind the front desk. Franky kept the details of her whereabouts vague, promising an update in the group chat later this evening. Pippa sighed.

"Be honest with me," she said. "Do you believe it?"

I considered the snarl I had gotten myself in, debating my next move. "Yes and no."

"And did you really see it?"

"I think I did."

Pippa seemed content with this, happy with my emphasis on the word *think*. "And what about Stasia? She seems intrigued by it all."

"I don't know," I admitted. "She's unpredictable."

"She's buying it?"

"She's curious," I amended. "I think she'd agree to investigate just about anything if it gave her an excuse to use her little theories and calculations."

Pippa nodded, satisfied with this. "You two add a fun dynamic," she admitted. "Brings some spice to old Franks and me. We were getting bored with each other."

"Old married couple."

Pippa was debating a better comparison when our phones buzzed, a new message in the group chat.

GORE GIRLS

FRANKY

polly's diner tonight at 7?

I checked the time. Quarter after six. Pippa and I were both off at six-thirty, which Franky knew, since she made the schedule. We both texted back confirmation, making plans to carpool. Pippa and I dicked around at work for a bit before arriving early, strolling into an overzealous jungle-themed diner. Bamboo branches lined the booths, cartoon animals staring down at us from the walls.

I was in the middle of making a jungle-themed joke when I was cut off by a crash nearby. A blonde waitress froze when she saw us, staring in terror over a mountain of shattered dishes. I watched in confusion as she stormed up to us, ghost-white and shaking with nerves.

"Is Franky coming?" she asked Pippa, glancing anxiously over our shoulder.

We watched a clean-up crew assemble, picking through the glass. "She'll be here in fifteen."

"Alright, I'll take my break early." The girl nodded, taking off her apron. "Thanks, Pippa. You guys can sit wherever, I'll send over coffee."

We found a secluded corner booth, sitting across from each other on sticky red vinyl. Classic rock played softly from the radio, warm lights dim. I stared at Pippa in confusion, waiting for an explanation.

"Her little sister was one of the victims," Pippa said mildly, looking through the menu. "Victim Number Three, to quote Franky. Cecilia Blint. She had just graduated high school, was planning to move away for fashion school." She forced a weak laugh. "Guess she'll never leave Mistaken Point now."

"Christ."

Pippa hummed in agreement, shifting uncomfortably. The waitress incident set her on edge.

"Does she blame Franky?" I gestured to the waitress.

"No." Pippa shook her head. "Just finds it hard to be around her."

"Because of her dad?"

"Because of her monster."

"Have you ever seen anything?" I asked, mostly for the hell of it. This town had a strange, eerie energy. Monster aside, something felt off.

"Never," Pippa answered curtly. "I don't know if I would, though. What kind of business do I have seeing a monster?"

"What do you mean?"

"I don't talk to men."

I blinked at her. "What?"

"It's a man thing, Lawrence," Pippa said, shocked by my shock. "Oh, come on. Don't tell me you haven't noticed. Franky's all up in arms about her monster hunt, but she hasn't realized that it only shows up around scary men? For such a devoted conspiracy theorist, she sure missed her biggest connection."

I considered this, chewing on my bottom lip. Pippa came across as both silly and dismissive. As if she found Franky's terror childish.

"But isn't there something to that?" I prodded. "Regardless of the whole, you know, freaky supernatural angle she's taking. Don't you ever feel unsafe here?"

Pippa gave me a strange look. "Not really."

"But you—"

"I don't know if you heard, Lawrence, but the big bad wolf has been arrested. The amount of decapitated women in the streets has really plummeted since then."

"It doesn't have to be so dramatic," I pushed back. "It can just be a feeling."

"If you're talking about the whole scary man thing, the only guy I spend any time with is my ten-year-old brother, and he's hardly a weapon of mass terror." Pippa grinned. "Though maybe Franky would disagree with that. He did set her pants on fire once. Hell, maybe that's where this whole monster thing came from. She did really love those pants."

For the first time, I found it difficult to talk to Pippa. She lived in a bubble that was faraway and safe. She categorically refused to let me pop it.

"Alright," I conceded, if just to end the awkward silence. "I guess the things she's saying just make sense to me. In a weird, abstract way."

Pippa sighed, glancing around the diner. People who were once staring at us scrambled to avoid her eye. There seemed to be an unspoken understanding between us, at Pippa's exhausted smile. She seemed to acknowledge that there might be some truth, a *crumb* of truth, in the manic ramblings of Franky Delores, but she took the alternative approach of wondering *what does it matter, anyway?* It wouldn't change a thing. The talisman of violence was on death row, and pointing out its continued existence just made us look crazy.

"I'm like a pariah by association," Pippa joked humorlessly, letting the moment between us drop to the floor.

"Glad to join the ranks." I glanced over my shoulder.

A group of older men were watching us, muttering to themselves over stained coffee cups. I didn't like their energy, but Pippa's complete disregard had me second-guessing myself. I pulled my flannel tighter around me, attempting to hide exposed skin. But it was too hot to be wrapped up like that, so I sat sticky and miserable, fanning myself with the menu.

"Do you resent her?" I asked finally.

Pippa read through three pages of the menu before she responded, loose smile pulled tight.

"She's my friend," she said, as if that answered it all.

"But that doesn't mean you have to—"

"I know." Pippa grabbed a napkin, started shredding it. "Sometimes I wish I could resent her, wish I didn't care so much, because I still feel so much grief. And we could've worked through it together, but she doesn't want to. She wants to play pretend and push people away and—and I feel sick to my stomach whenever I see Penelope on that stupid fucking board—" Pippa cut herself off, anger uncomfortable.

She was quiet for a while, coaxing herself back to normal. I gave her space, unsure what else I could possibly do to make this any easier for her.

"Franky doesn't know what to do with her grief," Pippa mused quietly, staring down at the mountain of napkins. "It makes her irrational, convinced there must be some larger trend or purpose. But you didn't know the victims, Lawrence, they . . ." She sighed. "When the police told Mom what happened, her first reaction wasn't sorrow. It was *relief*. She was worried about Penelope for so long . . ."

I watched Pippa deliberate, chewing her cheek.

"I think she was relieved that the bad thing finally happened."

We sat in a comfortable, contemplative silence. The blonde waitress circled back only once, gathering Pippa's shredded napkins and giving her a soft squeeze on the shoulder.

"Coffee's on the house," the waitress murmured.

I watched these two different women, meeting in the middle of senseless violence. I gave her a small smile, but she didn't look at me. She accepted Pippa's warm gratitude and disappeared out the back exit. I wondered what Cecilia Blint was like. Was she trouble, like Tiffany Summers and Penelope Hawk allegedly were? Was Pippa right in thinking that Franky was inventing the fanatical to give her grief a purpose?

Franky arrived shortly after, wearing a fleece for Mistaken Point's rare cold day. It had a beautiful pattern, and I stared at it and wondered who Franky used to be, *should* have been. People spoke of this "new Franky" as if she were a husk, a grotesque transformation, rather than the natural evolution from trauma. The horror of being changed by the horrors that happen to you. The horror of externalizing this pain, of refusing to swallow down the sharp, prickly anger, when it was all she had left. How utterly unfeminine of Franky.

How much more comfortable would it be for people if Franky could move on and pretend it never happened. If she lived her life in an attempt to sever herself from her father's crimes, rather than shackle herself to the base and refuse to be cut down.

Maybe I should give Pippa more credit. She wasn't wrong. In fact, she was being entirely too generous. I tried to imagine what I would think of Stasia if we were in this position. Maybe I'm discrediting myself, but I felt uncomfortable with the certainty that I would've given her up ages ago. Maybe that's for the best, though. Pippa's resentment sat at her feet like a dog.

"Is Cecilia's sister working today?" Franky asked, sharp voice cutting me from my thoughts.

Pippa and I shared a complicated look, a strange moment of silence.

"Haven't seen her," Pippa said.

"She's probably out back. I might try to go talk to her."

"Franky," Pippa said, exhausted. "Don't."

"What?"

"You can't bother people at work."

Franky played with the sugar packets, sulking like a scolded child. "She never answers my calls."

"Then stop calling her."

Franky grumbled to herself, ignoring Pippa as she turned to scan the diner. Her roaming eyes reached the group of men still staring at us, and she snarled at them, eyes sharp like shrapnels. They met her fury and matched it tenfold. A few of them stood up, gesturing angrily. The diner had all but cleared out at this point, the few remaining patrons side-eyeing Franky suspiciously.

"Franky . . ." I warned. "Take it easy, okay?"

"Can you guys stop telling me what to do?" Franky snapped. "I'm *trying* to investigate."

Franky's version of investigating seemed to be terrorizing the locals. At least her attention was focused back on us, though, rather than the rowdy men now packing their things. Small victory.

Stasia pushed into the diner as the men were leaving, shoulders hunched to her ears. She nearly jumped out of her skin as a man brushed his hand against her back, eyes wide with discomfort. She scurried to our table, throwing herself into the booth beside me.

"Are you okay?" I asked.

Stasia tried to brush me off, finding she didn't have the strength to.

"I'm fucked." She grabbed my coffee, chugged it. "Piece of lab equipment was broken last night, worth *ten-thousand dollars*, and my supervisor is blaming me."

"Did you do it?" Franky asked.

"No, I wasn't even *there* last night. I bet it was Jordan or—or fucking *Kyle*. I know one of those fuckers forgot to modify the settings. I was always reminding them, always—" Stasia let out a rattling breath. "They're letting me take the fall. No one will listen, it's like I'm defending myself to a brick wall."

"What's going to happen?" Pippa asked. "Will you have to pay for it?"

"No." Stasia sighed helplessly, trying to flag down the waitress. "I'll just have to deal with my supervisor making my life a million times more difficult, and I'll never get a good reference from him now, because of the target on my back. My whole future is in the hands of a man as temperamental as a toddler." She cut herself off, losing steam. "It's the exact same shit as my last lab," she continued softly. "What am I doing wrong? Why do they always do this to me?"

"It's not you, Stas. Can't you see that this pattern isn't you?" I grabbed her hand. "You bend over backwards to accommodate them, but they still won't respect you."

"Are you the smartest person there?" Franky asked, cutting into my ranting.

"By no means—"

"She's the most promising," I interrupted. "Don't be humble, Stas. Your research is miles ahead of what those clowns are playing with."

"Well there's your answer. The men are intimidated, and your supervisor doesn't respect you enough to protect you."

"And this is my life?" Stasia asked, sorrowful and steeped in thought. "Disrespect and—and undermining and—"

"Unless you can find the one place on earth free from it," Franky brushed her off, turning in her seat to try to see into the kitchen. "I think I should try to catch Cecilia's sister."

"Who?" Stasia blinked, struggling to keep up.

"I bet she's back there," Franky ignored her. "She's the only one I haven't spoken to, and I know she's seen things. All the family members have—"

"Franky!" Pippa chided. "No! No, I will not let you bother that poor girl. She's been through enough."

"And she could help me stop it from happening to someone else."

"She has no obligation to," Pippa said. "If she doesn't want to be involved, don't force her to be involved."

Sensical advice, but Franky crossed her arms, pouting. I was worried about another blowup, but Stasia cut in, mitigating the tension.

"I've been asking around about Maxine," she said. "A girl on my softball team knew her."

It was a genius diversion. Pippa turned away while Franky's eyes lit up, pulling out her notebook.

"What'd she say?"

"Same thing as your research. Telling people she felt unsafe, mentioned feeling *watched*." Stasia spoke slowly, watching Franky write. "Everyone seems to think it was the ex-boyfriend."

"I never understood what she saw in him," Pippa said. "He was always such a dick."

"Where's the ex?" I asked.

"Still in town," Franky said. "He's an engineer, works at the plant. I managed to corner him yesterday, and his story lines up. He said he hasn't spoken to Maxine since she got a restraining order against him after that party last month. Remember, Pippa?"

Pippa shuddered. "*Such* a dick."

"The police have already cleared him, not that I trust those clowns, but he seems to have a solid alibi." Franky snapped her notebook shut. "And get this, girls: she saw the eyes."

"Really?" Stasia leaned forward.

"I spoke to her mother today—"

"*Jesus*, Franky," Pippa cursed.

Stasia seemed equally horrified and impressed by Franky's determination.

"—and Maxine kept talking about 'yellow dots' in the backyard," Franky continued. "Yellow. Dots. Sound familiar?"

Stasia whistled, and Pippa grumbled under her breath.

"She seemed to think it was a flashlight," Franky said. "She was convinced that someone was back there, trying to look in her window, *watching* her. So I showed her mom the picture of the eyes, the one Lawrence saw, and it seems to line up."

I shifted uncomfortably, trying to stomach the severity. Pippa met my gaze, strange understanding.

"The common themes are there, same as the other victims," Franky continued. "Feeling watched by some*thing*, that inexplicable sense of danger. The monster has Maxine, no doubt in my mind. Knowing its pattern, it's definitely killed her, but it hasn't displayed anything yet. Why?"

Infinite girl with her one-track mind. Her multitudes were mind-boggling, but she sharpened herself to a point, determined to be singular. I glanced up, finding her eyes on mine. "Maybe it wants our attention," I suggested softly.

Attention. What a novel concept. Franky considered me, staring through a sea of fog. Could she feel my heat? The intensity of my gaze? I wanted to be her monster, I wanted her attention. Dangerous girl, red flags scarlet like sunset, I would've accepted anything she threw my way, as long as she was looking at me.

"Attention." Franky hummed, eyes on mine. "Funny that even a monster just wants to be witnessed."

Stasia paid for a round of milkshakes, then took off early to head to the lab. After running out of things to talk about, Franky disappeared into the night while Pippa brought me home, a moody melancholic number playing through gritty speakers. We were quiet for a while, contemplating the events of the day. I wondered what Pippa was feeling, if anything.

"She's complicated," Pippa announced finally, stopping at a red light. She avoided my eye.

"She's nothing but."

"So you see where I was coming from, when I warned you—"

"When you tried to save me from her reign of terror? Yeah, I get what you were saying." I laughed, crashing quickly. "I can't believe she spoke to Maxine's mom."

"She's done worse."

"I can believe it." I sighed. "You were right, about her Frankyworld. She can't see anything but her monster."

"It's her escape," Pippa said, voice slow, rattly. "The only way she can stomach being her father's daughter."

And how could I hold that against her? My trepidation had already melted into fond empathy, sticky with softness for the unbearable girl.

I hummed, shaking my head. "I still really like her. Is that stupid?"

"Very stupid." Pippa smiled, reluctantly amused. "But I understand. She's very lovable, once you get past all the . . ." Pippa waved her hand around vaguely.

"Yeah," I grinned, staring out the window to watch the world pass us by.

It was a strange afternoon, made stranger still with each piece of Franky I collected. Her fascination with the fanatical, the preoccupation with placing her grief. A grief that she and Pippa shared.

"Are you okay?" I asked, turning back to her. "I know it must be hard, to—"

"I'm alright," she interrupted, pulling in front of my apartment. "Don't worry about me, Lawrence. I've been dealing with Franky's nonsense for a long, long time. *You're* the one we should be worried about."

"Me?"

"Oh, absolutely. It's been ages since Franky couldn't scare someone off. Penelope was the last person who handled her so well, but even Penelope had her limits." Pippa smiled sadly. "Who knows how strange she'll get in the safety of your support."

TERROR

I had the next few days off work, left to pace around the information left at my feet.

Life went on otherwise; Franky's monster all but in the back of my mind as I went about my days. With every Maxine avenue leading to a dead end, the group chat gradually pinged with more jokes than investigations, and Franky seemed surprisingly okay with that. She even responded sometimes, in her classic Franky way, curt, amused, dripping in irony.

Relieved with the change in pace, I got home late from class and bustled around my apartment, messaging a stranger I planned to buy a motorcycle from. We negotiated prices as I tidied the kitchen, listening to a podcast about cryptids. Franky had sent it to the group chat earlier today, recommending we read up on other mysterious entities as we chased down our own. I think she just wanted an excuse to talk about her favourite conspiracies.

The host rambled on about footprints as I circled the apartment, mindlessly working through overdue chores. I was digging through the pile of clothes on my bed, slowly folding and putting them away, when I heard a loud crash in the kitchen.

"Stasia," I muttered to myself, laughing. I turned down the volume of my headphones, in case she wanted to pop in and chat.

Five minutes passed without another sound. Shrugging, I tried matching odd socks, humming to myself as I wondered what Stasia was up to. Maybe she—

CREEEAAAKKKKKKK.

I froze, mismatched socks still in hand. I backed away from my bed until I could see the small crack in my barely open doorway. A sliver of light. I glanced down the hallway, pausing the podcast and stilling my breath. I didn't see anything, slowly edging out the door to investigate. The apartment was dark, streetlights reflecting in the kitchen window. Circles of light at the edge of the hall. Shadows were playing funny tricks on me, the sounds of nails on linoleum. The crunching of broken glass.

Broken glass?

Knocking some sense into myself, I backed into my bedroom and gently shut the door, twisting the lock shut. Pulling out my headphones, I tossed my phone on the bed and forced myself to laugh, certain that Stasia must be out there, acting strange. Maybe a long day at the lab, or she just—

CRASH.

I jumped, rushing back to the door. This one was closer, in the bathroom between my and Stasia's rooms. It, whatever it was, was out there, just in the hallway. Another creak, another scrape. Close, closer still.

One palm flat against the door, the other holding the latch, I couldn't help but think about what a stupid way to die this was. I could imagine the headlines: *Creature Commits Break and Enter. Kills Girl While at It.* It would make Franky happy. Not my death, per se, but another red string. She'd bubble wrap my corpse in it, tie me to that silly bulletin board until the end of time. Another clue to keep her going, another crumb to a meal I hardly believed in.

Creeeeak.

Quieter now, cautious. Nails scratching, heavy breathing. Sniffing, air thick with condensation. I clutched the doorknob tighter, innards freezing with the reminder of yellow eyes, inches from mine. Yellow eyes empty, empty, emptier. A vessel for hunger, a vessel that wanted me stuck inside it forever more. I choked back a sob, choked down an anxiety attack. Whatever was out there, it was on the other side of my humidity-warped bedroom door. And it hated me.

In. Out.

SCRRRAAAATTCCHHHH.

A nail, one long nail, running down the length of my doorway. I heard every inch of its journey, felt the vibrations as I pushed harder against the door.

Something pushed back. Pressure meeting me halfway. The doorknob slowly wiggled in my fist, fighting to escape my grip. *It can open doors*, I thought distantly, bile bubbling in my throat. Is there anything scarier than a monster that can open the door?

I cycled through affirmations to myself: *You will not throw up. You will not cry. You will not let the scary monster into your bedroom to eat you whole.*

With every ounce of strength, I held onto the knob for dear life, pushing, pushing, pushing. My palms stuck, fingers sweaty, desperate to hold on.

Creaaaakkkkk.

A loud snarl from the other side. With a grand slash, the creature tore at my door, ripping nails into the wood. Shocked, I jumped away, crying out in fear as I lost my position. Scrambling back, I watched in horror as the knob twisted open, the door slowly cracking an inch towards me.

I breathed in. Out. Waited. Another inch. Tentative scratches, something sniffing the air. I squeezed my eyes shut, paralyzed with fear.

Further away, the front door opened.

"Lawrence, are you—?"

Stasia!

"St-Stasia—" I croaked, opening my eyes to watch the bedroom door. The inching open had ceased, door frozen in place.

"Lawrence?"

"R-RUN!" I howled, dragging my body backwards until my back pressed against the bed, rolling beneath it in terror. Door be damned, I wheezed as I heard Stasia's footsteps, her panicked inquiries, that terrible, terrible creaking sound. A gut-curdling scream.

"STASIA!" I sobbed, hands over my head, ears buried in the sand. "STASIA—"

Creaking, screaming, scuffling. Something being thrown, something crashing against the wall.

I shook my head back and forth erratically, shaking the possibilities out of my mind. I muttered affirmations to myself: *I will not find Stasia's body. I will not be ripped to shreds. I will not find Stasia's body. I will not be ripped to shreds. I will not find Stasia's body. I will not be ripped to shreds.*

Minutes passed. Hours. I didn't hear a thing over my wailing chorus of *no no no no no no.* I was a coward, a fool, I had lost my best friend and would surely follow shortly behind.

"Jesus *FUCK*," someone muttered above me, sandaled feet pacing back and forth in front of my bed. "Lawrence? Are you in here?"

"Down here," I whispered weakly.

Stasia kneeled in front of me, bread knife brandished like a sword. "What," she hissed, "the *fuck* was that."

"You met the monster," I responded weakly, frantically wiping away tears. "Congratulations. Franky will be stoked."

GORE GIRLS

STASIA

I saw it.

FRANKY
rock n roll
i'll be there in five.

Ever true to her word, Franky was indeed here in five. She must've launched herself across town like a rocket.

Shockingly enough, the first words out of her mouth weren't theories, interrogations, or manic ramblings. She kneeled in front of Stasia, letting her hand cup the top of her head like a cap.

"Are you okay?"

Stasia let out a shaky breath, burying her head in her hands. "That was fucked up," she said in an accusatory tone.

"I know honey."

"It hated me. It hated me so much, I—"

"I know."

"I—I never wanted that. I was—" Her voice broke, expression crumpled. "I was scared."

"I know." Franky gulped, eyes catching mine. Nonverbal conversation, words passing without a sound.

Franky piled another blanket on the mound that cocooned Stasia, sitting on the other side of her. We stared into space, silent. What was there to say?

"We won't let that happen to you again," I lied. Of course it was a lie, but what else was I supposed to promise?

I was hoping to sound calm, cool, and collected in front of Franky, but mostly I tried to keep it together because Stasia was my best friend and it scared me to see her like this. She was my rock, the sister I never had in my own. I selfishly needed her to remain as such.

Stasia looked to me, hair rumpled, scar on her cheek. I could tell she thought I was full of shit, but it was unprecedented for her not to call me out on it. The shift in her was palpable; the monster hunt was no longer an interesting project, it had become personal. Stasia was scared.

"Why me?" Stasia asked, voice breaking. "Why *us*?"

"I don't know," Franky answered honestly, clearly at a loss. Concern and safety attended to, it was hard to hide her manic excitement. She had gone rogue.

"We're safe," I announced, unsure who I was supposed to be reminding. Maybe I knew that this would send Franky out of orbit for a while. Give her something to lose herself in for a few days.

"Thank God," she mumbled. "I'm sorry guys. I wish it happened to me, instead."

From anyone else it would have been sincere, touching, a knight-like gesture of love.

From Franky, it sounded like a child upset that she missed the big show.

ICE

Stasia was acting strange.

To be fair, she had almost become monster chow mere hours ago, so I guess that would make anyone neurotic. Especially a person whose general baseline is wired as all hell.

The morning after the attack, I heard strange sounds coming from Stasia's bedroom, poking my head in to find her neck-deep in research on werewolves. It took ten minutes of coaxing to calm her down, gently shushing the manic ramblings on full moons. Pliant as she's ever been, Stasia was agreeable to the suggestion that she go back to bed, hands shaking as I tucked the covers around her ears.

I left her with a cup of tea and strawberries, persuading her to spend the day relaxing. Pippa promised that she would pop by with treats as soon as she was able, so, content with this plan, I set out on my day of errands.

Amidst a strange, horrifying night, I had somehow agreed to buy a motorcycle from that internet lady, a manic purchase if there ever was one. I followed the directions she sent, looking for an old-timey butch named Bobby. Allegedly, this was her place of work and residence.

Tunnel of trees crisp like crab apples, I sidestepped slugs and thought of brighter, more innovative ways to manipulate Franky's eyes onto mine. She never flirted with me when the monster was active, which was admittedly one of my biggest incentives to get rid of it. I kept walking aimlessly until I hit the last of the landmarks, a brand-new mailbox sitting strange in a sea of secondhand. A small house sat at the edge of my journey, nestled between a creek and a coven of trees. The air smelled like smoke, powerlines criss-crossed overhead. Stepping through smog, I went to the garage out back as instructed, finding a pair of legs sticking out from beneath a car, sweat-stained overalls rubbed raw with grease.

"Hey," I called out, "I'm—"

"Lawrence!" the car answered, clattering and bangs following my announcement. "Hold tight, I'm just—*damnit.*"

I waited awkwardly off to the side, checking out a Beach Babe calendar displaying the date thirty years ago. Miss July was a real bombshell.

"Sorry about that." Bobby rolled out from beneath the car, cleaning her hands on a rag. "I'm never prepared for guests."

Bobby clearly wasn't intending for this to be a stop and shop kind of visit; I hardly had a word out of my mouth before she rambled on.

"You're a newbie in town, right? One of those college kids?"

"Grad school," I confirmed. "Moved here . . . a few weeks ago, I guess?"

Six weeks. I've been chasing Franky's whim for six weeks, now. We met on Mars, our time together orbiting slower.

"How're you finding it?"

Bobby was gentle, good natured and curious. Lacking a mother figure and gay friends over the age of thirty, I warmed to her immediately.

"I'm liking it. It's a beautiful spot."

"Make many friends?"

I wondered if she was asking because she knew. It's a small town, people keep tabs on Franky.

"Oh, yeah. I moved here with my friend, Anastasia. And I met some new friends through work, the arcade—"

"Funhouse? That must be how I recognize your face." Bobby tapped her forehead, leaving a smear of grease. "Franky."

Aha. Seems I've found a fellow snoop. "The big boss," I joked. "She around a lot?"

"Yeah." I nodded. "In and out, usually, but. . ." I debated pledging allegiance to Franky to a stranger I just met. Apathetic as always, I rambled on. "I've gotten close with her."

Thankfully, it seemed Bobby was one of Franky's rare allies in Mistaken Point. The shift between us was palatable. A friendly introduction at once became intense, indulgent.

"She's a good kid," Bobby said mournfully. "A real good kid. I'm glad someone sees that."

"You know her well?"

"Hard not to in a town like this. She helps me out around the garage sometimes. Has since she was three apples high." Bobby appraised me, studying my value. Finding something worthwhile, she continued slowly. "It's a real shame, what happened to her."

"Do you mean her father?"

"No." Bobby shook her head. "*Her.*" She paused to think, lost in a memory. "Her father was a good man until he wasn't. I'm sure you know all about that."

I was wondering if she meant that I knew about the murders, or the irreconcilable fact that to have a good father is to have a ticking time bomb.

"I know." I answered both.

"This town loves Franky. She's not the things her father did. None of us are."

I thought of Deidre, the blonde waitress, Pippa's resigned sadness. I couldn't help but wonder how idealistic Bobby was, overestimating the grace that people could scrounge up for Franky. The town did not love her, it hardly stomached her. The people ran far and wide to avoid the ramblings of an uncomfortable victim.

"Franky never talks about it," I said. "All anyone's ever told me is that her dad was nice, and her mom wasn't. Isn't that funny?"

"Not at all." Bobby grinned. "But it makes sense."

"Did you know them?"

"Know them? I grew up with Franklin." She paused, crumpling and uncrumpling the rag in her hand. "No one on earth seemed to know Catherine, though. She was on an island alone."

I chewed on this, confused. "A lot of people seem to hate her."

I watched Bobby think, preparing myself to hear the renowned fables of this woman of terror. It had to be horrible, to dominate the narrative her ex-husband left behind, and to be star of the show despite her disappearance. What the hell did she do?

"She was an icy woman," Bobby said finally. "Icy, icy woman."

Right. Seems I would have to work a bit harder to get to the bottom of this.

"Did she grow up here?"

"No, and I guess that's part of it. She was an out-of-towner from the big city. Had a real complex about it, too."

"How'd she end up here?"

"Reluctantly." Bobby forced an empty laugh. "Her and Franklin met when he moved away for this fancy college, seemed like a real whirlwind affair. She accidentally got pregnant months into dating, so they had to marry and move back here to get help from his mother. She kept saying it was temporary, only temporary, but then it wasn't. Franklin's mom died, then Franklin inherited the house and opened the arcade, so they just . . . stayed."

The current of life can be an undertow for some people. It almost was for me, too.

"I never blamed Catherine for being unpleasant." Bobby misread my pensive silence as judgment and scrambled to fill it. "Hell, I felt bad for the woman. She got swept into housewife jail with a man she hardly knew."

I thought about the life I was almost trapped in, the life my mother wanted for me. I wondered when the first cracks in the relationship with Franklin began to show. Did Catherine see his violence? Was she afraid? Did she stay to protect Franky, or leave to protect herself? Was everyone right in claiming Franklin was the victim of a woman who wanted her own life, rather than the one set out for her over centuries?

"That sounds horrible," I murmured, trying to keep track of the narrative. "So she just packed up and left?"

"The very second Franky graduated. There was always something so strange about it." Bobby was quiet for a moment, thoughtful. "Felt too clean."

"Maybe she saw something in him that no one else did."

I wondered if I went too far, watching a slice of pain break across Bobby's face.

"I don't know, kid." She sniffed, staring down at the rag clenched tight in her hand. "I didn't live with them, I only ever got pieces."

She sounded defensive. It perplexed me. I wasn't blaming her for anything.

"All I know . . ." She paused, struggling. "All I know is that Franklin was my friend."

"He never . . . ?" I trailed off, wary of pushing her too far.

"Never tried to kill me, if that's what you're getting at." Bobby said gruffly. "I mean, he could be angry. Sure, he was angry. Got into trouble sometimes. Fights with the guys, banned from bars, domestic disturbances. Typical stuff like that. But I never thought—" Bobby clenched her jaw, turning away so I couldn't see her eyes fill with tears. "I found one of them. One of the girls."

My mouth ran dry, words failing me.

"I'll never forget it," Bobby lamented. "For as long as I live, I'll never get that image from my mind. It'll haunt me forever."

"God," I muttered, horror struck.

"Little Genie Templeman." She shuddered. "She used to ride her bike past my shop every morning, always waved hello. I—I found her arm in my mailbox."

"*God*," I parroted. "God, I'm really—"

"Eh, save it kid." Bobby waved me off, wiping away tears. "I'm just dumping all of this on you when you only dropped by to buy a bike."

"It's okay," I rushed to soothe her. "Seriously, it's fine. Franky's an anomaly. I'll take anything I can get."

Bobby gave me a knowing look. She seemed charmed by my tactless curiosity, my search for clues. "She's more than this, I hope you know that. And she's doing good for herself, despite the circumstances," Bobby said. "I'm proud of her."

Curiosity got the best of me. Doing good? Her delusion perplexed me, it sounded like she was trying to convince herself.

"Do you know about Franky's . . ." I debated how to frame this question. "Do you know what she's been up to?"

Silence. I *definitely* went too far this time. Definitely, without a doubt, hit the one spot Bobby wouldn't speak on.

"I know about her monster hunt, if that's what you're hinting at." Bobby forced an awkward chuckle, paling beneath a smattering of grease.

She was defensive again. I couldn't figure out why.

"We've all seen strange stuff." Her voice came out squeaky.

"You have—?"

"So I don't begrudge the girl for trying to find something to do, in such a small town." She bulldozed on, ignoring my previous question. "Why not? Kid needs some levity."

Bobby's anxiety fascinated me, but it felt fruitless to try unpacking. She hardly knows me; her guilt is her own.

"She sure does," I surmised vaguely, letting the conversation taper to a close.

Bobby waited, worried I'd pull another question like a rabbit from a hat. She deflated with relief when I just stared back in silence. I noticed her hands were shaking. She kept checking over my shoulder.

"She's a good kid." Bobby paused, mouth crumpled with pain. "It hurts to see what this horrible ordeal has done to our Franky."

Our Franky. Under guidance and ownership of the town. I tried to picture the past that shadowed her; I was staring at a cluster of stars, trying to find the constellation.

"She's good," Bobby insisted, "I can tell you that right now. No matter what, Franky is good to her core. Nothing could ever change that about her, and of that I'm certain."

I was lost on how to respond, unsure what else I wanted to hear.

"Franklin used to be everything to us. Had his finger buried in every single pie in town, but he was good. I thought he was good. He . . ." Bobby paused, sitting on the brink of letting me go. "Her father built this town, but destroyed it just the same. She inherited a wasteland."

PHANTOM LIMB

I called Stasia the second I left Bobby's, standing beside my new bike as I was sent to voicemail fifteen times. She finally picked up on the sixteenth attempt, barking out a short, "*What?*"

The conversation went as expected. She snuck away to the lab the second I left, denying any previous mental breakdown, trying to gaslight me into believing that she was just overtired and over-researched.

I let it slide, knowing better than to put up a fight. If Stasia wants to remain a repressed creature, teetering the brink of a nervous breakdown, that's her prerogative. I waved goodbye to Bobby and fired up the motorcycle, spending the morning riding aimlessly around town, chasing side roads and smoke.

I texted our group chat about the bike when I stopped for coffee, circling back to the apartment to grab lunch. Stasia was out, presumably still hiding at the lab.

Franky texted back first, not acknowledging my news, but inviting us over to her pool when everyone was free. We agreed to meet up at two o'clock, killing time until then. When Stasia got home, we headed over together, riding my bike through hot asphalt streets. She was curt in her greeting, refusing to entertain talks of anything but school or investigative work. When I asked if she was okay, she stared blankly, fixating on the practical parts of the case rather than the elements that could hurt her. It reminded me of Franky, in a way. Begrudgingly recognizing that Stasia wasn't ready to talk about her feelings, I let her be. It was exhausting pushing back when she was in Brick Wall Mode.

I parked outside Franky's place, going straight to the pool. Franky threw an armful of floaties in after us, and I claimed the doughnut, circling under the sun.

I hadn't seen Franky since Monster Night, hadn't spent time with her since the diner. Sensing the distance, Franky climbed onto the floatie beside mine, summer skin sweet as lemonade. She was wearing the prosthetic arm today. Hair tied up, necklace caught in her moss green bikini straps.

"Your necklace is tangled," I observed before thinking better of it.

Franky's eyes fluttered open to catch me staring, face bright with amusement.

"Attentive girl." She clicked her tongue. "Wanna fix it?"

I made a garbled sound, cheeks flushing rum red. Head thrown back in laughter, Franky splashed me, eyes sparkling. I followed the line of her throat like a disciple, aching at her alter.

The other two joined us eventually, chatting away in the simmering sun. We walked wide circles around Stasia, intuitive enough to know she didn't want to talk about the attack. Ever the empath, Pippa prattled on about her stolen mailbox, perplexed years later by the mystery.

"I still think Penelope stole it," Franky said, seemingly shocked by her own slip-up.

She had nothing to worry about. Pippa's eyes brightened with the mention of her late cousin.

"I forgot that was our leading theory," Pippa said softly. "We even took her to court, trying to get to the bottom of it."

"*Pretend* court," Franky corrected, laughing at Stasia's incredulous look. "Penelope was always fucking with us. We must've brought her to court once a week, but we never managed to actually prove anything."

"It was during my crime show phase," Pippa said.

"And you were always hitting me with that damn gavel Penelope gave you."

"The gavel!" Pippa exclaimed, smiling sadly. "I should find that. I bet it's still somewhere in the playroom . . ." She laughed to herself. "Man, Franks, we had a lot of good times that summer. It's no wonder Penelope wanted to be a lawyer."

"She got awfully good at defending herself," Franky said. "Lord knows we gave her lots of practice."

Stasia and I observed quietly, trying to find a trace of the former trio, one-third of which was dead and buried. It shocked me to hear Franky speak of Penelope so frankly, with such fond remembrance.

"Did she go to law school?" Stasia asked cautiously.

Pippa shook her head. "My family doesn't leave Mistaken Point. We have to look after each other."

"She was doing online courses for a bachelor's degree," Franky interjected. "She was working towards it."

"While working two jobs. Always annoyed me how *impressive* she was."

"She was the busiest person I'd ever met." Franky grinned. "Yet still had time to steal your mailbox."

Pippa broke into laughter, bittersweet as it was, bubbling with grief. I felt my eyes well with tears, turning to blink up at the sun. It broke my heart. My innards struggled to digest the raw, uncompromised grief, sopping wet with undiluted affection. The aftermath was complicated, but the emotions were crystal clear. They loved each other. They would always love each other. Franky and Pippa were as haunted by this love as they were alive for it. Penelope would always be the girl they played with on lazy summer afternoons. She would always be their friend.

By the time I was composed enough to turn back to the group, Pippa had floated away, soaking in a complicated sort of nostalgia. Franky watched her with a fidgeting affection, guarding her space like a watchdog.

I caught Stasia's eye and gave her a small smile, an acknowledgment that we were outsiders out of our depth. She sent back a gentle smile and adjusted her floatie, moving so that her head blocked the sun from Pippa's eyes, allowing her to comfortably stare into space without squinting. We continued like this for eons, spending time together in small movements, incremental acts of affection. I felt Pippa's warmth surround us, felt Franky's eyes on me.

In the heat of the sun, I could almost remember being ten years old again. The last time I felt truly comfortable in my own skin. One summer before I was forced to wear a T-shirt over my bikini at sleep-away camp, two summers before I caught my aunt's boyfriend staring at me strangely.

In the tenderness of Franky's backyard, I became a fluid, genderless creature, body like a board. There was no witness, no watchful eyes, hyperaware of nothing but Franky's sun-kissed skin, so close to mine. Eternal summer, sunny days forever. Franky left to ponder a lead, staring at her bulletin board with goose-bumped skin, but she circled back eventually. I found myself starting to trust the fact that she always would.

We followed her like a pack of stray dogs, but she followed us, just the same.

After an hour of floating, Franky and I were elected to go inside and order Korean food, wearing oversized band tees, dripping onto the hardwood.

"Do you like my new motorcycle?" I asked, trying not to puff up my chest.

She hummed, phone to her ear as she was put on hold. She had a quick, friendly conversation with the woman at the local Korean spot, placing our order and turning back to me.

"It's cool," she answered finally. "Where'd you get it?"

"Bobby."

Franky's eyes flashed.

"We talked about you," I admitted, overcautious against her hypersuspicion.

"What did she say?"

There was an edge to her voice I didn't expect. I knew I was pushing buttons, risking an appearance of Boiling-Hot Franky, but I didn't want to lie to her.

"Not much," I rushed out. "She just . . . told me a little about you. And, um . . . your mother."

I traced the frantic rise and fall of her shoulders. The simmering, the comedown. She looked at me in a moment of shocking tenderness, Vulnerable Franky somehow at the wheel.

"Are you okay?" I asked. "I'm sorry I spoke to her about you."

Franky took a deep breath in. Long breath out.

"Come here to me," she uttered, eyes soft and pleading. "C'mere."

Marionette on strings, I walked to her, not smart enough to be suspicious.

"You're investigating me," she stated simply, fingers reaching out to pull on the strings of my swim shorts. "Still paying such close attention."

"I—I'm not, I—"

She looked at me, yanking harshly on my strings. I propelled an inch forward, an inch closer. We were toe to toe. Her eyelashes fluttered low, long and spindly like spider legs.

"Okay." I melted. "I am."

Franky nodded. "Why'd you ask Bobby? Why didn't you ask me?"

"You wouldn't tell me."

"Wouldn't I?"

I considered that. Was Franky closed off and faraway, fervently refusing to talk about her background? Or did I just assume she was, so never bothered trying?

"What was your mom like?" I asked recklessly.

Franky nodded once, twice, amused as ever by my audacity. Bravado Franky flickered like candlelight, and I allowed myself a small moment of hope, nerves raw as she rubbed against me.

"Sweet girl." She grinned to herself. "You're funny. I'll give you that."

I felt feverish. "Yeah?"

Franky laughed, considering me. She tugged harshly on my shorts strings, at once punishing and rewarding my insolence. There were inches between us. I watched her lips and waited.

"My mother was not a well-liked woman," she said at last.

"I've gathered."

The words spilled out. I was afraid they'd make her angry, but she just threw her head back in laughter.

"I don't know what you've heard," Franky said, "but she wasn't as bad as people make her out to be. It took me years to realize that. She was just . . . *stuck.* She acted like a caged animal because she was one."

Caged. I thought about what Bobby said, the horror of being a woman trapped by your fate. Your fate which has been predestined for centuries. I'm part of a newer generation, but I can still recognize the implicit horror, the sweeping current I almost fell prison to, had my mother got what she wanted and locked me into the modern version of stay-at-home mom: the girlboss that works forty hours a week and climbs the corporate ladder and smiles politely at every man attempting to undercut her success along the way and somehow still has time for two-point-five children, a husband (hah!), a mortgage, barbecues with annoying neighbors, church Sundays, eternal dieting, turning down the things you want, food especially, placating small talk, somehow remembering every stupid name of your coworkers' every stupid child.

I thought of Franky's mom with a sharper pang of empathy. Local housewife wants more. The sheer terror.

"Were you close?" I asked.

"We weren't anything."

I didn't know Franky's life pre-monster, but I did know that trauma does not always make people closer. Sometimes it makes loved ones scatter like shotgun shells.

"Do you . . ." I read her carefully. "Do you guys keep in touch?"

Franky shook her head, expression complicated. "We aren't anything."

I chewed this information into a fine paste and swallowed it to the pit of my stomach, precious context to my precious Franky. So she outgrew the internalized misogyny that made her resent her mother, but she still doesn't have a relationship with her. And for what reason? It felt too daunting to get in to while pruning and chlorinated and waiting for takeout; it felt like something bigger than what Franky could easily explain in one afternoon. I gave myself time to digest the offered information and tried not to be greedy. It was hard, because Franky's trickle-fed affection felt like torture, some days. She gave me pieces, bite-sized so I never choke, but didn't she know that I wanted to be full of her, filled to the brim like a cookie cutter?

I look at her and I listen and I crack her open inch by inch and I want and I want and I *want*. I want to eat her. I want to treat her kindly. I want to tell her about my mother, my months underground, my sleepwalking stupor. Barely awake, barely alive, and God, I used to be so *tired*. The endless wheel of girlfriends, jobs, classes, roommates. One door closed, another one locked. I was so tired of being me, so desperate for anything, but she brought me back to life. Her stupid quest, her salacious smile. I ached for her like a phantom limb.

I reached out to hold her prosthetic hand, an easier intimacy.

Franky looked down. She didn't move, but her expression was complicated. To be held at the site of violence and hardly register the tenderness. I trailed a gentle finger along the place her skin met plastic, feather light.

"I don't like it," she said, studying the connection. "It's like grieving twice."

"Sorry, I—"

"Not you." She grabbed my hand to stop me from pulling away. "The prosthetic."

I tapped it twice, a silent request. *Keep going*.

"It doesn't take away the lack," she murmured. "When I see it, all I can see is loss."

I was quiet, walked my fingers up to her elbow.

"It hardly even makes other people more comfortable. That's the only reason I wanted it."

"I've never known you to care about other people's comfort," I wrapped my hand around her arm, right above the cutoff point. Tenderness at the site of violence. I was frantic, feral. I wondered if she'd be mad if I ate her raw.

"I used to." Franky let out the tiniest laugh, shaking her head. "It used to be all I could see."

"How feminine."

"You look surprised."

"I've never known that version of you." I tightened my grip on her skin. Warm, sticky. I wanted to drag my tongue along every inch of it, salty and sweet.

"Would you like to?"

Was she fucking with me? Flirting? I stared at the skin of her neck, wondered if she'd be mean. Wondered if she'd break for me, soft and slow, hard shell crackling like bubble wrap. Mouthy, sour thing she was, I bet I could make her sweet—

I swallowed hard, staring at her. So I've got pieces, pieces offered with the reverence we both knew they deserved, but there was still so much left unsaid. The sharp pieces of her, how she fractured herself to move forward. Would she let me draw connections, tape over the gaps between each Franky I so adored?

I was getting better at it. I was getting so good at weathering her storm. I wondered if my graduate program would allow me to do my thesis on Hurricane Franky. Wholly horrible in her whirlwind of horrors.

There was a knock at the door. The food was here.

I watched her head to the front door, chatting awkwardly with the delivery driver, someone she must've known from high school. I set the table, laid out napkins and drinks. Pippa and Stasia were still lounging in the pool floaties when I poked my head outside to call them in. We shivered under the frosty air-conditioning as we ate, dripping onto Franky's kitchen linoleum. I washed the dishes while Stasia and Franky helped dry and put them away, and Pippa set herself to work making strawberry daiquiris for us all.

We ended up back in the pool. The daiquiris were surprisingly sweet, if a little too strong. I went back to floating, mind lingering on Franky's skin, so warm against mine.

Stasia connected to the Bluetooth speaker as the sun settled slow, casting an orange haze on our pruning skin. I glanced down at my body, wondered if my stomach looked weird, worried about my thighs. The four of us had wildly different body types; I couldn't help but compare. Franky's wiry shape. Stasia's dense muscles. Pippa's curves and contours.

"I like that bathing suit," Pippa said, splashing me to get my attention. "It makes you look like a banana."

I laughed joyfully, enchanted by the simplicity of our friendship. I have a body and that gives me trouble every minute I'm alive, but it doesn't have to. Pippa doesn't think my thighs or hips look strange, cellulite ridden, or disproportionate. She thinks my yellow bathing suit looks like a banana.

I was laughing so much, overcome with childlike glee, that I hardly noticed Franky staring. Staring at me like maybe, just maybe, she might want pieces of me, too.

Franky hardly gave us a break from the mission, ushering us back into the living room the second we grew bored of swimming. Barely dressed and dreary from the heat, we sat on the floor around the whiteboard, staring up at her.

"Stasia," she probed gently. "Do you want to say anything?"

Pippa and I exchanged a wary look, carefully watching Stasia. Fruitless caution, she dove in with clinical apathy.

"I found a hair sample," she announced, counting details on her finger, like reciting the periodic table. "Something galloped at me, it broke our living room window." She deliberated for a moment, chewing her cheek. Her voice came out thinner this time, subdued. "I've never been so scared in my whole life."

Franky captured this snapshot in jot notes on the whiteboard. *HAIR, GALLOP, SCARED.*

"It *gallops*?" Pippa asked incredulously, wrinkling her nose. "You guys are just fucking with me now."

Stasia shifted uncomfortably, forcing a smile to appease Pippa.

"I don't see why it can't gallop," Franky said. "We don't even know what it is, yet."

"Stas thinks it's a werewolf," I said. "All I've ever managed to get a clear view on are the eyes."

"Yellow," Franky said, nodding. "Stas, this is huge."

Pippa chewed on a hangnail, expression complicated. I nudged her knee with mine, giving a sympathetic smile. It was easier for me and Stasia to apply a fanatical monster to fictional women. I could tell Pippa struggled to fit her grief into the equation.

"I should head out." Pippa stood, giving Stasia a gentle squeeze on the shoulder. "I, um, have work early tomorrow morning. And need to shower, after the pool. Um . . ."

Stasia opened her mouth to speak, eyes flicking back to the whiteboard. Her own account glaring back at her.

"I should head off now, too," she said, straightening her shoulders. "I'll bring the hair sample to the lab. See if I can figure anything out."

I watched everyone watch each other, sitting inside the insurmountable intensity. *How does it end?* I wondered, standing to follow Stasia, dry clothes sticking to damp skin. *How can this possibly resolve itself?*

Franky followed us to the front door, a lost puppy left to her own devices. We waved goodbye to Pippa in the driveway, parting ways as I brought Stasia home on my bike. Still insistent on shelling up, Stasia disappeared into her room the second we crossed the apartment threshold, dressed to disappear to the lab moments later.

"Hey." I grabbed her hand as she walked by, grip tight so she couldn't escape. "Don't run away from me, okay?"

Stasia considered me, remembering the months I spent hiding from her. I felt her hand slack in my grip, tension melting from her body.

"Okay," she mumbled, shrugging off her coat. "Okay, I'm sorry."

I squeezed her hand, knowing there was nothing more to say. Stasia spent the night beside me on the couch, occasionally shocking me by referencing the attack.

"It really scared me," she said. "I thought I was going to die."

"I thought you were, too," I replied honestly. "I was terrified."

She nodded, accepting this. Finally finding common ground, we considered the events of the past two months, grinning despite ourselves.

"I can't stop thinking about it, what almost happened," she murmured.

I glanced up from my phone, tucked it away to show I was listening.

"I bet it's like trying to sleep when you have upstairs neighbors," Stasia mused, speaking to herself. "I bet dying and being buried is just . . . *hearing*. Footsteps circling above you, unintelligible conversations. I bet it's just as annoying as having upstairs neighbors."

"Hearing forever," I considered. "Would you still speak to me?"

"Del, if you die, I'm dying, too," she promised. "Unfortunately, we're a package deal."

"But would you *want* to come?"

"Sure." Stasia shrugged, more easygoing than I've ever given her credit for. "But it's hardly about what *I* want."

"What's it about, then?"

"How you'd drag me to hell if you wanted company for the journey."

Unfair and full of truth, her assessment of me. I always was her mother's worst nightmare, and with every passing day, I can't help but concede that there might be some truth to that.

My own mother's prophecy, just as callous and calculated and true: that I've spent every day since Creation trying to make the world burn.

BITTER

A million days of summer sun, I woke late to a thundershower, rain beating against the windowpane.

Dejectedly rubbing my eyes, I rolled out of bed and gathered up my sheets. I had the day off school and work, so decided I'd throw on a load of laundry and do some cleaning. Maybe grocery shopping if I could find an umbrella.

Stasia was out for the day. There was a note on the fridge, pinned there by a crab-shaped magnet, simply scrawled *lab*. I shivered, pulling at the edges of my tank top. It was cold and humid, the worst imaginable combination. Changing into a sweater and shorts, I set about my day, boiling the kettle for tea and starting the laundry. I was halfway through cleaning the bathroom when my phone buzzed, interrupting my rainy-day playlist.

GORE GIRLS

FRANKY

any news?

I waited to see if anyone would answer, peeling off my yellow cleaning gloves.

STASIA
Haven't found a match for the hair.

PIPPA
Are we sure its not lawrence's?

ME
:/

STASIA
She's still a prime suspect.

ME
excuse me
i did not GALLOP towards you

PIPPA
We can't be too sure

Franky messaged me privately.

FRANKY
new missing poster outside the arcade
seems to be a tourist, last seen at a b&b on
the edge of town

ME
uh oh
have the police said anything
about a possible connection to
the serial killings?

FRANKY

of course not.
they'd rather the illusion of safety rather
than actually admitting there's something out there

I chewed on this. Couldn't help but wonder if the missing posters cropping up was the work of a copycat killer, coincidence, or maybe victims that were late to be missed and never found. The unidentified dead, ghosts in both realms. Sometimes I wondered if Franky's dad did it. Sometimes I wondered if Franky wondered that, too. She never mentioned him, and I struggled to understand how he fit into this puzzle. Was the monster continuing Franklin's legacy, or the actual source of it?

ME

we'll figure it out
i promise

GORE GIRLS

FRANKY

meet up later today?

PIPPA

Im free

STASIA

Sure.
I'll leave the lab, call my therapist, then be over lol.

ME

see you guys then

Stasia and I grabbed the coffee order, ambling across town together. Franky and Pippa were lazing on her patio set, encased by trees and discussing a rude customer from work. Pippa cheered as we deposited a fruity fizzy thing in front of her, looping us in by circling back.

"Customer tried to kill us today."

"No shit?" I laughed, checking Franky for a reaction.

"Some kid tried to hack a pinball machine," she explained. "Thought this could be done by, like, fucking around with the wires. Almost sent us into orbit."

"Not the first assassination attempt at Funhouse," said Pippa.

"And certainly not the last." Franky grinned.

"Anyone else have any riveting news?" asked Pippa. "Stas, you were almost murdered this week. How're you holding up?"

Stasia grimaced, taking a long sip of her black iced coffee.

"She's okay," I answered, nudging her knee with mine. "Landlord replaced the window, and we invested in some sturdier door locks."

Franky hummed, clearly unconvinced that this would work, but unwilling to trigger Stasia's fragile mental status with a debate.

"If you think of any safety precautions for the dangers of Funhouse, let me know," joked Pippa.

"Sounds like an issue to take up with the boss." I grinned, relaxing as I saw Stasia smile.

"Eh, she's useless." Pippa dodged Franky's punch, jokingly winding up her fist like an old-timey cartoon.

We all grinned and lazed in the emerging sun, Franky and I sipping matching iced matchas. Pippa excused herself to raid Franky's kitchen, bringing back an armful of assorted snacks. We were picking through the options when Stasia broke the silence, faraway eyes and razor-thin mouth.

"The police didn't listen to me," Stasia mumbled. "They didn't care."

"About what?" Pippa asked. "Did you tell them you saw a fucking *monster*?"

Stasia jumped, clearly jostled by Pippa's intensity. "Of course I didn't." She looked offended. "They didn't ask me *anything*, is my point."

Pippa made a strange sound, leaning back in her chair. She shifted farther away from Stasia, staring into her drink. It was interesting, to watch the ways their interactions differed since the attack. Stasia's horrible experience made her blind to Pippa's horrible past. Our unique relationships to pain kept overshadowing each other.

"They didn't question you guys?" Franky asked.

I shook my head. "Police only spoke to our landlord, who passed on the info. Apparently, there's been a string of break-ins, they just recommended we get better security."

"Fuckers," Franky muttered, angrily chewing a pretzel.

The silence was tense, this time around. We were halfway through the snacks when Stasia's phone rang, making us all jump.

"Easy girls," she said. "It's just my mom."

I clenched my jaw, trying to subtly give Pippa and Franky a warning look. Futile.

To be snared into Stasia and Mrs. Lanes's orbit was a tumultuous, terrible occurrence. It was a web of precarious passivity, aggression bubbling beneath a performance of polite Catholic sensibilities. I could only imagine growing up in a house like that; Mrs. Lanes was a nightmare. A paraben-free, grass-fed, disorder-fueled nightmare. It's a wonder that Stasia survived.

"Hi, Mom," she answered, giving me a smile. "Yeah, I'm just with friends. Yeah, Delores is here." Pippa and Franky exchanged a look. "Well she—yeah. No, I just—okay. Sorry. Okay. I wasn't trying to—okay. Sorry."

I gritted my teeth, heart racing with secondhand anxiety. I never spent much time around Mrs. Lanes, Stasia wouldn't allow it, but I knew she didn't like me. I've been blamed since the dawn of time for turning her daughter gay. And what a bragging right that would've been, if Stasia and I had a breadcrumb of chemistry beyond second-grade curiosities.

"I didn't see that," Stasia murmured, turning in her chair to face away from us. "No, I—I'm sure I was, I've just been so busy with—okay . . . okay."

Pippa and Franky examined their drinks, politely giving Stasia space. Closest to the situation yet furthest away, I watched Stasia stumble. Generally put together, the last week had been rough on her. Monster attack overlapped with lab troubles, adding her mother to the mix was one straw of hay too many.

"Okay," Stasia's voice dropped to a whisper. "Okay, talk later."

Without a word, Stasia hung up the phone and left the patio, burrowing into Franky's house to hide out. I held up a hand to stop Pippa from chasing her, shaking my head resolutely.

"Let her go for a second," I said. "Her mom is intense. She just has to cool down."

"How intense are we talking?" asked Franky.

"I'm sure she'd prefer round two with the monster, rather than another call from Mrs. Lanes."

Stasia was gone for a long fifteen minutes before we decided to chase her, marching single file into Franky's living room. Stasia was lying on the multicolored rug, staring up at the ceiling fan with an emptiness in her eyes I haven't seen since grade school. Pippa sat on the floor beside her, pulling black locks of hair into her lap to gently braid. Franky gave me a complicated expression, grabbing those sour candies Stasia liked and laying them on her stomach like an offering.

I watched the three of them, straddling a simple line between intimacy and uncertainty. Pippa's short nails combing Stasia's hair, not an inch of skin touched. Franky cautiously watching us all, sitting on top of her stone wall like Humpty Dumpty.

I wandered into Franky's kitchen, grabbing a cream soda and watching a bluebird flutter through the branches. Took a sip.

Thought about the instinctive space we knew to give each other in moments like this. In moments when we were daughters and had to grapple with that.

"Hey guys," I called, circling back to the living room. "I have some thoughts."

Stasia blinked, fog around her growing thinner. "That's a first."

I grinned, pleased with her attempt at banter. "It's more of a thought exercise."

"My two least favorite things," Pippa joked, glancing down to make sure Stasia smiled.

"Don't think, just answer with the first thing that comes to your mind," I instructed, standing in front of the whiteboard like a drill sergeant. "What have your mothers given you?"

"An eating disorder," Stasia answered.

"Internalized misogyny," said Franky.

"IBS," Pippa joked.

I wrote all this on the whiteboard, marker squeaking.

"Alright," I said. "And what have your fathers given you?"

The room fell silent.

"I like my stepdad," Stasia said. "He, um, he was always nice."

I wrote *NICE* in big block letters. We stared at it in silence.

"He was—he—" Stasia paused, lost for words.

We waited for her to fill in the gaps. I held the marker an inch from the whiteboard, awaiting another adjective.

"He was nice," she finished softly, face crumpled.

"I never met mine," Pippa said. "But I hear he was a real asshole."

I wrote *ASSHOLE* on the board. Pippa grinned.

Franky was notably silent, staring into her lap. We never spoke about her father. Our entire lives revolved around his crimes, yet we never spoke of him. I watched her curl in on herself, hand shaking. She did not want to speak of him.

"My dad was nice." I put myself on heat to protect Franky. "Mom was . . ."

She was

The sentence trailed off forever, no end in sight. She was everything you could possibly imagine. It was too much, her stifling endlessness. She made me feel small, drew tighter circles around my parameter to make sure I never outgrew her.

My mother and I have always had a tumultuous relationship, whereas Dad was more like my coworker. Present in the sense that he brought in money, sat at the dinner table, drove us places. He got to be the fun parent, the reprieve.

My mother was Abraham, and she would've sacrificed me to the God of Reputation every single day if it guaranteed her salvation. I was wrong because I ruined myself, she was wrong because she gave me the handbook.

Step one: Be born *Wrong*.

Step two: Never find an explanation for this.

Step three: Let your mother shove you into the wrong mold. Never fix this.

Step four: Become a warped, grotesque creature, growing nastier with each and every day. Let your limbs curl like ribbons as you wander further from home. Melt yourself down, remake your outline. Find out that you cannot remake your outline, suffer under a half undone, half rewound fabric of being. Find out that you cannot undo what your mother has done. Live your entire life suffocating under what your mother has done. Debate killing yourself, never find the nerve to actually do it. Try to forgive your mother. Pretend you don't know that you can never forgive your mother.

Step five: Never escape.

Twelve minutes passed before anyone spoke again.

"What was your mom so angry about?" Pippa asked Stasia, adding a lilt of comedy to her gentle tone. A real buffet, the way Pippa approached people. She gave you an endless selection and let you pick her intentions.

Stasia responded well to this sort of behavior, a clicking into place I've long tried to balance. I was always too sincere, too genuinely invested for her taste. I was relieved to see Pippa's feigned detachment pry her open.

"She asked why I wasn't invited to some softball party," Stasia answered softly. "I didn't know how to tell her it was because I don't have a boyfriend."

The room fell flat. We stared at her, waiting for more.

"I don't make sense to them. No matter what I do, they just can't place me. I'm like—*God*, I'm like some sort of alien to them or something."

Franky chewed her bottom lip, finger running back and forth along the shaved notch in her eyebrow. Pippa responded similarly, clicking her tongue and nodding with a resigned understanding. It was at my disgruntled expression Stasia continued, realization dawning over her face as she watched us.

"We're all ostracized from womanhood in different ways," Stasia murmured, studying each of us with razor precision. "Why?"

I understood her bitterness. She bent over backwards to be a woman, to be seen as one. Femme, polite, poised. She was the patriarchy's perfect girl, but someone forgot to hit the "likes men" switch on her way out. In result, everything else fell off-kilter. She was always on the outside looking in. Excluded from her teammates' events, ostracized, unable to sneak in. I know it was a mystery to her. She saw these things happen to me and consoled herself by the fact that I was obviously wrong because I wore the wrong clothes, had the wrong haircut, said the wrong things. She followed their script like a robot, and yet.

"It's men," I answered simply. "The basis of correctly performing femininity is men. Attraction to men, subservience to men, coddling of men. Twisting yourself like a contortionist to appeal to men and setting yourself apart from the indistinguishable blob of 'other women.' We fucked up. We can never be part of this exclusive club."

It was a lecture I've given her countless times. In the more dangerous years of youth, Stasia viewed her lesbianism as a malfunction. She's not as self-hating as she used to be, but the roots remain. I think they'll always remain.

"She's right," Franky said. "Our unwillingness to factor men into our lives, it's like a second head. I've felt it for as long as I've known what it means to be a girl."

"It's an otherness," Pippa observed. "I never even had to come out, because I was always just the funny, ugly one, who none of the boys would ever go after. They must've smelled it off me. *Eau de Lesbian*."

"I had a 'not like other girls' complex,'" I admitted, accepting a chorus of booing and laughter. "I don't anymore!"

"The pendulum swung far in the other direction," Stasia joked.

"Because I opened my eyes! I realized there is no 'other girls,' no monolith of the female experience; just women who have been socialized into shaping their lives around male approval. They keep each other in line, but we can never be kept in line. We'll always be on the outside looking in."

Stasia stared down at her lap, eyebrows furrowed. "It's just unfair," she murmured. "It's unfair that we either have to brainwash ourselves into submission, or live life on the outskirts because we don't make sense to people." Her voice broke, cheeks red with anger. "I should make sense to people! I try so hard, I—"

We watched her trail off, frustration clouding over.

"Stas, you make sense to us," Pippa said gently. "Yeah, we're on the outside, but we're on the outside together. We're free."

Stasia's eyes watered, still staring down at her lap. She let Pippa hold her hand, smiled as I gently nudged her shoulder.

"Isn't this so much better than a softball party?" I joked, gesturing around us.

Stasia broke, blinking back tears as she choked back laughter.

"Much better," she admitted softly, shaking her head. "You guys make sense to me, too."

I watched us all, our reflection and ultimate contentment. We're different, we're all so different, yet united beyond a doubt by this one factor. Pippa, an Indigenous woman supporting her family. Stasia, money like a hazmat suit, nothing ugly ever touching her. Franky, orphaned and incidental business mogul. And me. More education than brains, mean and spiteful and calculated and warm. Runaway child, failed capitalist.

"I wouldn't trade it for the world, you know," Stasia said at last. "I really wouldn't. Loving women is the only thing that's ever made sense to me."

"It's the only sensical thing you've ever done," I joked, nudging her gently.

We all laughed, gently moving away from the topic. The day rolled on, but I kept wondering about Franky and her relation to the discussion. She didn't share much, yet likely had the most complex situation among us all. Her relationship to men was nonexistent, yet she revolves her life around her father. If the roles were reversed, would he be doing the same? Would he live as her inverse, occupy the space she left behind like a stray dog, desperate for meaning? Would he chase a monster to set her free?

Maybe not, I decided, watching Franky stand to make coffee. I've been here for almost two months now, and I don't think he's called her from prison once.

Pippa and Stasia left shortly after, with Pippa driving home and Stasia heading to the lab. She muttered complaints about her supervisor, hands shaking as she waved goodbye.

I stayed behind. I didn't offer a reason, excuse, or even ask permission. Franky was tidying up the living room, and I just helped her, motorcycle keys dangling from my carabiner.

"Do you wanna go for a ride?" I asked, shaking my hips to make the keys jingle.

"Buy me dinner first, Lawrence," Franky responded dryly.

"I meant my *motorcycle*."

Franky finished loading the dishwasher, turning to me with a grin. "You just want to show off."

"And . . ." I lowered my voice an octave, leaning against the counter. "Would it work?"

"Does it work on all the other girls?

"What other girls?" I swept my hand around. "It's just you and me. C'mon."

Just me and her. I wondered how Stasia was doing, wondered what Pippa was feeling. I was loyal to Franky, but sometimes that meant being disloyal to everyone else. Franky noticed this sacrificial tenderness and moved closer.

"C'mere," she said, gesturing for me to follow. "I want to show you something."

She led the way out the backdoor, crossing her backyard to disappear into the tree line. I chased her trail, shoving on a random pair of boots with cold hands deep in my pocket. I tripped over tree roots and spindly bushes, swatting away flies in the late evening sunset. We walked through the forest for a long, long time, ending up in a stranger's backyard. She stopped a few feet ahead, turning to find me.

"Here," she murmured, waiting for me to catch up.

We stood in a small clearing in the trees, large house looming in the distance. The moss-covered ground hosted a small, handmade swing set, initials carved in old wood. *FD.*

"Dad built this for me when I was five," Franky said, gesturing to the swing set. "I used to hide out here whenever he and Mom would fight."

I watched her, finding a small girl lost in a memory.

"Once, I stayed out here for hours, 'cause I wanted to know how long it would take them to look for me. No one . . ." She swallowed. "No one ever did. I just went back home the next morning."

I reached out to hold her hand, and she flinched away like I hit her.

"Sorry, I . . ." She sighed, shifting closer. "I haven't been out here in a decade, but I wanted to show you."

I let her track my movements, slowly reaching out to rub a gentle hand on her arm.

"When I was small, he would bring me out here and push me for hours," she whispered, leaning into my touch. "I used to think he could push me to the stars."

"I could give it a shot?"

Franky smiled, circling the space. The trees like a wall around us. She sat on one of the two swings, rusty chains creaking in protest.

"And I know you might . . . I know you might have certain ideas about who he was. Pippa said you asked about me."

"Snitch."

"Loose-lipped," Franky corrected.

"Bastard. She didn't give me much."

"You knew about his arrest."

"I know what she told me."

"What you pried out of her." Franky grinned. "You wanna know something funny?" She laughed. It sounded forced. "I used to think you were only trying to get close to me to learn more about the murders."

I reran our early interactions, smiling incredulously at the context. "Has that happened often?"

"No." Franky coughed, squinting down at the ground. "No one's tried to get close to me in a long time. I . . . I forgot people could want that."

"Franky . . ."

She waved me off.

"All I've ever wanted is to know *you*," I pressed. "I hate that people assume that means your father."

"Their version of events means nothing to me, anyway. Whatever happened, it's *mine*," she insisted. "I know what people say around town, what they talk about on the forums, but they don't want to listen to me. They never did."

"How long have you been trying to tell people?"

It was a complicated question. She stared up at the sky, considering her answer.

"I've been seeing the monster for a long time, Lawrence," she started slowly. "A long, long time. I didn't know what it was at first. I just knew it hated me, and nothing I did could ever change that." She circled her past, considered it like an archeologist. "Every now and then I would try testing the waters, mention a small incident or sighting, but I could tell it made people uncomfortable, so I always dropped it. But when Mom left . . . that's when I really started trying to tell people. I guess I got pretty intense about it, 'cause everyone scattered. I stopped being invited places, or maybe I stopped going out. I don't know. A few stragglers checked in, but I scared them off, too, with my desperation to be listened to." Franky inhaled slowly, fidgeting with her necklace. "I just wanted some way to ease the guilt," she murmured. "I should've tried earlier, *really* tried. I let people shut me up, and now I need to live with that. It's just hard, knowing I could've saved those girls, if only people believed me."

I recognized her guilt, her fury at being made a witness. It reminded me of Maxine, of Stasia. How my only impulse when faced with women in danger was to run and hide.

"And I know that makes me annoying," she continued. "I know that people don't like me anymore. They only liked the version of me that lived in their comfortable world of delusion, but I can't do it anymore. I can't pretend. And now look at me, I have no one left." Her voice lowered to a whisper. "I hardly even have myself."

Oh, Franky. The saddest girl on planet Earth.

I sat on the swing beside her. The forest moved around us, the humming of insects, the rustling of branches, but Franky couldn't offer a sound. She just swung side to side, gently bumping her hip against mine. Left, right, left, right. When she bumped me again, I grabbed the chain of her swing, keeping her close.

"I like this version of you, you know."

Franky raised her head, regarding me cautiously.

"I like it when you're annoying," I said, "and sanctimonious, and insane."

"Hey," Franky protested weakly, smiling despite herself.

"I like that you're so determined," I continued, "and I like that you care so much it makes you crazy. And I . . . I understand that guilt, that grief, but it's not yours to hold, Franky."

"You don't understand."

"Then make me."

Franky's lips quivered, staring at mine. She was a hair's width away. I had to be careful, so careful. One wrong move and she'd scatter.

"People keep telling me that you used to be different, but I like who you are *now*," I pressed softly. "I don't get what's so wrong about being changed by what happened to you."

Her face crumbled, blinking quickly. Ah, *fuck*. Wrong move.

"Of course they would say that," she scoffed, muttering suspects under her breath, old friends, estranged ones. She pickled herself within seconds, once soft surface pruning with bitterness.

I didn't try to chase her, she was out of orbit. Better luck next time.

"Franky," I interrupted her rambling. "*Franky*."

She shook herself, standing to stretch. "It's going to start raining soon," she observed, looking to the sky. "We should go."

Go where? I ached to ask, but she was already leaving. I stood to follow, chasing her trajectory through the forest, across her backyard, standing side by side on the shadowed back porch.

"I'll see you later," she murmured, not meeting my eye.

"Okay."

I stared at her as she stared at her feet. I was so close I could almost taste her.

Sensing my reluctance to leave, Franky reached out for me, hand lingering between us. It fell like a shooting star, dropping back to her side. Another lost shot.

"See you," I said, stepping away.

I felt the tether between us stretch, malleable like putty. I wondered if she'd call out, chase me, pull us close for a cliché kiss in the rain. But the rain hadn't started, and Franky let me walk away.

I heard the screen door shut behind me, and when I turned, she was watching from the window. I turned to a pillar of salt as I looked back, anxious to dissolve in her, itching to make my way into her secret heart. Forcing myself away, I walked home in silence, thinking over my failure. I had locked the door behind me when a new text chimed in.

FRANKY
thank you for saying all that.
sorry i got distracted

ME
you're always distracted

Was it possible for a text to sound resentful?

FRANKY
im sorry
i like talking to you
sometimes theres just too much on my mind.

It was a red flag. I hit the gas.

ME

can i be on your mind every now and then?

She didn't answer for a while. Twenty-two minutes, to be exact. I was tucked in bed half asleep when she finally answered.

FRANKY

go to sleep, lawrence

Slippery, slippery girl. She evades me once again.

ACOLYTE

The semester picked up, so I got to ignore my failures with Franky for a little while, absent under the guise of scraping through midterms.

A week went by, and I still hadn't reached out to her. The few times I went into work, Franky was nowhere to be found, and the group chat had fizzled out.

It could've been over. I could've backed away slowly and went on with my life, maybe found a new hobby, or better yet, a new girl. One who was uncomplicated and open with affection. But I was drawn to Franky like a fool, and, glutton for punishment, I chased her down the second I summoned the courage. Even brought her a sea of offerings.

With my last midterm submitted, I spent the morning at the library, then rode my bike to Franky's house after lunch, wind-swept trees whistling a wailing melody. Headphones bobbing against my chest, I knocked on her door and tried to look intimidating. Sheep in wolf's clothing.

Franky answered with a suspicious grimace, emotions flicking across her face like candlelight. She seemed . . . hurt?

Offended? I was perplexed to parse through the Rolodex of feelings.

"Hey," I greeted softly, leaning against the doorframe.

She nodded stiffly, scratching the back of her neck. "So, you're back."

"I had midterms," I said, shifting the tote bag on my shoulder. "Can I come in?"

Franky stepped back, but just barely, forcing me to brush past her to get into the front porch. Elated with the opportunity, I didn't step away. Stayed pressed against her, tilting my head with a patronizing smile.

"Were you lonely?"

Franky bristled, slamming the door shut harder than necessary. "It was *peaceful*," she bit out, not stepping back. "I got some work done for once."

"Is that so?" I hummed, moving away because I knew she didn't want me to. Franky moved to chase me, but then seemed to catch herself, burying her hand in her pocket and planting her feet.

I led the way into the living room, shock stopping me in my tracks. It seemed that in my absence, Franky dove into her mission with a scattered ferocity. The house was a wreck, papers covering every inch of space.

"Is your printer okay?" I asked, running a finger along documents taped to the wall.

"I ran out of ink three times."

"I think you've inadvertently committed deforestation, Franky."

"Recycled paper." She scowled, hilariously offended. "It's old Funhouse documents."

"Let's hope those weren't important."

I traced the length of the room, turning to find Franky scowling beside her whiteboard, fingers tapping her mouth. Ever emotional, she felt almost volatile, today. I stood beside her, head tilted in question.

"Everything from the case, it's all redacted," Franky said, explaining her sour mood. "Redacted, redacted, redacted. I'd have easier luck tracking down Bigfoot."

"Ever considered changing hobbies?" I joked with little success. "Alright, kidding. I'm here because I found something."

She hardly gave me a second glance.

"It's really good."

"Hm." She spoke into her bulletin board, practically inside of it, snarled in string.

"I stole government documents."

This got her attention. I put that fact in my back pocket, for future reference. Guess I'll have to steal the *Mona Lisa* if I ever want her to go steady with me.

"What'd they say?"

I resented her skipping over my incredibly impressive tale of thievery, so decided to circle back of my own accord. "So, I went to the library this morning, just snooping around for some general information," I said. "I figured, hey, if there's a monster in Mistaken Point, maybe there's *always* been a monster in Mistaken Point. Can't hurt to check out the history of this place, right?"

"Mhm." She continued scribbling away on her whiteboard.

"And, um, and I noticed there was archival evidence of sketchy stuff from the past hundred years. Old newspaper clippings, zines, stuff like that. It was under lock, though." I soldiered on. "So I distracted the librarian, sent her on a wild goose chase for a book that doesn't exist, and I stole the key."

Franky continued scribbling on the board, standing back to consider a pinned-up photo of a footprint.

"And—and then, with the key, I unlocked the archives and took them." With this grand finale, I shoved the stack of papers in her hand. Old conspiracy zines, newspapers with unexplained crimes, strange sightings documented in old diaries.

Franky stared down at the stack, placid. "This is cool, Lawrence. Thank you."

I was dismissed. More than dismissed, I was disregarded. She flicked through the folder for a moment before losing interest, laying it on a nearby coffee table before turning back to her board.

"Franky?"

She hummed, hardly an acknowledgment.

"Seriously? That's it?"

She wrote on the board for two more minutes before turning to me, expression flat. "Are you mad that I'm not paying enough attention to you?"

It was meaner than she had ever been, cold and cutting. A jolt ran down my spine.

"Excuse me?"

"You interrupted me to essentially declare that you robbed a library."

"I robbed a library for *you.*"

"Did I ask you to?"

Speechless, I walked in circles around the living room, mouth gaping like a fish.

"Do you think you've brought something new to the table?" she snapped. "I've *seen* all this. I have—" she grabbed a thick binder from the floor, "an entire *folder* dedicated to this."

I thought of her detached grimace, the frost coating her every move. She had been so strange the last time we met. The hide-and-go-seek she played with her heart. I haven't seen her since. I wondered if she was lashing out, emotionally exhausted, or maybe just plain sick of me.

"Are you okay?"

"Why would I not be?" she asked. "At my peak am I usually falling to your feet in rapture?"

Ouch! I clutched my heart. "Why are you—?"

"I just don't get why you're *nagging* me like this," she said. "Can't you see that I'm busy?"

"I'm trying to help you."

"Maybe I don't need it anymore," she hissed. "So how about you go back to being too busy to see me?"

Huh. I scratched my head, watching her. She was hurt, lashing out like a scared dog, but why? Was she afraid that I was going to leave her?

"Is that what this is about?" I marvelled, gesturing to her frost. "Do you think . . ." I rerouted. "I'm not going anywhere, honey, I—"

"Maybe you should," she interrupted, voice shakey.

I froze. "You want me to leave?"

"Seems like *you* want to leave."

"I was busy for one week, Franky." I gritted my teeth. "I'm sorry I triggered your abandonment issues, but—"

"*Abandonment issues.*" She barked out a laugh. "Don't psychoanalyze me, Lawrence—"

"A *child* could come to that conclusion—"

"I'm not stupid," she interrupted. "I know you agree with what everyone's been telling you about me, and that's why you ran off and disappeared. I bet you think I'm some"—she waved her arm around—"some insane person or something. Am I entertaining you?" Her voice grew higher, meaner. "Could you pay for a show this good in the big city?"

"Do you think I'd be putting up with all this just for the sake of some entertainment?" I forced a laugh, thin patience pulled taut. "You have no idea what you're talking about."

"Don't I?"

"No! You're insecure, and you're lashing out at me instead of just *talking* about it—"

"*Insecure*?" Her eyes lit up. "How could I possibly be insecure when I have you as my fucking shadow—"

"You love it!" I accused her. "You love the attention I give you."

Franky froze, inhaling sharply and bouncing back, as if struck. She didn't deny it. Cheeks flushed, lips parted, she looked incapable of denying it.

"You want to be worshipped? Well, baby, I'm on my knees."

Franky choked at this, thrown off her game.

I reached forward and grabbed her chin, thumb smudging her pretty, brown lip balm. Chocolate flavored. I ached to lick it off her.

"Bet you'd like me down there," I speculated, voice low.

Franky gritted her teeth, brown eyes on fire. I wanted to sit behind them and warm my hands. They were freezing from the months I've spent chipping away at her cocoon of ice.

"You have no idea what I'd like," she spat back.

"Why don't you tell me, then?"

Franky grabbed the hand holding her chin to pin at my side. There was an undercurrent of control that surprised me. I struggled against her, smile sparkling. Finally. *Finally!*

"All bark," I rasped. "Any bite?"

The teasing unstuck her. She backed away from me, hand clenched at her side. I had reached her limit, saddened that it was so soon. We considered each other in silence.

"You'd never be interested in me," I speculated in a low voice. "Because I age." I tried for a joke, tried to add a lilt of humor, but it was true. I couldn't gloss over my sharp edges, my meanness. "Your wall of perfect girls, flawless and unreachable. They're twenty-three forever; they'll never give you trouble, never let you down, because they'll never change."

Stuck in a dreamworld, she couldn't handle something real. I was too fleshy for her. Too complicated. I tried to make myself a fabrication, a fable, a folktale, but it wasn't enough. She'd only love me if I was mythologized, only look my way if I was on her stupid board.

"I hope they love you back, Franky," I said at last, heading for the door. "I hope they give you a fraction of the attention I do."

I watched her turn to the board, lost and faraway. Resigned, I left and let the door close behind me, stubborn hope burning low.

I was foolish to think I could ever measure up against her monsters.

I sat brooding in my bedroom, regretting what I said, wishing I had done more to catch her eye.

Futile, I reminded myself bitterly, letting my yo-yo drop to the floor. Reeling it back in. I reminded myself that I hadn't said one word of a lie, my haze of anger stating pure facts. She was attracted to me, might even *like* me, but she would never care about me, at least never as much as she cared about her monster hunt. I knew that going in; it was stupid of me to expect any different.

I checked my phone, saw that Stasia would be at the lab until late, saw it was heading on ten at night, saw an old message from my mother, questioning my sanity. I let my finger hover over the notification, aching for her voice like a child. I missed home so much, or maybe I just missed coming home to something. Food on the table, someone to fix my fuckups. I didn't know how to fix this. My home wasn't home anymore, I remember realizing that on my last visit. I couldn't remember when I stopped going, when I cut myself off. Probably when I realized that if I went back, I would never leave.

I let my head fall, glancing at my phone. No new notifications. I didn't know what to say to either of them, Franky, my mother. Narrative foils, a total cliché. One withholding, the other overbearing, I wasn't sure which I was compensating for.

I opened the text chain with my mother. It had been one month since I answered her.

ME

i'm sorry I had to leave but i can't be around you anymore it makes me too sad

(deleted)

i only exist in relation to you

and it was too hard, becoming
your ghost
i couldn't sever myself without one of
us bleeding out. i'm sorry i chose you
for the sacrifice

(deleted)

New message from Franky.

FRANKY
there's so much violence in getting older
but those girls will be 19 forever
surely that's not preferable.

ME
maybe it is

FRANKY
maybe.
perfect girls never age

I stared at our messages. Tapped my thumbs together over the keypad.

FRANKY
sorry I freaked out on you
i was being a dick. & you were right
i was insecure & i am obsessed with the case.
im sorry about that

I watched my ceiling fan spin round and round. Wondered how much she wanted of me.

Drunk on power, I decided to give it all. She could pick through the excess for a picture she preferred.

ME
i wish i had half the appeal to
you as that board

FRANKY
don't sell yourself short, lawrence
you're plenty fascinating to me.
maybe just a bit easier to figure out

ME
i'll surprise you yet, delores

It was heady and strange, to call her my name. Franky Delores. My mirror. My inverse.

FRANKY
looking forward to it

Just as I was certain we decided to go to sleep, my phone buzzed again.

FRANKY
hey lawrence?

ME
yea?

FRANKY
do you actually believe in the monster?

I stared at her text. I didn't know how to tell her that I believed like an acolyte, worshipping at the pew of her every word. That I saw it, that I kept seeing it, but no matter what the truth was, all that mattered was that *Franky* believed in the monster, and her conviction was as magnetic as it was horrifying. Her unquestioning, cult-like devotion to this conspiracy. It was real because she wanted, *needed* it to be. And that's just another level of reality, to believe in something so much, you make it real. To believe in something so much it becomes the only thing on this green earth that really matters.

ME

i do

i saw it, remember?

FRANKY

yeah

yeah i remember.

thank you for seeing it

ME

anytime

And I meant that; I'd see the monster in all its horrible glory every single day, as long as it gave us something to talk about.

Stasia and I had Debriefing Night over pad see ew, closing by return. Her neurosis was on high gear, insisting we pick up the food ourselves rather than ordering in, insisting we do a perimeter sweep of every entered room. Her voice was shrill, shoulders straight. I was exhausted with her anxiety by the time we reached home, answers short and stilted. She sensed my annoyance and gave me wide circles to resent her for a few moments. We ate in silence.

"It's been a weird week," I announced, finally on the other side of my anger.

"Just this week?" she joked weakly.

"It's been a weird relocation," I amended. "This place is making us strange."

"Just this place?"

I grinned, gently reaching out to hold her arm. It was hard to compare her to Franky, to Pippa. Hard to draw firm lines around her border. She was growing stranger, I thought, in her insistent attempt at conformity. So much to be accounted for, endless artifacts to be excused.

I sometimes thought that I hated Stasia's mother, maybe more than she ever could. Not only because of the fucked up little creature of shame she left behind, but because of how goddamn annoying her trauma made her. If Mrs. Lanes was just a normal, nice mother, I wouldn't have to jump through so many hoops to keep Stasia sane.

"I'm grateful you're here," Stasia said, sensing my circling spite.

I softened, reminding myself that it's hard to love people, harder to have patience for them. But who on earth has more patience than Stasia? The one person who ran away with me.

"I'm grateful you're here, too," I answered, reaching forward to hold her hand. "This is a pretty depressing Debriefing Night."

"We've gotten ourselves indoctrinated into a pretty depressing way to pass the time."

I laughed, shaking my head incredulously.

"God," Stasia snorted, squeezing my hand. "I hate to give you credit, but you were right. I thought you only got us into this whole mess for a girl, but it turns out she's not as crazy as she looks."

"Well." I smiled. "Let's not go too far."

"I guess I'd be crazy, too," Stasia mused. "If all I had to show for my trauma was a monster that no one believed in."

CURSED

Slug season. Franky picked me up from class with the cops hot on her trail, backwards baseball cap and low-slung sunglasses.

"Tuck and roll, Lawrence," she said in lieu of a greeting, eyeballing the shadows.

My classmates watched us with piqued interest, watching as I climbed into her vintage truck with a smug smile.

"What's going on?" I asked, buckling up.

Franky had texted me in the middle of class, demanding I meet her in front of campus. Disoriented and dazed, I tossed my bag in the back as she sped off, pushing hair away from my face.

"Cops are tailing us," Franky reported, checking her mirrors. "Bastards have been at it all morning. I can't shake them."

I glanced behind us, seeing a white SUV with blacked out windows. "Why would they be following you?"

Franky shrugged. "Why does anyone do anything?"

"Did you break any laws?"

"Is asking questions against the law?"

"*Franky.*"

We blew through a yellow light, swerving to catch a last-minute turn. Franky glared at her side mirrors, changing lanes and turning down a dirt road. I turned in my seat, finding there were now two white cars trailing behind us.

"I've been asking the police when they plan on making details from the Frankenstein Killer case public."

"By asking, you of course mean—"

"Relentlessly calling every hour, yeah." She grinned. "I couldn't make the trial, so there's information I'm missing." She checked the mirrors again. "Must've put me on a government watch list or something."

"It makes you look suspicious, but I'm unsure if it warrants a high-speed chase."

"Threatening an officer might."

"*Franky!*"

"What? I just said if they don't tell me, I'll figure it out myself. Might've thrown some insults in there, too. But they had it coming!"

I groaned, pinching the bridge of my nose.

"They should be thanking me," she murmured. "For giving them something to do for once."

"You're a piece of work." I laughed, reaching back to dig through my bag. "Do you want a cheese stick?"

Franky held out her hand, letting the cheese stick dangle from her mouth as she erratically changed gears. We sped up and skidded to the side, turning a corner with thicker trees. Branches clawed the side of the truck, tunneling closer. I peeled off a string of cheese, checking behind us as we chewed.

"Still there?" Franky asked, pressing her foot to the floor.

"We're losing 'em."

The truck's wheels spun, stubborn and cranky in the mud. Franky swore under her breath, checking the rearview mirror. The two cop cars were spinning out behind us, desperately losing speed. Franky put her arm across my chest like a second seat belt, shooting me a warning look as she drove with her knees. With a sacrilegious string of words, she jerked the wheel, nearly flipping the truck with the speed of the turn. Pushing through a near nonexistent road, we bumped along a tiny trail, drowning in forest. The police were abandoned behind us, cars too wide to fit in the narrow space that Franky pushed her old beater through. Manically glancing behind us, she kept driving until we hit a patch of light. Slowing to a stop, Franky pulled her arm away to put the truck in park. We had ended up in her backyard.

"Francesca Delores," I exclaimed with a laugh. "You're fucking nuts."

"You're a great partner in crime, Lawrence." She laughed despite herself, chewing on the cheese stick. "We should do this more often."

We landed in Franky's living room; she sprawled across the floor while I made us matcha. Cups steaming in front of us, we sat facing each other on the shaggy carpet, slice of light breathing through the window. We texted the group chat and invited the other girls over, promising a hilarious story to entice them.

"You and Stasia make a funny pair," Franky commented, staring down at Stasia's curt group chat response. "Pippa said you two used to date?"

"Oh, God no," I squeaked, making a mental note to murder Pippa. "We kissed once in elementary school. Been friends ever since."

"Do you start most friendships with making out?"

"I try to." I gave her a purposeful look.

She scoffed, staring into her matcha. "She came all this way with you," Franky mumbled. "Why'd she agree to that?"

I swirled my matcha, anxiety beating like a heart.

"I think she was worried about me."

Franky glanced up, catching my eye. I looked away, but she kept staring at me.

"I was in a bad place, before coming here," I explained, voice soft.

Franky leaned closer to hear me.

"Why'd you leave?" she asked gently.

I sometimes wonder what's too far, what can't we come back from. Monster hunts, childhood trauma, screaming matches over iced matcha. She gets every piece of me. Which one will finally be enough?

"I ruined myself," I answered honestly. "I ruined my name in the field. I can never work in it again."

"Why?"

"My mother." I felt guilty for blaming her, but all I ever did was blame her. "She pushed me into this career, pushed me into wasting years of my life. I just wanted her to have one thing. One thing about me that she could love." I caught my breath. "But it was too much . . . it cost too much, to try to be what she wanted. I couldn't take it anymore. I had a mental breakdown. Debated—" I swallowed. Squinted out the window in case I cried. "Debated killing myself. Chickened out. Ran away so she couldn't make me feel guilty about ruining my life to save it."

"Lawrence." She nudged me, big eyes brimming with sincerity. "I'm sorry she made you feel like you had to do that."

I hummed in acknowledgment. We both stared at a blue jay, picking seeds out of the bird feeder.

"I do understand," Franky said, "if that's worth anything."

"You do?"

"I have the same name as my incarcerated father." She grinned, giving me a sideways look. "Every news article detailing the crimes has my name. So, yeah." She laughed, "I understand well enough, the domino effect of a parent ruining your entire life."

"What about—" I swallowed, building courage. "What about your mother?"

"Mom?" Franky blinked in shock, sitting up straighter. "Mom, uh—God, Lawrence. My mother never wanted me. I ruined all her expectations already, on the day I was born."

I waited for her to say more but waited in vain. "She sounds like a fool," I said finally, knowing Franky would turn apocalyptic if she sensed pity.

"She was a lot of things."

I hummed, watching the blue jay hop from branch to branch. We were quiet for a while. I would've stayed quiet forever if that's what Franky wanted.

"I researched you, you know," she commented, throwing a grenade like a weather statement. "I was curious to see what you were running from."

I grinned, too flattered to feel anything else. "You could've asked me."

"I could've," she agreed. "But then I wouldn't have seen those old headshots."

I cringed, remembering the fluorescent lights, the Token Woman talks. The endless cycle of award ceremonies. Hometown articles praising me as the next It Girl of the Corporate Stratosphere. I always hated my hair in those pictures. The beachy waves made me want to rip my eyes out.

"I researched you, too," I admitted. "And found fuck all."

"I'm low-key."

"You're a ghost."

Franky shrugged, sipping matcha.

"Seriously, how are you nowhere?"

She laid down her mug to pick at her hair. Shivering as she dodged my eye.

"I couldn't testify," she murmured, staring at her hand. "And with the courtroom closed, I became this open secret. Sometimes people mentioned '*Franklin's daughter*' in interviews or documentaries, but they rarely bothered 'cause they weren't allowed to talk about the things that actually made me interesting. Like . . ." She swallowed thickly, curling in on herself. "Like how I was the last person to see Lily alive."

Lily. I glanced up at the murder board looming above us, scanning the list of victims: Adelaide Smith. Penelope Hawk. Cecilia Blint. Darcy Briggs. Caroline Hale. Tiffany Summers. Genie Templeman. Sammy Hayes. Lily Thorman.

The last victim.

"What happened that night?" I asked, trying to remember the pieces she told me at the party, ages ago.

Franky shrugged again, fidgety and weird. I sat in silence until she caved, words coming out chunky at first, then thick like honey.

"Me and Lily . . . Did you know we used to date?"

I shook my head, leaning closer.

"We broke up over three years ago, but kept seeing each other, because who the fuck else would we see? It wasn't emotional anymore, but I liked her." Franky paused, taking a deep breath. "It was her last night, and she wasn't listening to me about the monster. Or . . ." Franky glared at the floor, lips tight. "Or my father."

"You—?"

Franky shook her head, unable to elaborate for a moment. "He was acting strange," she mumbled, speaking slowly. "*Really* strange, and I was worried about it."

I wondered what *strange* might look like, for a man like Franklin.

"I was in the middle of asking Lily's opinion on it when he came home from work early," she continued. "He threw himself onto the couch between us, staring at Lily, asking her these weird questions. He was usually pretty good at controlling himself around strangers, but it's like he just . . . lost it. I got fed up and demanded he leave, but then Dad started playing the 'poor me' card. Accused me of being manic, delusional. Said I haven't been the same since Mom left, and got all tearful, saying I must blame him for it. You should've seen the performance. *God*, it was almost comical. But then—" Franky stopped. Struggling to move forward. "But then Lily took his side, I'll never—" She clenched her fist. "I'll never understand why she took his side. She was always so nonconfrontational around men, always wanting to keep the peace, so I called her out on it. We had this massive fight right in front of him, and I told her to leave me alone. But that's when I saw the monster."

I leaned forward, bated breath.

"It was right outside the living room window, staring in at me. Staring at *Lily*, with that insatiable look in its eye." She took a moment to compose herself. "I begged Lily to stay, but she wouldn't listen to me. Kept saying that if I wanted her to go so badly, she would. Then Dad offered her a ride home." She shivered, sick to her stomach. "I begged her not to go, begged her not to trust my father, but she . . . she wouldn't believe me." Franky slumped in on herself, exhausted by the memory. "I never saw her again."

To be believed. I thought of it as my first mark of devotion to her. I wonder if she felt the same.

"*Jesus*, Franky."

She shrugged, faraway. She did not want my pity. She hardly seemed to want acknowledgment that I listened and processed and remembered.

"That's heavy," I said, trying to keep my voice light. "Really fucking heavy. How do you carry that?"

"I don't," she lied, eyes cold, lined with tears she stubbornly blinked away. "Lily was a dick, but she didn't deserve to die. None of them did. Nothing . . ." She trailed off for a moment. "Nothing more to say than that."

Infinitely more to say. How complicated, how complex. My ex-girlfriends accused me of being emotionally withholding and manipulative. Franky's ex-girlfriend accused her of delusion and died in her backyard. I guess we both bring some baggage to the table. I thought of the weights I lifted, preparing myself to take the infinite grief from off her back.

"You're really strong, Franky," I said. "I'm sorry life hasn't been kind to you. You deserved kindness."

Franky waved me off, cheeks red, eyes brimming with tears.

"I'm serious. I'd take every second of pain away from you if I could."

Too tender, but terribly truthful. Franky fidgeted under my flayed heart, struggling to digest it. We sat in silence for two minutes.

"I'm glad your journey led you to my arcade," she said softly, "but I'm sorry it went like that, too."

I turned to her, finding a thoughtful expression. Sincere.

"Yeah?" I asked, probing for more. Insatiable for her attention. A million years under her careful eyes would feel like a second.

"Yeah." She smiled shyly. "You're—uh. You're something special, Lawrence."

Something special. I thought of her alleged long list of lovers, chronically non-monogamous, serial heart-eater. I wanted to ask if I could be her favorite, if I could change things. She lived on the other side of town. I wanted to walk her home. Then have her walk me home. Then walk her home. Then have her walk me home. I wanted us doomed together, cursed, Sisyphus and his beloved rock.

"You are, too," I said. "But you already know that, don't you?"

Franky's eyes lit up, expression deliciously delighted. I wondered if she'd let me eat her whole. Stasia and Pippa arrived before I could do something stupid like ask her.

DOOM

Every summer, at the end of August, Franklin's Funhouse would throw a cowboy-themed carnival, missing not one celebration in thirty years. Heckled by locals to bring back the festivities, Franky begrudgingly gave in, cranky as all hell to do something she had agreed to. The date was set, promotion spread, and it was set to be a real rager. Franky spent the week arranging rentals, her usual intense aura now radiating migraine.

Franky was insistent, if a little stubborn, about pulling this off, bribing us with overtime if we agreed to help manage the sea of crowds. Pippa perched on the front counter as I sat behind the desk, helping her with a beaded necklace. Franky tornadoed around us, muttering to herself about cotton candy and helium.

"You're going to give yourself a heart attack," Pippa commented calmly, not looking up from her beading.

"I hope so," she bit back.

I couldn't help but laugh, dutifully passing Pippa a bead.

"Something funny, Lawrence?" Franky snapped at me, bite of her bark softened by a silly smile.

"Just having a blast at Funhouse, as always."

She misread my sincerity, eyebrows sharp. "You guys could've said no to the overtime."

"And miss spending quality time with you?" I couldn't help myself.

Franky rolled her eyes, pausing her pacing to lean against the desk.

"I'm serious," I insisted. Stopped myself from saying *Franky, I want to do everything with you, and I'd do anything for you.*

Pippa caught my subtext, snorting to herself. Franky had resumed her pacing, growing bored with my noncommittal attempts at affection. I could hardly blame her. I was even tiring myself out.

"Do you need help with anything else?" I asked.

Franky checked her watch. "No, I should be fine. You guys can head out now."

"What time do you want us here tomorrow?" Pippa asked.

"Try for three o'clock. I'll pull an early morning to set up and should only need help with some last-minute rental things."

"You sure?"

"Yes." Franky gave me a look. "Now shoo. I'll see you both tomorrow."

"Bright and early, boss." Pippa saluted, gathering her things.

I hung back, feigning interest in my file folder.

"Lawrence?" Franky asked, nodding at Pippa as she left.

I stared at her lips, painted brown by tinted lip balm. Her soft brown eyes, heavy curtain bangs tangled in spidery eyelashes. She was wearing moss-green eyeliner the color of her coat, and I felt like asking her if she knew she didn't need a jacket today. If she noticed anything outside of whatever fixation could keep her busy. Monster hunt, Cowboy Night, would she ever let me join the long list of things she did to distract her?

"How was your day?" I asked weakly, edge of desperation.

Please, Franky, please, just tell me about your day. I'm begging you, pleading you, tell me every minor, minute detail. Creature you are, creature of complications, prickly self-loathing and tempestuous terror. Don't you know that you're my everything? Please. Please, just tell me about your day.

Franky stared at me, eyebrow quirked.

"Please?" My voice broke. I was sick of Cold Franky, sick of being sent in circles. I wanted her attention like a child.

At my desperation, her expression shifted. She paused her pacing at my precocious begging.

"It was okay." She fixed me with an intense stare. "I got stuck on the phone with a disco ball rental company. Did you know those even existed?" Franky traced her collarbone with her pinky finger, appraising me. "How was your day, *Delores*?"

"Legal name!" I laughed, feeling shy from her sudden heat. "It's been fun. I really like working here."

"And why's that?"

I stared at her, shocked by the earnest expression. Her taunting smile.

"I, um, like to hang out with you?"

"Was it a question?"

"N-no. A statement. I like to hang out with you."

"Just me?" she teased. "Not Pippa?"

"You *and* Pippa," I corrected myself, stammering. "Of course Pippa, too."

Franky leaned across the desk, looking down at me. "You look pretty today. Did anyone tell you that?"

I almost fell out of my chair. She reached her hand out and tangled a finger in my hair, tugging gently. She was waiting for an answer.

"No. Just you." My throat was dry. "Why do I look pretty today?"

She pulled on the strand of hair again, pulling me closer. "You look pretty every day. I decided to tell you today."

"Why?"

Frustration flickered across her face. Lightning quick, like every emotion she's ever had.

"Because you asked so nicely."

Before I could respond, her phone rang, cutting us short. She gave me a strange smile, staring a moment too long. I waited, always waited, but she just nodded and grabbed her phone, pulling away to answer. I watched her trail, overheard negotiations on bulk disco balls. I kept staring until my phone buzzed.

PIPPA

Please tell me you aren't still there simpering over frank

I watched Franky walk in circles, kicking a pile of cowboy hats like they had personally wronged her. A tassel stuck to one of her platforms, and she almost toppled the photo booth trying to free herself.

I grinned down at Pippa's text, tracing the swirls in the carpet as I headed to the door. Guts and moxie meant nothing in this town. I would make do on admiration alone.

Cowboy Night came fast. Pippa and I carpooled to the arcade, grabbing an extra matcha on the way for Franky. She was buried in a sea of cowboy memorabilia, some as old as she was. The arcade had been transformed since we left last night. Franky must have pulled an all-nighter to pull this off.

"Christ, Frank." Pippa whistled. "Very subtle touch, you've got."

I laughed, examining the prop booth, Wild West decorations, ceiling full of disco balls, twirling to catch the glimmers of fluorescent lights. Even the front desk had been transformed into a stable, fake wood paneling lining the exterior.

"Last theme night was a wreck," Franky said. "I'm trying to wipe the slate clean."

Pippa gave me a meaningful look, as if encouraging me to log that anecdote to memory. I did her one better, chasing Franky down to heckle for more information.

"What happened last theme night?" I asked, accepting a stack of wanted posters to chase behind her as she tacked them up.

"My father was arrested," she answered, pushing through a doorway of streamers into the "saloon." The party room had been decorated like an old-timey bar, with boxes of root beer packed on the floor.

"At Cowboy Night?"

"No." She grimaced, stealing the switchblade from my pocket to cut into the boxes. "It was our Valentine's Day event, room full of roses and my father in handcuffs."

"Just . . . in the middle of the event? While everyone was there?"

Pippa trailed in behind us, munching on pistachios. She caught my eye and nodded solemnly, carefully watching Franky's reaction.

"Yeah," she said. "It was the last victim, Lily, they . . ." She shook her head, shivering. "It doesn't matter."

Pippa mouthed a string of words I couldn't make sense of, but I already knew what Franky was avoiding. They found the last girl on Franklin's property.

"I thought you and your dad missed the Valentine's party?" Pippa asked lightly, giving me a meaningful look.

Franky clenched her jaw, digging the switchblade into the boxes a little harder than necessary. "I don't know."

She struggled to open the next box, unable to gain any traction without another arm to hold it steady. She swore, bead of sweat trailing down her cheek. I looked closer, shocked to realize it was a tear.

"You never made the party, you two were downstairs," Pippa reminded her softly. "That's where they found him."

Franky shuddered, jumping to her feet and tossing the switchblade to the side. "It doesn't matter. I don't remember any of it, anyways."

"Franky."

"Drop it. Seriously." She gave us both a grave look, kicking a box of bottles as she stormed from the room.

Pippa and I watched her tear away, angry and sparking with sadness. Pippa's failure was remarkable; Franky was clearly suppressing something and was determined as all hell to keep it that way.

"There's a basement?" I asked, taking over Franky's job of unpacking the root beer bottles.

Pippa nodded, moving to join me. "The doorway is right next to your office. It's usually locked."

I hummed thoughtfully. We worked in silence for a few moments.

"What happened down there?"

Pippa shrugged. "No one knows. But that's where they found her dad. Dragged him upstairs covered in blood, and carried Franky off in an ambulance out back. No one knows what happened. Franky and her father are the only two people on earth who do."

I glanced over my shoulder, listening for Franky. There was a faint ding of the microwave; she must've stormed off to the kitchen.

"It's really fucked down there, dude," Pippa said. "Maze of old games, flickering lights, real horror movie vibes. I've only been down there once." She checked over her shoulder, too, lowering her voice. "Franky keeps it shut up for a reason."

"Why?"

Pippa kept stacking root beer bottles behind the saloon, glass clinking as her hands shook. "I don't know," she whispered, "but I think it has something to do with her hand."

Franky had simmered down by the start of the party, dolled up in her cowboy gear to greet the tidal wave of locals. Her hair flared beautifully beneath a black cowboy hat, matched with a cow-print vest and chaps, over jeans and a wifebeater tank top. A red bandana was tied around her neck, reminding me of the fable the girl with the green ribbon. I wondered if she would stay upright if I untied the knot.

Pippa and I were strung out manning the ticket booth, managing the nonstop flow of people for about an hour. The lineup clogged for a moment with the arrival of a balding man and his daughter at the front desk. She couldn't have been any older than seven and seemed to be having the worst night of her life. Stomping feet, belly-screams, big production. The man reached down to pull on her arm, propelling her forward. She fell flat on her face with the force of it, clutching his ankles as he kicked her away. People in the lineup behind them politely avoided the spectacle, some even smiling indulgently.

"H—hey!" I stammered, voice breaking. "Don't—"

"She's in the dramatic phase!" a random woman interrupted merrily. "My husband wouldn't go *near* our daughter in those years."

Pippa chewed her cheek, anxiously scanning the room for Franky. The man muttered something about how the child gets the attitude from her mother. The whole lineup snickered.

"Hey," I addressed the little girl. "Hey, do you want this?" I awkwardly held out a teddy bear from the gift counter, trying to convey too much through a simple stare.

She blinked up at me through tear filled eyes, suspicious and sad. The dad tore her away before she could respond, pulling her back outside to stomp to his truck. The next person in line sidled up to the front desk, laughing low.

"What an angel, trying to bring that little girl out." The woman shook her head. "I'd hate to see how she treats her future husband!"

Pippa and I stared blankly at her, too perplexed to take her money. She shrugged and let it clatter to the desk between us, gesturing for the group of preteen boys with her to run inside.

They gave us an oily look and dissolved into laughter, pointing at Pippa's fake cowboy moustache. I heard them mutter a smorgasbord of slurs, seemingly terrified that women exist outside of pornography.

Pippa ripped off the fake moustache and tossed it into the nearby garbage bin, sighing heavily. "Man, I hate customer service."

Stasia arrived an hour later, just as the crowd started dwindling. She listened patiently to our tales of horror, passing a box of doughnuts behind the counter.

I watched Franky buzz around as the crowd ebbed and flowed, watched her micromanage the teens running the bar and photo booth. Pippa and I waited for her word to abandon post, grinning guiltily as she finally approached us.

"Anyone new?" she asked curtly, clearly sitting on some lingering anger.

"Not for at least twenty minutes, my liege," Pippa responded, trying to coax a smile from Franky.

"You guys can go into the crowd and keep an eye on things." She stood straight-faced, didn't budge. "Just make sure one of you is always keeping an eye on the front."

Stasia watched this exchange with a confused smile, holding open the saloon doors for Pippa and me to escape. Franky stormed off as soon as we were on the same side of the desk, putting at least fifteen feet between us at all times.

"What's going on with her?" Stasia asked.

"She's mad at us," I said, the same time Pippa responded, "She's pissy with me for forcing her to address her trauma."

"What trauma?"

Pippa and I shrugged. "We didn't get that far," I answered.

"How you two get anything done is beyond me." Stasia sighed. "Fill me in."

We explained what happened, with Pippa filling in the blanks, clinically explaining her perspective of the Valentine's Day party. Franky and her dad were no-shows, leaving Pippa to manage the event on her own. There was a horrendous scream from the basement, so Pippa rushed to the door, just to find it locked from the other side. Someone called the cops, and they showed up just as Pippa tried kicking the door down to find the source of the horrible, endless screaming. They restrained Pippa and beat the door down. Franky's dad was led up through the crowd, covered in blood and gore. Franky was nowhere to be seen. No one answered Pippa's frantic inquiries into her whereabouts until a low-tier officer took pity and told her that Franky was headed to the hospital. Franky almost died from blood loss, half of her arm gone forever.

"Jesus," Stasia said, as I let out a long line of more colorful expletives.

"Yeah."

"Her dad . . . ?"

"I think," Pippa whispered, scanning the room. "Anyone here can tell you the same story. It was fucking gruesome."

I stared at the corner of the room, the hallway that led to the basement door.

"We should go down there," I said. "See what we can figure out."

"Are you insane?" Pippa hissed, struggling to stay quiet. "Franky will kill you if she finds out."

"Then she won't find out," Stasia said. "You'll keep watch, make sure everything up here goes smoothly, and Lawrence and I will scope out the basement and look for clues."

"*Clues*?" Pippa threw her hands in the air. "Are you two the Scooby gang, or something? Do you expect to find her hand down there?"

I shuddered, but Stasia soldiered on.

"We're going down, whether you help us or not."

Pippa groaned, scanning the room until she found Franky, buried beneath customers at the saloon. "Okay," she surrendered. "I don't expect you'll even manage to get down there, but if you do . . . be quick."

Stasia and I saluted, slinking into the crowd. We made a sharp turn down the employee hallway, ducking through the barricade blocking the general public. I stopped at the basement door, realizing I walked past it every day and never took note of it. I remembered assuming it was just a supply closet, not seeing the signs of damage on the wall, the replaced door and hinges. The locks lining the parameter.

"Jeez." Stasia whistled, running a finger along the fresh paint on the doorframe. The line of bolts and locks.

I opened the outside locks and tried the knob. No luck. With a sigh of resignation, I turned to leave, confused when Stasia grabbed my arm and started digging through my hair.

"Huh?"

She unearthed a bobby pin, fiddling with it until it broke. She inserted one of the buckled pieces in the doorknob, twisting and maneuvering the lock around until she heard a soft *click.*

"Excuse me?" I asked. "Since when could you—"

"No time to explain. I get bored sometimes." Stasia pushed me aside, glancing around us as she slowly pulled the door open. The new latch was smooth, silent. We both snuck into the room and shut the door softly behind us. Phase one of our plan was complete.

"Now what?" I asked, staring down a rickety set of wooden stairs into an abyss of darkness. I strained to hear, tricking myself into believing there was a strange sound from somewhere down there.

"We explore," Stasia answered, grabbing my hand.

She slowly led us into the darkness, feeling along the walls for a light switch.

"No light?"

She shook her head, pulling her phone from her pocket to turn on its flashlight. She swept it across the room, exposing exactly what Pippa described: an endless maze of old machinery, games, and boxes stacked to the ceiling. She kept surveying our surroundings until she found a light switch at the bottom of the stairs, turning it on to reveal a string of faint yellow light bulbs, barely brightening the room. They flickered every few seconds, drowning us in darkness in terrifying increments.

"Spooky," Stasia joked, bracing herself as we entered the labyrinth.

"I don't know if we . . ."

"Shh!" Stasia froze, swiping her flashlight frantically in front of us.

I strained my eyes, hearing nothing.

"Must've been from upstairs," she muttered, continuing on with a wry laugh.

Desperate to believe her, I took the lead, taking out my own flashlight to investigate. The games lining our path were prehistoric, coated in a decade-old layer of dust. Our path diverged into two trails, one seemed to open up into empty space, and the other followed the wall. We chose the latter, figuring we could circle back.

The basement was cold, dark, and dusty. Not yet revealing any secret murder schemes or sites of mutilation. A text from Pippa chimed in on my phone, two words: *any luck?* I ignored it for now, silencing my notifications so they wouldn't distract me.

Somewhere nearby, a few rows over, a cardboard box tipped over, eliciting a loud *crash.* Stasia and I jumped, huddling closer together as we kept walking.

"Must be the wind," I joked, shivering in the frigid air.

"How is it so cold down here?" she asked, stopping to examine the name of an old arcade game, *Fight the Fire!* She swiped a hand through the dust on the screen, finding a permanent error message. "How is it . . . ?" She glanced around us, as if to verify we were in the center of the space. "There must be an outlet beneath it."

I hummed in agreement. Her explanation sounded nice, reasonable. I didn't want to entertain anything but.

We continued on, cringing each time the lights went out, worried they wouldn't flicker back on. Stasia checked every game, perplexed to find that only *Fight the Fire!* seemed to be alive. We reached the end of our journey, finding ourselves in a small corner of empty space. Something large had been removed, fairly recently, too, judging by the scrapes on the concrete floors. A large rectangular space of flooring, free from dust and dirt. It was a strange scene, splatters of maroon seeped into the surroundings.

"Look." Stasia pointed, hands shaking.

A sign far above our heads, warning workers on the danger of operating a garbage shredder. I thought back to the ones I saw in office buildings, the narrow opening, a hungry mouth. I connected the dots slower than Stasia, putting pieces together as she threw up in the corner.

"Oh my God," I mumbled. "Oh. Oh, oh my God. Oh my God."

Something crashed behind us, a freefall of footsteps. The basement door.

Stasia and I were locked in, the only way out was back the way we came. We stood together, resigned. Stasia wiping vomit with her sleeve.

Franky appeared before us, expression stony and complicated. "What are you two doing down here?" she asked icily, studying the scene. The empty space, the sign, the puddle of bile. "You . . . What are you—"

"I'm sorry," Stasia rushed out, blubbering through silent tears. "I'm so sorry."

"I don't know what you think . . ." Franky failed to speak, failed to explain. Her eyes were fixed on something to the left of us, tracing the top of the machines. She was frozen in horror. Stasia and I turned at a sharp scuttle, the sound of nails against metal.

The creature was directly above us, perched on top of an old arcade game. I couldn't help but notice the name: *Doom*.

We all stood in silence, frozen as glass. The monster was horrific this close, ghastly white in yellow lighting. Its skin stretched tight and translucent over sharp, sinewy bones. It had the shape of a werewolf, the face of a distorted human. Large eyes, empty and yellow and terrifying. There was a strange sadness in them, an expression of terror. It clashed against its wide, beak-like mouth, curved into a permanent smile. Pointed yellow teeth grinned back at us, two holes in its face sniffing the air. I watched its talons grip into the game, lowering its face to the empty space we stood beside. It appeared interested in the site of Franky's trauma, drawn like a shark towards blood.

Franky gulped, reaching forward to grab my hand. With a deathly grip on my skin, she uttered one word before dragging us along like ragdolls: "Run."

The monster took a moment to notice our attempted getaway, its descent slinky and slow like a cat. It kept pace with us, pointed mouth moments behind us. Franky led us through the maze, never once stopping to think, not saying a word as we wheezed behind her. Our hands chained together like a string of kindergarteners, we desperately scrambled through the sea of machinery, too consumed with terror to notice the games flashing to life, illuminating our path.

Franky made a sharp right, then left, pulling us closely behind in her attempt to trick the monster. We kept running, listening for the scrape of its claws against the pavement, stopping to breathe when we noticed them growing farther and farther away.

Franky scanned the space in front of us, evaluating exit routes. "I think it's this way," she whispered, eyes frantic with fear. Sweat-slicked hair stuck to her forehead, chest rapidly rising and falling.

Stasia and I didn't have the space to argue, we merely let ourselves be pulled along again, heartbeats on fire. The scrape of nails, the banging of machinery, the continuous beeping of each game coming to life. We reached a fork in the maze, spinning around a corner to find ourselves backed into a dead end.

Franky swore. "I went the wrong way. We were meant to take a left, not—"

She stopped short at the sound of a horrifying howl, sharp and high.

Chased to a dead end, we backed down the tiny hallway and crowded close, goose-bumped skin sticking together. Cold chills sentient like a spider, I watched a shadow turn the corner, heard curled nails and a harrowing shriek.

Franky desperately inched her way backwards, pulling the whole blob of us with her. "We need to run," she hissed, insistent whisper pushing past our expressions of horror. "We—we have to. We have to run past it to go the right way. We can't just wait—"

The creature stopped, sniffed. We stood at the bottom of a T-shaped hallway, the monster must've been a few feet away. Our options were to await death or run. I felt the illusion of free choice, the icy terror around both corners. I couldn't envision a world where we got out of this.

"We're getting out," Franky insisted, grabbing my hand. "Follow me. For the love of God, just follow me. Don't look back."

Stasia and I hardly had a chance to protest; we were propelled forward by the Force of Franky, spinning behind her, pirouetting feet across concrete floors. We reached the end of the hallway, the division between two paths: the monster and salvation. We stood in the shadow of the monster for one millisecond, one tiny fraction of life, and then Franky took a sharp right turn, and we broke off running. Stasia almost tripped, dragged along by Franky with a broken yell. We scrambled up the stairwell, free from the labyrinth and bathed in neon lights. Franky shoved us ahead of her, heaving breaths and heightened heartbeat drowning out all other sounds. As we stumbled back into the arcade, Franky viciously shoved the basement door shut behind us, slamming each individual deadlock with terrified precision. She threw her body against the closed door, braced for impact. Unfrozen, Stasia and I tossed ourselves against her side, holding back the door with every ounce of our strength.

"Guys?"

We all turned to find Pippa standing before us, expression of confusion and concern. "Where'd you all disappear to? I was stuck manning the photo booth by myself, and you know I don't know how to work that thing."

"Th-the . . ." Franky trailed off, lost in a world that did not experience her monster.

The crowds of people continued milling about, children laughing, teenagers trading tickets, recent divorcées on first dates. A sea of cowboys, unaffected and alive.

"The what?" Pippa prompted.

The what, indeed. Whatever happened to us, whatever horrible thing we just endured, it was over. We stood in a room of people who would never believe us, would never care. It took the fabric of our experience and tarnished it with truth. Whatever happened was manufactured, make believe. I opened my mouth, throat dry from screaming.

A bloodcurdling scream erupted, hitting a near inaudible frequency.

Franky's eyes widened with terror, turning to the door behind her. There wasn't a sound, there hadn't been a sound.

"It's outside," she whispered.

"Wha—" Pippa began, cut off by Franky rushing past her.

She pushed her way through the crowd, thick and bubbling like a river current. We all wandered outside, every occupant of Franklin's Funhouse pushing and shoving their way to the source of the scream. Franky stood in front of us all, Moses parting her way to the dewy pavement, neon red sign illuminating the crowd.

It was evident immediately, placed in front of the door like a delivered parcel.

The body of my classmate, Deidre Valentine, lying in a pool of blood. Cheeks torn to ribbons, skin like a patchwork quilt. Gory, glorified, gushing violence. Franky rushed forward thoughtlessly, throwing herself to Deidre's side. She felt for a pulse, a flicker, anything. Tried first aid, tried CPR, tried to stop the bleeding. Her franticness was fruitless, a cowboy costume covered in blood.

My eyes welled with tears, tracing her sprawled-out form. It was over the shouts and cries and screams that I noticed it, noticed the key detail tying it all together.

Deidre was missing her left hand.

Pippa and Stasia sat on the concrete steps, watching me pace. Back and forth. Back and forth.

By now, it was a sealed crime scene, ambulance lights and police sirens fading into a fuzzy, far-off sound. Our interviews went quickly, they didn't care about us. Franky had been in there for hours, questioned beneath fluorescent lights. I stared up at the Franklin's Funhouse sign, stared at the place where Deidre had been. There was a spot of black on the gravel, blood pooling into the earth. I'd have to hose it away, convince Franky to put in pavement. I'd have to get rid of it for her.

"Can you stop pacing?" Stasia snapped, letting her head hang back. "You're making me motion sick."

"It didn't chase us."

"What?" Stasia asked. By now, she had filled Pippa in, politely ignoring her polite disbelief. Pippa had sunken into a stunned stupor, staring at the pavement.

"It didn't chase us," I repeated, retracing the thought that had been on my mind all night. "When we were in the basement, when we ran for it, the monster, it . . . it didn't chase us."

I can't tell Franky, I'll never tell Franky, but I looked back. I looked back into the darkened, dusty hallway, the hallway of the monster. And all I saw was a black void of hunger, a creature of temptation, a creature of terror. Yellow eyes blinking back at me, yellow eyes framed with the widest smile. Teeth sharp like pinpricks, claws clicking against concrete. I'll never forget it, I'll never forget it for as long as I live, because for a creature so desperate to kill us, it let us live. It stood watching, calm and curious, as we careened away.

"It wanted us to find Deidre," I realized, voice soft with wonder. "It didn't want us dead. If it did, we would've been dead already. No . . . no, it wants us to *witness* it. It wants—"

I was interrupted by the bell above the door, front porch creaking as Franky stepped out into the moonlight.

She looked like hell, eyes sunken like potholes in the snow. Her hair was in disarray, cowboy costume rusty red, teeth chattering despite the muggy air.

"Franky." Pippa stood, rushing to meet her. We trailed behind, letting her stand before us like a prophet. "Are you okay?"

Franky considered this, glancing down at her shaking hand. There was blood beneath her fingernails, dirt and grime from the basement coating her arms. She looked up at us, brown eyes soft with sadness. We waited, bated breath and heavy hearts.

"At least I'll never have to host Cowboy Night again," Franky said finally, bursting into violent tears, endless as the cool summer rain.

VICTIM

We arrived back at Franky's house, beet red and heaving. Franky latched every lock and deadbolt, checking the windows and closing the curtains. We stood in a circle in the living room, staring at each other in a silence occasionally broken by aborted attempts to debrief. After about five minutes of this, Pippa buckled over with her hands on her knees, rattling breaths shallow.

"I'm gonna have a fucking panic attack," Pippa announced, shaking herself to start pacing the room. "What was that? Franky, what—what was that? What happened? What happened? What happened? Christ, what happened? What happened? What fucking *happened*?"

"I've been telling you, Pippa, I—" Franky seemed equally lost for words, waving her hand around. "I told you that we're not safe! I told you there's something out there, and now another girl is—is—"

"Is *dead*, Franky!" Pippa snapped. "She died in the exact same way as the others, dumped in front of your property and—and Jesus, are we just moving in circles? What *happened* back there? What happened?"

"I don't know," Franky broke, pleading with Pippa. "I don't know what happened. I was in the basement with—"

She stopped herself, but we all knew what she was going to say. She was with the monster. Could it have killed Deidre, then tracked us down to witness its crime? Was I right, when I guessed that it wanted us to find her?

"I thought we were safe," Pippa said, eyes angry to hide her tears. "Why . . . why aren't we safe now? We should be safe. I paid the price, I—" She shuddered, hands shaking. "The bad thing has happened. Why is it still happening? Why is it—"

"Because it doesn't work like that, Pippa." Franky cut in, simultaneously frustrated and consoling. "I told you, it was never going to be as neat and clean as you wanted. They can't just lock one man away and pretend that makes it all better. Things have been *happening*, they keep happening. Everyone loves to brush me off and call me crazy, but I knew the monster would strike again. I made the connections, I saw the signs." Franky caught her breath, turning clinical too fast. "And the victims, they—"

"Don't fucking call them that, Franky!" Pippa exploded, stress-spent and as scared as I've ever seen her. "They were my family, my friends, my—we *knew* Deidre! My aunt used to babysit her, I sold her a joint once. Now she's . . . now . . ."

Pippa broke off, grabbing an empty soda can to throw across the room. She responded to pain like a child. It was too big for her to hold.

"I knew her, too," I spoke up, gently breaking the silence.

Everyone turned to me at once, surprised by my random intrusion.

"We were in the same sociology class."

Pippa froze, reign of terror running tepid. "I didn't know that."

"She was always really nice to me," I said. "She once told me about her friend, Tiffany Summers."

"The missing head." Franky nodded, wandering over to her bulletin board.

"No." Pippa pulled her back, grip tight. "She was the girl who outed you in middle school, remember?"

Franky blinked in shock, staring at Pippa for a long moment before breaking into a strange, sad laugh. "You're right. That motherfucker."

"Deidre defended you, remember?"

"Yeah." She nodded, mouth pinched. "Yeah, she was always cool." Franky broke into a shy smile. "I used to have a crush on her."

"Frank, you dog!" Pippa exclaimed, the same time I inexplicably yelled, "*Hey!*"

"I liked how angry she was," Franky admitted. "This was before I realized that you can't have *two* crazy people in a relationship. One person should at least be a little chill."

"And as a side note, I'm always saying how sane Lawrence is," Stasia joked.

We laughed, and Franky gave me a secret smile. We simmered slowly and turned back to the bulletin board in tandem.

"So." Pippa clicked her tongue, staring up at Franky's notes with startling sincerity. It was her first time reading the evidence. "The monster."

Franky shifted, uncomfortable under the scrutiny. That damn board was like her heart. "If you have any questions, I can . . ."

Pippa held up a hand to stop her, wandering to the section labeled *TESTIMONIALS*. A shaking finger reached out to trace the board, drawing a line between every scared woman who wasn't listened to.

"I didn't realize she said that," Pippa whispered, frozen in front of a sticky note labeled *Penelope*.

I walked closer, reading over Pippa's shoulder.

"It's like there's something lurking around every corner. Having fun feels strange when those invisible eyes are watching me. Mom insists that she doesn't know what I'm talking about."

The quote was dated a month before Penelope's death.

"She said it when we were driving home one night, right after we dropped you off," Franky mumbled. "Baseball practice, the summer before it all started."

Pippa hummed, outstretched hand clenching into a fist. She pressed her knuckles against the board like she wanted to punch right through it.

"She knew," Pippa said, a soft revelation. "She *knew* she was being watched, and she told people she felt unsafe."

Franky's expression held a level of sadness words could not contain. It made my stomach churn.

"I . . ." Pippa started speaking, stopping to hug herself for a moment. "I'm really scared. This has been going on for almost a year now, but I've never felt this scared before. I just . . ." She sighed. "Even during the murders, I never thought it would happen to me, because it *didn't* happen to me. I thought that meant I was doing something right, that I . . ." She trailed off. "I guess I never realized until now that I'm not special or exempt from whatever these girls did wrong, I just got lucky. There's no reason I'm here except I'm just a little bit luckier than they were. I—I always thought that Penelope must've done something wrong or wasn't paying enough attention to the signs of danger to protect herself properly. But she was." Pippa let her hand fall to her side, then reached up to clench at her heart. "She knew something was wrong, she did everything right, but it didn't change a thing."

I blinked back tears. We gave Pippa space to stew.

"There is no intelligence or alliance that keeps you safe," Franky whispered, near inaudible. "It's just luck. I understand why you didn't want to see it that way, but it's the truth."

Pippa stayed frozen by Penelope's testimony, while Stasia and I stared absently at our own evidence. The Maxine situation, our monster break-in, the minuscule moments that made a petrifying picture. Deidre hung heavy over our heads. She joined the constellation of victims, a smattering of stars that painted the saddest picture: she paid attention, she protected herself, but it still wasn't enough. It would never be enough. And even those who weren't smart enough, quick enough, cautious enough, they shouldn't have had to be. They deserved the right to be reckless. They deserved a life without looking over their shoulder.

It was too much to bear. I felt hopelessness curl inside me like a clenched fist. Minutes passed that felt like hours. None of us seemed to understand a way forward.

"Can I . . ." Franky started, breaking the silence. "Can I say two things?"

Pippa stepped away from the board, wiping tears from her eyes. "Sure."

"Okay," Franky said, "so we're scared."

It was a statement, but we all nodded like she asked us a question.

"Right." Franky nodded pensively. "I think that's smart, considering the circumstances."

Dedicated pupils, we kept nodding, on edge for whatever she'd say next.

"Second thing: Does everyone like lasagna?"

The three of us stared blankly, lost for words.

"Um," Stasia said, raising a brow. "Yeah."

"You know I do," Pippa said.

"I'll eat anything."

Franky nodded somberly, considering us like a general might study battle-weary troops, mid-war.

"Then I'll make lasagna," she said at last, holding her hand out to me. "Lawrence, can you help me out?"

I slipped my fingers between hers and followed Franky to the kitchen, leaving Stasia and Pippa in the living room to pick through the evidence. We didn't speak much. She pulled out a recipe book and started gathering ingredients, and I stayed close like a shadow. I watched her ponder, picking through pasta and chewing her cheek. She set me to work grating the cheese.

"I didn't realize you knew Deidre," Franky said softly, cautiously.

I laid the grater down, turning to stare at her. She was bathed in syrupy light, a soupy yellow that bounced off her high cheekbones and furrowed brows. She always looked so intense, dark eyes, downturned lips. I thought of the multiple Frankies, the boxes I put her in to make sense of the shifts. Tonight, miraculous night, she seemed to be every Franky at once. She was vulnerable, intense, faraway. But staring at me in that soft, charming way that made my insides churn like butter.

"She was the only friend I made in class," I said. "I always thought she was going to get herself in trouble. She was just so angry."

Franky seemed stumped by this, humming noncommittally and avoiding my eye. She stirred the beef, poked at the boiling pasta. I gravitated to her side, cheese long abandoned, and pulled on a strand of her hair, begging her to meet my eye.

"Franky?" I prodded. "What are you thinking?"

She turned to me, kohl eyes sad and scared. I let my hand cup her head and finally, *finally* felt grounded for the first time on this mournful, morbid night.

"I don't know why I'm still here," Franky whispered, leaning into me. "Why I keep surviving, when girls like me . . . when I'm the one who . . ." She chewed her lip, shaking her head. "I don't know. Looking into the victims has always felt a bit like looking in a mirror. Is that selfish?"

"No, honey, it's smart. Most people feel the opposite way because it's easier."

Franky shivered, stepping away from the stove. She stayed close to me, though, my hand still tangled in her hair.

"I think you're really brave," I continued, "for not letting fear stop you, for seeing things how they really are."

"And how are they?"

"Fucking terrifying." We laughed for a moment. Sharp like thunder. "I'm serious. I came to this town and felt exactly what you've been talking about; watched, hunted, *afraid*. And it was so lonely to try and make sense of it on my own. Then I met you, and I . . ." I felt overcome, suddenly. Embarrassed and reaching for words. "You brought me *relief*," I said at last, throat thick.

"You did that for me, too, you know," she murmured. "I feel crazy a lot of the time, and maybe I am, but you never made me feel that way. You just listened. You always listened."

"I wanted to hear."

She hummed, considering me. I wondered if I looked even half as beautiful to her as she looked to me.

"You're so warm," Franky mused, reaching out to grip the edge of my T-shirt.

"Temperature wise, or—?"

"No." She shook her head. "*You*. You're like a heated blanket."

My girl was introspective tonight. She considered me with rapt focus, viewing me under her strange Franky-lens in her nonsensical Franky-world.

"You're like my flashlight," she announced at last. As if this made perfect sense.

And maybe it did. A laugh bubbled up in my chest, sweet like cotton candy. "What's that supposed to mean?" My voice cracked.

"That you make me feel safe," Franky said, pulling at the hem of my T-shirt. She carefully slipped her hand beneath it, warm fingers splayed against my hip bone. "Is that sensical enough?"

"M-makes perfect sense to me."

"I haven't felt safe in a long time, Lawrence. I don't know if I ever have. But you?" She let her hand drop to my waistband, middle finger hooking through the belt loop. "You give me that feeling. It's warm and . . . and *comfortable*. You keep the monsters at bay."

My fingers twitched, skin warm under her fluorescent attention. "Franky . . ."

She sensed my desperation like an oncoming storm, and it seemed to sober her up. She pulled at my belt loop once, twice, giving me a crooked smile that said, *I will eat you whole one day, but I'm not hungry, yet. My appetite is preoccupied. Please try again later, and please, please, please be patient with me.*

"Go grate more cheese," Franky rasped, gently shaking me off. "We'll need the calories. We still have a monster to catch."

Oh, that volatile, voracious girl. I fought the urge to grab her hand, to hide inside her countless nooks and crannies. Slug season, a sea of mosquitos, I'd know you anywhere. Moth to the fire, Lawrence to the Franky. I wanted to hold her steady, hold her still. Hold her down, crawl beneath her and place her hands around my neck. I wanted to scream that we can slow down, that there's time. There's always time. Finding the monster, putting her hips on mine, what's the big rush, anyway? What's your big idea? Trap the creature? I'm your monster, you can lock me in that big dumb cage forever if it pleases you.

"Okay," I surrendered, always surrendering. "I'll grate more cheese."

And I grated the cheese. And I watched her from the corner of my eyes, so sad and scared and complicated. I would wait for her forever, wait like a dog until she has the space to want me in that insatiable way I want her.

We didn't speak, but I felt content in her presence. Warm in her sunlight.

I watched her, and same as ever, same as we've always been, I felt her watching me right back.

With my one task completed, I was quickly dismissed from Franky's kitchen, softly reprimanded for being "in the way." Hands high in surrender, I went to rejoin Stasia and Pippa, finding them in the back garden by the fireplace. Stasia's phone illuminated both of their faces, eyes glued to the screen as they swatted away mosquitos.

I crossed the yard and settled beside them, leaning closer to see they were scrolling through the online forum Deidre mentioned a million years ago.

"How'd you guys hear about this?" I asked, voice shaking.

"Mom mentioned it once, ages ago," Pippa murmured, eyes locked on the "Local Anecdotes" thread. "But I didn't think it was worth looking into. Then Stasia mentioned—"

"My lab mate sent the link to our group chat," she said, "You recognize it?"

"I heard about it a while back." I paused. "Deidre told me about it at the party."

We all stared down at Stasia's phone, falling silent. The most active thread, the one nearly crashing the site with constant pings of activity, was a board dedicated to Deidre. Stasia's thumb hovered over the link for an agonizing moment, before shutting off her phone and tossing it to the side. I exhaled with relief. The color slowly returned to Pippa's cheeks.

"Thank you." Pippa exhaled, "For not looking at it. Tonight has been too much, man." She forced a laugh. "I don't want to keep thinking about how hated I am."

She was a brand-new Pippa. Raw and jumpy, eyes like a live wire.

"Are you okay?" I asked gently.

"I'm a lot of things. Don't know if 'okay' is on the list, but I'll certainly add it to the agenda."

"Pippa," Stasia implored, hand on her arm.

"Sorry." She sighed, shifting uncomfortably. "I don't mean to make it a joke, I'm just triggered, I guess. Triggered and traumatized. Can't even go to therapy, cause the only therapists in Mistaken Point are my old high school classmates. The ones that survived, that is."

Stasia shuddered, as if shaking something icky off her back. "I can't even imagine . . ."

"Stick around this shithole and, apparently, you won't have to."

I opened my mouth. Closed it again. Stasia stared down at her hands. No one had anything else to say, so we didn't say anything. A long ten minutes passed in silence, then another five. Pippa stared up at the darkening sky, chewing on a tangly thought, one that seemed difficult to unravel.

"Those monster hunts as children," she started, "the séances and booby traps and Big Foot expeditions. The ghost was always Franky's dad in a sheet. I just assumed this was the same thing." She was quiet for a while. "I'm still kind of hoping it is."

"Have you changed your mind at all?" Stasia asked gently. "Since seeing the evidence and, um . . ."

"Another dead body?" Pippa asked bluntly. "I don't know, Stas. It took me long enough to accept that a human being could be committing those crimes. Now I need to fit a *monster* into the equation?"

"You struggled with his identity," Stasia observed, seeing through the attempted levity.

"*His*," Pippa parroted, smile sharp. "Franky's not here. We can say his name. Franklin fucking Delores." She laughed humorlessly. "Mr. Mistaken Point."

Stasia and I shared a look, neither of us knowing how we could possibly navigate this topic.

"STASIA!" Franky called, poking her head out the sliding glass door. Her intrusion cut our premeditative attempts short.

"YEAH?" Stasia called back.

"Do you know anything about wine?"

Stasia quirked a brow at us, turning to face Franky. "Yes?"

"Can you come help me with something?"

Stasia stood up and dusted off her pants, giving me a meaningful look that seemed to say, *Ask her about it*. She grabbed her phone from the grass and crossed the backyard, disappearing into the house with Franky.

Pippa sat in silence, while I wondered how to ask her about our friend's father. It felt like a universally taboo topic, even in the best of circumstances.

"I don't know how to light the fire," Pippa announced, voice soft for once. "Its mechanisms are beyond me."

It was the kind of propane fireplace I had back home. I fiddled with the knobs, gifting blue fire like Prometheus.

"Thanks, kid," Pippa said dryly, still not meeting my eye.

"Hey," I murmured, hand on her arm. "Hey."

She turned to me. Her eyes were rimmed red, sunken creatures holding back tears. It broke my heart.

"Can we talk?"

Pippa inhaled. Nodded. Exhaled slowly.

"You've been here your entire life," I started gently, "And you're the only person I trust to tell me the truth about Franky's father."

Pippa turned away from me, fixated on the fire. I was wondering if she ever planned on answering at all when she cleared her throat.

"I . . ." Pippa swept her hand through the fire once, twice, three times. "You shouldn't trust my opinion on it."

Strange detour. I furrowed my brows. "Why?"

Pippa gulped, shaking her head. I leaned forward to catch her eye, surprised to find that she looked guilty.

"Because he just seemed like a normal guy to me."

I thought about the testimonies from the town; the claims of Franklin being nice, laid back, *normal*. I thought about Bobby finding a hand in her mailbox.

"*Normal*?" I clarified incredulously.

"Have you ever met a psychopathic serial killer?" she snapped, softening the sharpness with stumbling laughter. "I mean, what do you want me to say, Lawrence? That he was manipulative?

Antisocial? Violent to animals? I—I don't know, man, he wasn't! He was just . . ."

"Normal?" I supplied.

She shot me a sharp look. "I don't want to talk about it."

She never did. A summer of friendship spent spinning in circles. I stared at Pippa, understanding her avoidance, but past the point of accepting it.

"I need your context, Pippa," I pressed softly. "I need it if we're going to help Franky."

She shivered, picking at a scab on her knee. I watched and waited until she was finally ready to talk. Voice sharp and distant.

"I don't know what sort of magical insight you think I have," Pippa muttered. "I mean, I noticed that he stared a lot. Said weird shit sometimes. Jokes, inappropriate comments or questions. He got kicked off of coaching the hockey team, 'cause he was creeping the girls out."

"And this was normal?"

"Don't—" She frowned. "Don't give me that shit, man. Do you think *you* would've figured it out? You read what he did and you picture a monster, but do you have any idea how hard it is to reconcile the fact that it was just Franky's dad?"

She was ablaze; Bobby's defensiveness mixed with Deidre's delusion.

"Would *you* have clued in?" she pressed hotly. "Would *you* have made the connection between 'friend's angry father' and 'serial killer madman?' I guess you're the Franky expert here, right? So maybe *you* would've understood the signs. Would have noticed the bruises, the injuries, the way she was so . . ." Pippa hugged her knees against her chest, bottom lip quivering. "The way she was so *scared*. She was really scared of him, Lawrence. Would you have noticed? Would you have . . ."

Her anger boiled hot, but it could not simmer forever. The memories of a younger, more fragile Franky brought Pippa back to earth, righteousness crashing down alongside her. She was quiet for a long time. I watched the stars as Pippa's shuddering breaths slowly evened out. "I'm sorry," she swallowed, voice rough. "I'm not angry with you, I'm angry at myself. I should've known."

I wanted to protest, but she wouldn't allow it. She gave me a silencing look, holding out her open palm. Her hand was warm.

"It's just hard," she said. "To look back and see the trajectory. I understand why Franky made a monster. I guess I went too far in the opposite direction." She smiled sadly, hand shaking in mine. "I made a normal man."

I squeezed her hand, letting her think out loud.

"I just wanted it to be over," she whispered. "I wanted it to be over so badly. I—I don't want to live in Franky's world. This monster shit, her insistence that there's still something out there . . ." Pippa paused. "Why has it never seemed to scare you?"

I considered this question, gave it the attention it deserves.

"I've always . . ." I started slowly, carefully picking my words. "I've always been on the parameter of what she's saying. I have the freedom to understand it, I guess. I don't have to ignore it for career reasons, like Stasia, or for peace of mind like you might be. I've never been as extreme as Franky is, but maybe she's the smartest among us, for recognizing how fucking scary it is to be a woman in this world. She's seen violence, she's experienced it. It's unbearable to recognize the pattern and realize that it's not a one-off situation, it's a system, a creature that hates you. I don't blame people for ostracizing Franky, and I've never blamed you for being unable to face what she's saying. I can't fully stomach it myself, some days. But she's right, Pippa. I wish I could feel safe in ignorance, but she's right."

Pippa was quiet for a long time, digesting what I said, turning it over and around in her palm until it was smooth as a marble.

"You're the first one who's ever believed her, you know," Pippa said. "In every single way, you're the first person. And I'm sad it wasn't me, but . . ." She squeezed my hand. "I'm glad it was you."

I leaned forward, pressing a gentle kiss to Pippa's shoulder.

"You've been a good friend to her," I insisted. "Don't fight me, I'm telling the truth. You've saved her life a million times by being there and not giving up on her."

Pippa shook her head, smiling sadly. "I love her, Lawrence. I love her like family. I just wish I did more for her when it really mattered."

Pippa looked like she wanted to say more but was distracted by movement inside the house. I followed her line of sight to find shadowed figures rushing around. I squinted, seeing what looked like Franky's lithe shadow, waving her hand around. She moved like a comet. I smiled despite myself.

"You care for her in an uncomplicated way," Pippa remarked, watching me watch the window. "You just take whatever she throws at you. That's not easy, but you've never seemed to mind."

I considered this. Considered the Franky I knew, the Frankies I missed out on and could never meet: Hockey Captain Franky, Belle of the Ball Franky, Traumatized-but-Committed-to-Hiding-it Franky.

"She just makes sense," I said. "She's always made sense to me."

"You and you alone." Pippa grinned, shaking her head as she stood up.

I turned off the propane fire and stood up beside her, staring up into the stars. I felt the pull of Franky, my gravity, my North Star. I let it lead me back home.

Pippa and I rejoined Stasia and Franky, finding a perplexing picture.

While Stasia muttered to herself over Franky's wine glasses, giving us a distracted smile, Franky stood in front of an insane selection of alcohol, bottles spread out like a buffet. There must've been fifty lining the countertop.

"Let's get drunk," Franky announced. "Belligerently so."

"Franky?" Pippa exclaimed, lost for words. "Did you two rob a liquor store while we were outside?"

"It was Dad's," Franky said, turning to busy herself with cutlery. "It's the only thing I brought from his house, because what the fuck was I going to do with heirlooms or family photographs?"

There was a pregnant pause, all three of us wondering what to say as she brought fourteen knives and two forks over to the table. Stasia chased her with two more forks, taking away the excess knives.

"Alcohol makes sense," Franky continued, hand on the table. "That's an inheritance I can work with."

Oh, this girl. I ached.

"Don't just stare at me like that," she said, annoyed by the pitying pause. "Dig in!"

We shifted awkwardly, unsure what to do with ourselves. Pippa was the first to break, reaching for the closest bottle of alcohol.

"You can't do white wine," Franky reminded her softly. "Gives you the spins."

Pippa hummed in agreement, laying down the white to pick up a red.

"That one is the oldest," Stasia commented, glancing over her shoulder. "Super expensive brand."

"Perfect." Franky grabbed a bottle opener. "Let's drink that first."

Franky gifted us each a glass of wine like a priest giving communion. Settling around the dining room table, we dug in. The food was delicious, and while too unbothered to care about fancy liquor, I could admit that Franky's collection felt smoother than the bargain brands. Maybe it was just the company, though, and the near-delirious state of exhaustion.

We left Cowboy Night around eleven, and no one thought it was strange when Franky started cooking supper past midnight.

"It's been a horrible night." Franky raised her third glass of wine midway through the meal, liquid sloshing on the tablecloth. "So. Cheers to that."

We all murmured in agreement, glasses clinking.

"And . . . and I want to put this one out to my girls," Franky continued sloppily, holding eye contact with each of us. Eye contact as intimate as an organ transplant. "My girls who stick by my side . . . my girls who I love."

"*Whom* I love," Stasia corrected.

"Exactly!"

Stasia smiled, shaking her head fondly.

"Cheers to us," Pippa concluded, refilling our glasses for the toast.

Clink.

We chugged the wine, sweet liquor spilling down spent cheeks. We sunk in on ourselves, strange atmosphere akin to the wake before a funeral. Dead body in the next room, city of mourners pretending not to notice the stench. But *God*, did it keep catching up to us. When the food was gone, we loaded the dishwasher and we sat back down at the dining room table. Silent space, we stared at each other.

"What should we do?" Stasia asked, glancing around the room.

Loaded question.

"We're all too drunk to drive home," she continued. "I guess we could split a cab—?"

"Stay?" Franky interrupted, lightning hot and quick as an electric fence. "I mean . . . please. Please, can you guys stay? I have room, a spare room, and the couch pulls out into a sofa bed, and um . . . and please. Don't leave."

Pippa and I opened our mouths, glancing at each other, but it was Stasia that broke into Franky's desperate pleading, meeting her with a simple sincerity.

"Okay," Stasia said. "We'll stay."

And so, loaded with blankets and loaned pajamas and hastily made beds, we stayed.

We fell asleep to the sounds of distant sirens. A small town on fire, home to a million ghosts.

TRAP

We lived in a state of general unrest for three more days before anyone thought to do anything about it.

The days were hot, and we kept hiding away, hoping that someone would clean up the mess made of everything. Funhouse was on indefinite hiatus. As were Franky's nerves. She spent the morning at the police station going over her statement, and she returned soaking wet in a storm cloud of sorrow. She was fractured again, boiling hot. Unhinged Franky back at the wheel.

She summoned us all to her living room at half past three in the afternoon, bribing us with takeout coffees she bought on the drive home. Franky stood in front of the whiteboard, arms crossed like a drill sergeant. She wasn't wearing the fake arm today. Wasn't wearing much.

We settled in a semicircle in front of her, claiming our drinks and mirroring the first time we did this, so long ago. The three of us clueless as children, staring up at our ringleader.

"Alright, girls," Franky announced, commanding our attention. "We've leisured long enough, but now we need a plan."

"Right." Pippa nodded, sipping her coffee. "Of course. And I assume you have one locked and loaded?"

"Of course I do."

"Right." Pippa sighed, long-suffering. "Well let's hear it, Napoleon."

"Alike in both strategy and stature," Stasia joked, gently nudging Pippa.

"Not funny." Franky pointed at them. "But we're not here to give pointers on comedy. We're here to catch a monster."

"I don't see why we can't do both," Pippa said.

"My strategy," Franky ploughed forward, ignoring her. "Is a hostile takeover of the monster's territory."

We sat in silence, dumbfounded.

"The monster is a landowner?" Pippa asked incredulously.

"*No*, it—clearly, it's still at the arcade."

"Uh." Stasia scratched her head. "Why?"

"It's waiting for us," Franky announced simply. "So, we feed into its trap, trick it into thinking it has the upper hand, then *BAM!*" She smacked her hand against the whiteboard. "We trap it."

"We . . ." Pippa rubbed her forehead, dumbfounded.

"Why's it waiting for us?" Stasia asked.

"Because it wasn't finished," Franky explained impatiently. "I think it had more planned after the chase in the basement, but it must've left when the police showed up. Which is so typical of it, but if we follow through with my plan, we can finally show these assholes what I'm talking about! We can finally . . . We can show them! They can't ignore me if it's right in front of them."

I studied her franticity; defences triggered, hackles raised. "Did something happen at the police station, Franky?"

She looked at me like I kicked her. "Why would you ask me that?"

"You just seem . . ." I gestured to her.

"Seem what? Angry?" she snapped. "I *am* angry. I'm—I want it to be their turn. I want to bring the monster to the police station and let it scare the shit out of *those guys* for once. Let it stalk *them* and scare *them*." She was breathless, burning hot. "Let them finally see that I'm not FUCKING *CRAZY*—"

"Franky." Pippa interrupted, eyes soft and scared.

"I'M NOT CRAZY!" Franky shouted, voice cracking in half. Slow tears ran down her face, full body shaking.

"Franky." I stood, hand gentle on her left elbow. Right above the cutoff point. "Honey, what happened?"

Franky suffered through several wheezing breaths, shoulders curling inward.

"Did the police say something?" I prodded gently. "Did they—"

"They blamed me," she interrupted, soft and certain.

We were quiet.

"What?" Pippa's voice was hardly above a whisper.

"They said it's my fault for hosting a large public gathering months after the killings," Franky said. "They said I should've expected something like this to happen, seeing how I'm—" Her words caught in her throat like a bone. "Seeing how I'm Franklin's daughter."

Silence. Pure, shock-slick silence.

"Are you serious?" Stasia asked, the same time Pippa indignantly yelled, "That's bullshit!"

"They said there's no trend to investigate," Franky continued, far away. "They wouldn't listen to me. They said my investigation was childish. They told me I should go to therapy."

"I'll give them therapy." Pippa swung her fist around, cheeks red with anger.

"They . . ." Franky swallowed, her last confession clearly the hardest. "They laughed at me."

"Franky . . ." I drifted, lost for words.

Far-Away Franky hardly lasted a second. She wrung her sadness out like rainwater, shaking me off to turn back to her board. She returned to irate intensity like an old lover.

"So we need to trap it," she said, trying her best to be feral again. It didn't have the same bite as before. "We'll trap it and—and we *show* them."

Her tirade was interrupted by a dinging from Stasia's phone.

"They have to see it," Franky continued. "They won't listen to me, but they *have* to—"

"Um," Stasia murmured, eyes scanning the screen. "Guys . . ."

We turned to her, shocked by the sheer terror on her face.

"They've arrested a group of teen boys for Deidre's murder," Stasia said, showing us her phone screen. "Apparently, they were radicalized by that conspiracy board. Wanted to copy the Frankenstein Killer's method, but lost their nerve after chopping off her hand."

I could barely breathe.

"They got a confession from one of them," Stasia read, glancing up at Franky. "Said they targeted Deidre because she reminded them of the other victims. He gave a full statement and turned himself in." She turned off her phone, hands shaking. "It was a bunch of random kids, not . . . not a creature. Your monster has been acquitted, Franky."

Still as death, we turned to her, waiting for the reaction with bated breath.

Franky's face crumpled, hand trembling by her side. With a shuddering breath, she ran from the room, shoulders shaking with tears.

She was only gone for three minutes. Which is evidently how long it takes to collect a knife, hammer, and taser.

We stood to meet her, stopping in our tracks once we noticed the dangerous edge to her expression.

"Franky, are you . . ."

"The plan is still on," Franky barked, impatient and inconsolable. She tucked weapons into her belt loops.

"What do you—" Pippa stammered. "*What?*"

"This won't distract us."

Pippa blinked up at her, gesturing vaguely around us. "Distract us from *what*?" she asked incredulously. "They caught the bad guy. I'm sure whatever you saw was just those kids being weirdos, but that's over now. We're safe again, Franky."

"No we're not!" Franky exploded, anger boiling over. "It's a *monster* Pippa, not a bunch of fucked up teenagers playing copycat."

"But why does that matter?" Pippa pleaded. "Monster, teenagers, who cares? Why are you so—?"

"Because I will not let them pin this on one outlier again," she interrupted. "They want this to go the same way as last time, but I won't let them. One man will not take the fall for my monster."

We stared at her, lost for words. Her frustration bubbled like the tide.

"I've put so much work into building a case," she continued ranting, "but people just brush me off. Somehow a bunch of teenage boys slip into the space. They become victims of radicalization, distant mothers, and it becomes another fluke. People find reasons to feel safe again. It doesn't matter that they arrested those boys, it doesn't matter that Maxine is safe, we—" She stopped, frozen in the face of her own misstep.

"Maxine . . ." Stasia stared at her, lost for words. "Did you say she's safe?"

Franky shrunk, curling in on herself with guilt.

"Franky . . ." Pippa warned. "What do you mean she's safe?"

"She called her mother a few days ago," she admitted softly, staring at the floor. "Turns out she skipped town after her ex-boyfriend broke the restraining order. She was just waiting for things to settle down before she reached out to anyone."

We watched her. Shocked and silent.

"Why didn't you tell us?" Stasia asked, voice low with betrayal.

"Because then you wouldn't believe me anymore."

Franky, Franky, Franky. I chewed my cheek, sending Stasia a desperate look: *Please don't hate her.*

"All this . . ." Pippa muttered, burying her face in her hands. "All this for a made up monster."

"It's not . . ." Franky turned to me, frustrated and desperate. "Lawrence, you've seen it. Tell them it's real. Tell them Maxine doesn't change things. *Please.*"

I found myself caught in an uncomfortable middle ground. I've seen the monster, I was chased by the monster, but Franky's focus was so singular it scared me.

"I . . ." I glanced at the two of them. "I saw a flesh-hungry monster that wants to rip women to shreds. That can be—um . . ."

"Franky, listen," Pippa interrupted. "I'm sorry to ask you this question, but I have to. I have to know. The monster, are you . . ." She paused, gathering her courage. "Are you sure the monster isn't just men who remind you of your father?"

We all froze. We never spoke about Franklin's relation to the monster. We never spoke about Franklin, period. We lived our lives defined by his actions, but we refused to acknowledge him.

I turned to Franky, scared to see her reaction. A smattering of tears streamed down her face, her impossible contrast of vulnerability and fury.

"Why are you bringing him up?" Franky asked, voice shaking. "Why do you . . . why are you making me think of him?"

"Because he set the context."

"That's irrelevant—"

"Of course it's relevant, Franky! I can't tiptoe around this anymore. Your dad killed those girls. Do you know that? Will you just tell me you know that?"

Silence. Horrible space filled with nothing but heavy breathing. We watched Franky crumble, watched pieces fall off her, slow and terrible.

"I—I don't want—I can't—I . . ." she stuttered, hand shaking. She struggled to pull herself together. "I—I need to . . ."

Pippa reached out to her, pushed to the side as Franky stormed from the room. There was a slam, a crash, something shattering in a nearby room. The sound of an engine starting.

"Is that . . ." Stasia trailed off, ear cocked towards the front yard.

Pippa swore as we heard Franky's truck spin away, a long line of expletives. In any other circumstance, I would've complimented the creativity.

"That motherfucker," she hissed. "That *MOTHERFUCKER.*"

"Do you think she—"

"Of course she is," Pippa hissed. "Of fucking *course* she's gonna go off alone, and try to get herself killed by an imaginary monster—"

"It's *real*, Pippa," Stasia interrupted, voice sharp. "After everything we've all been through, are you not even afraid of the *possibility*?"

"You guys weren't *here*," Pippa shot back. "You don't understand where I'm coming from. I hope it's a monster! I hope it's this gross, woman-eating beast."

I put my hand on Stasia's arm, quieting her queued rebuttal.

"Because that would be easier!" Pippa continued. "It would be easier than knowing it's just a bunch of random men doing this. Ones you walk past in the grocery store, say hello to on the street. Isn't that scarier? Isn't it easier to forgive a creature who doesn't know more than what it was made to be?"

I gave Stasia a meaningful look, silently shaking my head.

"Okay," Stasia said. "Okay, I hear you. But can I say something?"

Pippa crossed her arms, body coiled with tension. She nodded once, movements jerky.

"I won't pretend to know what you've been through this past year, because you're right. I wasn't here. I don't understand how it feels, knowing that the people you grew up with are capable of such evil." She paused, letting Pippa digest her words. "And I know you're frustrated and angry at Franky, I am, too, but can you trust me on this?"

Pippa dropped her intense gaze, studying the floor between us.

"It's *real*," Stasia pressed. "And that thing, that monster, whatever it is, is fucking *terrifying*, it . . ." Her voice broke. "It's going to hurt Franky," she exhaled. "And Franky will let it, to prove herself right about the world."

Pippa softened slowly, studying us. Our fear, our frustration, our unwavering care for Franky. She scrubbed a hand over her face, lips pressed in a hard line. "I'm gonna be gray by the time I'm thirty," she muttered, storming from the room.

Stasia and I watched the empty doorway, glancing at each other. Her eyes were wide, rimmed with red. We were about to face the monster again, and she was scared. She was really scared. I opened my mouth to comfort her, to offer a way out, to promise I'd get her out of this alive, but it was all lost to a loud slam.

"Well?" Pippa re-entered the living room, tossing an armful of weapons onto the coffee table. Stasia and I cataloged baseball bats, hammers, knives, a smorgasbord of supplies. "Are we doing this stupid shit or what?"

I picked up a flamethrower, giving Pippa an inquisitive stare.

"Franky has an anarchist streak."

"Just Franky?"

"Ha ha," Pippa deadpanned. "Enough jokes. Pick your weapon, girls."

I stuck with the flamethrower, making a mental note to research how to use it on the drive over. I slung it over my shoulder, grabbing a hammer to tuck into my belt loop for good measure. Stasia chose a baseball bat, while Pippa kept it simple with two big knives she let dangle from her jacket, axe in hand.

We stared at each other, ridiculous in our army jackets, miscellaneous weapons, and matching Doc Martens. We bided time, bit back fear.

"Well," Stasia said, lip quivering. "I guess we should go . . ."

Pippa nodded, expression grim. "Carabiner up, girls. Let's go find that asshole."

ROT

Stasia sped across town, shaky behind the wheel of Pippa's decade-old car. The wheels wheezed on sharp turns, sunburns sticking on seat belts and peeling leather seats. It was hot out. It was always so damn hot out.

"Stupid idiot, so stubborn. Always running off on some wild goose chase, as if she doesn't get enough attention as it is . . ." Pippa muttered to herself in the passenger seat, as bitter as she was worried.

I leaned forward to place a hand on her shoulder, wondering what I could possibly say to comfort her. "She's very frustrating," I landed on eventually.

"Understatement of the century."

"Where should we go?" Stasia asked, rolling to a slow stop at the intersection in front of the arcade. "Do we have any ideas where she'd run off to?"

Ideas were not needed. I glanced out the window, finding Franky's pickup truck abandoned by the arcade entrance.

"Well." Stasia clicked her tongue. "That was convenient."

We turned into the parking lot, hands hovering over our seat belts. The front door hung open, lights flashing through the window.

"Any last words, girls?" Pippa asked, only half joking.

"If we make it through this, I think I'd like to buy a car," Stasia said. "I've been looking at them for a while now and always talk myself out of it."

Pippa nodded, solemn as a priest. "Lawrence?"

I sat, considered, and summed up the moment as succinctly as I could. "I hope we don't die."

"Poignant." Pippa nodded, kicking open the door. "Well, girls . . . it's showtime."

It was, it turned out, not showtime.

Our entrance to the arcade was unceremonious. It appeared quiet, empty, unharmed. Pippa tried the light switch by the door, shrugging when it wouldn't work. The flashing games lit the way, fairy lights weakly flickering. Franky was nowhere to be found.

"Any signs of struggle?" Stasia asked, investigating our trail.

Some of the games were tilted, moved from their long-inhabited spots, revealing patches of fresh carpet. We chased the movement, listening to the silence for sounds of Franky.

It was quiet, suspiciously so. What was Franky's big idea, anyway? I felt resentment growing as we walked in circles, a sentiment clearly shared by Pippa. She muttered profanities to herself, leading our way with an axe.

"If the monster doesn't get her, I will," she threatened, pausing when she turned a corner. "What the . . ."

Stasia and I rushed to her side, finding a platform loafer abandoned in a circle of flashing games. Pippa tiptoed forward, poking the loafer with her axe. It tipped over, and we all jumped back in fear.

"That doesn't feel good," Pippa observed. "Who leaves behind a shoe?"

"Maybe she was in a rush to escape," I suggested.

"From what, arcade tokens?" Pippa gestured around us, the confusing disarray.

I wandered forward, finding a bag of arcade tokens spilled across the floor. "Maybe so."

Stasia dropped her baseball bat and grabbed Pippa's axe, walking past me to the next corner. "I've lost my patience," she said, moving us along quicker.

Pippa and I shared an amused look, wondering when Stasia ever *had* this aforementioned patience. We followed obediently behind her; I held the flamethrower up in defense, while Pippa walked back on to me, knife in each hand.

"We look so stupid." Pippa laughed, bumping into my back, propelling me forward to crash into Stasia.

"Hey!" She whipped around, axe at the ready. "Can you try not to barbecue me, please?"

"Woah." I crashed backwards into Pippa. "Easy with the axe."

Pippa spun to face us, almost catching me with a knife. "What's going on back there?"

"Jesus, Pippa!" I cried, jumping back towards the axe.

"Really between a rock and a hard place, hey?" Stasia laughed, delighted when Pippa started riffing off her joke.

"*Guys*," a voice cut in from behind us, midway through Pippa's bit of chasing me with her knives.

We all turned to find Franky, hobbling along with one shoe. I pointed in the direction of the other, taking in her disheveled appearance. She had lost all her weapons except the long knife strapped to her chest.

"Jeez, Franky." Pippa whistled. "Did you get in a fistfight with the photo booth again?"

Franky snatched her other shoe, letting out a shaky breath. "You have no idea what you just walked into."

"You *led* us here."

"I didn't want you to follow!"

"You always want us to follow!" I cut in, tired and hungry and confused.

"I've never once asked—"

CRASH.

Franky stilled, our fight frozen midair. We all turned slowly towards the sound, finding nothing but flickering lights.

"Follow me," Franky hissed, falling over herself as she shoved her shoe back on.

She took off running down the corner she appeared from, checking over her shoulder to make sure we were following her. As if we would do anything but. Whatever was behind us was getting closer, the loud crashes became more frequent, overturned games circling us in. Franky led us to a dead end and cursed under her breath, raking her hand through her hair as she muttered schemes to herself.

"Is someone here?" Pippa asked. "Are you—what is all this, Franky? Is there—"

CRREEEEAAAAAASSSSSHHHH.

We jumped in unison, scrambling in another direction like a bunch of buffoons. Something jumped over our heads, a shadow illuminating our trail like a trick of the light. Stasia squealed, clinging tightly as we kept hot on Franky's trail.

BANG.

Franky paused, hand on her knee as she stopped to catch her breath. We looked around us, studied the rafters, the high ceilings, the tall games towering over our heads. Shards of glass were crushed into the carpet under our feet, games boxing us into a tiny circle.

The lights were blinking, with a looped audio of *Mortal Kombat* saying, "*FINISH HER!*" and "*FATALITY!*" We heard the monster prowl, circling the struggling games.

"It's here," Stasia hissed, gripping my arm.

"What?" Pippa shrilled, almost excited as she scanned the room. "What's here, the—the creature thing? Are you fucking *kidding* me? Where is it?"

"There!" Stasia hissed, pointing to our left. "Jesus, it's . . . there it is. *Jesus.*"

It was at her panicking that we saw the first glimpse of it together, as a group. It was received in silence, in awestruck horror, jumping on top of an overturned machine to stand before us. The glimpses of the past had nothing on this portrait, a full creature under the blinding neon lights. It was a quilt of body parts, a constellation of rotting girls. I felt bile rise in my throat at the smell, the tightness in which long-dead women were connected under its ghastly white skin.

"What the heck . . ." Pippa muttered, too scared to swear. "What . . . *what* is that thing?"

"Frankenstein," I whispered, gulping back vomit. "It's Frankenstein."

"*Frankenstein*?" Stasia asked, forgetting to stay quiet. "Come on, Lawrence. It's Frankenstein's *monster*."

"Really?" I hissed. "You're choosing *now* to—"

"She has a point," Pippa whispered, frozen in terror.

"Thank you," Stasia said. "If we're going to be on the brink of death, we might as well be accurate."

"For the love of God, girls, this is not the time to be fucking around," Franky hissed, trying to regroup. "We . . ."

I turned to Franky, wondering what cut her off. Her eyes were moonstruck in horror, focus pinpricked on a gray-white hand, growing off the monster's side like a tumor. Franky's hand.

"*Oh*," she exhaled softly, dismayed. "It's—"

Before anyone could cry or scream or attempt to offer solace, the broken *Mortal Kombat* game decided to play a long sequence of audio, catching the attention of the monster. We froze, staring it down.

Pippa slowly backed up, grabbing her way along the wall.

"Where are you going?" Franky whispered.

We turned to watch her dig through her pockets for change, messing around with the jukebox. "December, 1963" started playing a moment later, bubbly tune bouncing off the walls.

"Pippa?" I asked manically.

"I want to die to good music."

I barely had time to curse her out before Stasia grabbed Franky and me, trembling as the monster sniffed the air. It lowered its head, fear-stricken eyes trained on us, narrow with hate. We took a step backwards; the monster took a step forwards. Another step backwards. The monster jumped to the floor in front of us.

We all took off running, screaming at the top of our lungs. The monster did not take kindly to our flashy attempt to escape, clamoring over itself to follow our trail. Its new limbs made it clumsy, but it was still a hell of an opponent to outrun. Pippa grabbed a pinball machine and tipped it over, blocking a pathway.

"*THAT'S A BITCH TO REPLACE*," Franky yelled, breathless.

"*SO'S MY SKULL.*"

By some accident or perhaps hilarious sense of humor, the monster jostled the jukebox, changing the song to "It's Raining Men."

"If I die to a song about men, I'm killing myself," Pippa swore.

"It's pretty catchy," I whispered, singing along as we ran.

Franky kept glancing over her shoulder, fixated on the gray hand. I couldn't imagine what she was thinking, what must be going through her head. I squeezed Stasia's hand, sending a wordless message. *For the love of God, hold on to Franky.*

We turned a corner fast, finding ourselves careening down the back hallway. I wondered if Franky's dad ever accounted for a situation like this when he designed this labyrinth of games. Daedalus dooming Icarus, sabotaging his child through property design.

Franky was so focused on the monster, she didn't notice the loose wires snarled across her path, tangling up in one and falling to the floor. Pippa doubled back without hesitation, struggling to free Franky's foot from its trap.

"Go!" Franky shouted, trying to push us away. "Just—keep running!"

Stasia and I inched away, backs against the wall as we watched the monster slow to a cat-like prowl. Franky and Pippa freed her foot, frozen in terror on the glass-covered carpet. The monster pounced at Pippa, landing on her left leg with a horrific howl. Glass sliced her skin as she tried to escape. Franky instinctively scrambled backwards, eyes darting between Pippa's dropped phone and the monster.

She wants a photo, I realized quickly, blood running cold. She's debating between saving her best friend and taking a photograph.

Pippa noticed this internal struggle, deflating weakly. She resigned herself to her fate, wincing as the monster's claws dug into exposed brown skin. I watched in horror, paralyzed with ineptitude.

"*NO*!" Stasia screamed, charging at the monster.

I watched the swing of her axe, a high arch into the monsters head. But it must've been from a Halloween costume, because the axe bounced harmlessly against its skull, stunning both Stasia and the monster. They blinked at each other for a strange moment until Stasia threw the axe in the opposite direction, wailing in relief as the monster growled and chased it, jumping off Pippa's now blood-soaked leg.

We rushed forward, gathering Pippa and Franky and limping into the basement of Funhouse as quickly as we could. Franky dead-bolted the door behind us, hand shaking and eyes absent. It was morbid to end up here. Franky's plan had gone awry, and now we were trapped at the origin point of her horrors.

We all pressed against the door, awkwardly meshing together in an ill-fitting puzzle. We waited for a kickback, a hiss, a snarl, but there was nothing. The monster let us be.

Pippa cursed under her breath, clumsily descending the staircase to sit at the bottom, head between her knees. I heard her mumbling the steps to a breathing exercise, muttering about monsters.

"First timers," Stasia joked weakly, still pressed against the door. It was like she didn't trust its stillness, waiting for it to push back against us at any moment.

With wheezing breaths, I took stock of our surroundings, the same horrible basement from days before, now somehow our safe haven. Pippa was still muttering to herself, Stasia kept obsessively analyzing the door hinges, and Franky looked understandably harrowed by our new location. I clutched onto the dusty handrail, barely balancing on the top steps.

"I need to check the basement door," Franky muttered to herself. "That's probably how it got in on Cowboy Night . . . I need to check to make sure it's locked, I—"

"Okay," Stasia interrupted. "What should we do?"

Franky blinked up at her, shell shocked. "Um. You—" she stammered, struggling to come back to herself. "There's a knife hidden somewhere down here. I think in one of the boxes near the electricity panel. You guys can look for that?"

There were more than enough weapons for us to share, but the request seemed to be a make-work task to get us out of her hair.

"Okay." Stasia nodded, shooting me a look. "And the door will hold?"

Franky studied the locks, considering something. "Yeah," she murmured. "Yeah, it'll hold."

And what better way to put it to the test. Stasia and I watched Franky flutter off, turning back to the door in tandem. It was quiet. The monster was quiet.

"I think it likes us to feel safe, sometimes," Stasia whispered, leaning close. "This cycle of terror and false safety . . . it's like it relishes the chase."

"Makes our meat more tender."

"You know what they say," Stasia mumbled, stepping away from the door with a shaky sigh. "Scared meat tastes better."

PATRICIDE

Stasia and I were buried alive, picking through the fossils of Franklin's Funhouse.

Arcade tokens. Tickets. A million miles of receipt paper. No weapons, notably, but we kept looking, knowing that Franky needed her space.

While she wandered, we kept a close watch on the basement door. Every now and then Stasia or I would wander up the stairs, testing the doorknob and locks, just to be sure.

Pippa found the strength to join us eventually, sitting on top of an old pool table, head in her hands.

"I can hear it," Pippa muttered, words caught in her palms. "It's up there, sniffing, scratching . . . It seems to run away whenever you guys get too close, but it's going to come back soon."

Stasia and I exchanged a look. I kept picking through a box of old paperwork while Stasia joined Pippa on the pool table, sitting side by side.

"It will," she agreed easily, ignoring my befuddled expression. "But we'll be ready next time. I promise."

Pippa exhaled, slowly lifting her head from her hands.

"Franky was right," Pippa said, pausing to consider something. "She was willing to kill me for a photograph."

These were two separate statements, but their conjunction made me dizzy. So Franky was right about the danger, but she endangered her friend to try procuring proof. Sanctimonious girl, always so caught up in the details.

I studied Pippa. Her skin was sallow with stress, lips dry from screaming. Her leg was still bleeding.

I tore off my sleeve, kneeling in front of her to wrap the fabric tight around the gash. It was a surface wound, less dramatic than it looked, but I didn't know what to do about the massive gash Franky left on her heart.

"Are you—"

"It's a strange creature," Pippa interrupted, staring up at the ceiling.

Dust fell from the exposed beams like rain. The monster prowled overhead. I could hear the faint audio of the games it activated along the way.

"Strange, strange creature . . ." she continued. "It's like it let us escape."

"We hardly got away," Stasia reminded her. "You were hurt."

"Fatally so," Pippa joked. "But still. It could've finished us off if it wanted to."

"It's not always violent," I said. "Sometimes it's just scary."

"And sometimes it's both."

"Seems tonight it decided on both," Pippa grimaced, picking at the makeshift bandage. The place where the monster dug in its claws. Real or fake? Had she tripped? Fallen in the glass? Been attacked by something else? How did we all rewrite the same memory, and what is memory, anyway?

"Are you okay?" I tried again.

Pippa turned to me, smiling. "One of us should find Franky," she said at last, staring into the maze of machinery. "I'd offer, but I don't know what the fuck to say to her."

One of us clearly meant *Lawrence*. Amusing as it was to picture Stasia attempting the heart-to-heart.

"I'll go." I stood, scrubbing a hand over my face.

Pippa and Stasia exchanged a look, turning back to me with a complicated smile.

"Alright," Stasia said.

"Be careful." Pippa saluted me.

Careful. I smiled to myself, pushing away from the mountain of boxes to enter Franky's labyrinth. My melancholy minotaur, running from our golden string of fate.

The journey through the winding games was much calmer without a creature hot on my trail. I traced a finger along dusty pinball machines, poked a few broken buttons. I walked past Stasia's puddle of vomit from Cowboy Night, congealed and crusty. The footprints and shattered game pieces from our frantic escape. I was surprised to find Franky sitting in a clearing of dust, right below the warning sign for the garbage shredder. Her knees were buckled against her chest, arm wrapped around herself. She was crying.

"Franky," I uttered softly, slowly approaching her.

She wouldn't raise her head, wouldn't meet my eye. I sat beside her and waited. It must've been a million years before she found the space to speak. She rose like the tide.

"Do you . . . do you know where we are, Lawrence?" She gestured to the space around us. The sign above her head. "Do you know what happened here?"

I shook my head, wondering if this was some sort of test.

"My dad did this to my arm," she continued, curt and clinical, smiling at my signals of shock. "I know it's obvious, but can you let that be a big confession? I've never said it out loud, before."

There was no need to play pretend. I felt the air punched from my lungs, the ground melt beneath us.

"It's because I confronted him about Lily," she murmured. "I wasn't sure until her. *God*, I hoped I was wrong, but then it just . . .

it *clicked*. I know it was stupid, to confront him alone like that," she continued, "but I thought the event upstairs might stop him from doing something violent. I don't know why I thought that, it's not like that's ever helped me before." She let her eyes flutter shut, head lolling back against the wall. "I don't want to talk about what he did to me, I'm sure you can guess. H-he . . ." She shuddered, pulling her knees tighter against her chest. "He fucked my arm up so badly, I needed it amputated. It was distilled pain, every second I spent scared of him distilled into that one moment. I thought I was going to die."

I stared at her, lost for words.

"I guess I was screaming," she said absently. "Someone must've called the cops. Too little too late, guys." She laughed dryly, melting into a rattling cough. "*Decades* too late. They must've opened and closed my file a million times, a million . . ." She trailed off, eyes on the ceiling. "When the police found us and saw what he did to me, they pinned the murders on him, too. Guess they needed something substantial." She smiled sharply. "A life's worth of pain was not evidence enough."

"Franky," I pleaded. "You shouldn't have had to lose so much to be believed. It was never even your responsibility."

"Whether it's mine or not, I hold it, Lawrence. I hold it so tightly." She stared down at her amputated arm. The missing space, empty like a puzzle piece. "I was his first victim, and I feel the weight of every single girl who came after me, every girl I could have saved, if only . . ." She bit her lip, building courage. "If only I died."

"Franky—"

"It's true, I know it's true. If I died, they would've caught him sooner. Women are only believed when they're dead. I made the fatal mistake of surviving.

She was floating, faraway. I wanted to pull her back to earth, worried she might float away for good, this time.

"I survived him for years, and what good has it done?" She smiled, waterlogged and warm. "A *monster* makes more sense to me than my father's violence. That creature upstairs, that frightening fucking . . . that *thing* makes sense to me. It won't turn around and play nice with the neighbors. It hates me in a way that is pure and uncomplicated. It hates me because I'm here." Her voice broke, staring up at the ceiling. "I never really understood why Dad hated me. Maybe it's the same reason."

"He never should have hated you," I murmured, lost on what else I could possibly say. "He should've . . . he was supposed to love you unconditionally."

"I don't think that's something he knew how to do," she said. "He was . . ."

Franky's dad was a fictional man, a constellation of ideas and anecdotes. I wanted the truth; I wanted it from the person who knew him best. She watched me for three long minutes.

"He scared me," she said at last.

"I never got past the childhood fear of him, because he kept getting scarier. No matter what I did, no matter how careful I was, he hated me. I don't know why. I thought—" She choked out a sob. "I thought I was his little girl." Her voice, once soft and shapeless as water, turned sharp. Venomous. "How *stupid* of me," she spat. "How—"

"Don't say that," I interrupted. "You were just a kid—"

"I'm twenty-five years old—"

"You're still a kid, Franky! You're always going to be a scared kid, making up ghost stories to make sense of your father's anger."

The aftermath of Isaac and Abraham: Isaac becomes God.

"He's trapped you," I continued softly. "He's keeping you here, but you deserve to move forward. You need to believe me when I say that. You need to try and believe me."

She shook her head, hand over her ear. She wasn't listening, she didn't want to, and what could I do to change that? Nothing would erase her past, no meandering monologues, no confessions of love. So she's opened up to me, so I've climbed inside her rotting chest, locked up like Fort Knox, but what does it matter? All she cares about is her monster, her relics of rambling self-hatred, the only ways she could make sense of her pain.

Isaac and Abraham, reborn through the flames.

"Please, Franky . . ."

She stared up at me, and God, she made me so sad. I wanted to put her in my pocket. I wanted to kill her father. I wanted to hold her still and beg. *Please, Franky, forget the monster, I can play pretend and eat you raw instead. C'mon, Franky, let me hold your hand. Let me lie on top of you, writhe around like a worm. Taste buds covering every inch of skin. North Star to my endless summer rain, let me brush your hair. I'll orbit you round and round; I'll never get dizzy. Reignite me, kill me, spend years telling me about whatever crosses your mind. Seriously Franky, I'm chained to your whim like a bad dog, and I'll spend forever trying to tell you, trying to encapsulate it. Like trying to take a picture of the sun.*

"I care about you so much," I pleaded. "So much, Franky. Such a stupid amount. I met the worst possible version of you—"

She snorted, attention captured. "Gee, thanks."

"No, listen. I met the worst possible version of you, and I can't imagine liking you more. But the crazy thing is, I know I will every single day, the further away we get from this fucked up, horrible situation. You're beautiful, Franky. You're beautiful and you're smart and hilarious, and lovable, too, despite your best efforts. I'm with you every step of the way, okay? I always meant that." I ducked my head, forcing myself into her line of vision. "And I'm going to kill this monster," I continued. "Because we deserve better than the shit we got from our parents. Violent fathers, endless resentment pushed onto us by enabling mothers. I'll kill it all for you, Franky."

She met my eye, finally met my eye, and basked in my searchlight of sincerity, like a sailor lost at sea. I gave her everything I had and more. I let her take it all. It was always hers, anyway.

"Okay," she conceded, crumpling with exhaustion. "Okay."

"Okay?"

"Yeah." She let out a shuddering breath, grabbing my hand like a lifeline. "Let's kill it."

EVIDENCE

A resolution to kill a monster is infinitely easier than actually killing a monster.

Franky and I learned this fast, returning to Stasia and Pippa to find a half-hatched plan. They explained their scheme with figurines on a rotten Monopoly board, and I tried not to be offended when the one they chose to represent me was a tiny clown statue.

"The abandoned lot is our best bet," Pippa said, putting the figurine for the monster, the money bag, in front of the free parking space. "It's risky to lead it through town, but I think it'd be impossible to fight it here. The monster has the upper hand in this goddamn labyrinth. Unless one of you can climb walls and haven't thought it relevant to mention. Plus"—she jabbed the free parking space—"that part of town is abandoned, so there's no chance of witnesses. Which will be positive if we get our ass handed to us, I can't ruin my street cred."

"But we *won't* get our ass handed to us, because we have a foolproof plan." Stasia cut in, segueing into the second part of the plan. "We set it on fire."

Franky blinked, hand on her hip as she processed this.

"Okay." She pursed her lips, eyes red from crying. "Why?"

Pippa and Stasia shrugged. "Got any better ideas?"

Franky and I exchanged a look, eyebrows raised. I shrugged, and she scratched her head.

"So we burn it," Franky surmised, still stumped. "But what . . . what if we want it for evidence?"

Stasia, Pippa, and I exchanged a look.

"We can cross that bridge when we get to it," Pippa said warily, "but for now, let's be prepared for anything."

"Okay." Franky nodded, gnawing her lip. "This all seems too easy."

"It is," Pippa agreed. "And I look forward to us finding the one loophole and catastrophically fucking up."

"You give us too little credit," Stasia smiled. "I'm sure there's more than *one* loophole for us to slip into."

Pippa grinned, making the tiny horse representing her gallop a circle around the tiny doll representing Stasia.

"So, the abandoned lot is by the power plant, right?" I asked.

"Ghost city," Pippa confirmed. "Franky's dad bought the land last summer. He was in the process of developing it, but then . . ."

But then, indeed. That area of town was eerie half-built buildings rotting away in a sea of poured concrete, power lines, and little else. I always took the long way across town to avoid walking by. Even before the monster hunt, it always seemed to be haunted.

"Okay." Franky hummed, closing her eyes. "Okay."

Pippa grabbed the wolf figurine representing Franky, tapping it against her nose with a gentle smile.

"C'mon, Francesca," she leered. "If you can handle my mom's goulash, you can get through this."

Franky smiled, grabbing the little wolf to put in her front pocket. "Okay, girls." She took a deep breath. "Let's go eat that motherfucker alive."

We sprung into a strange, uncoordinated sort of action. Stasia was on monster duty, tracing its clumsy footsteps on the ceiling above us, while Pippa and I gathered and divvied up our weapons from earlier. Franky was doing . . . something. Pacing back and forth, muttering to herself, dictating the action in a manic, detached sort of state.

"Would eating the monster be cannibalism?" I asked absently, ripping off my other shirt sleeve. "Cause it has, um, human in it."

"You know what, Lawrence. I was wondering the exact same thing," Pippa said.

"Really?"

"*NO!*" She gestured around us, the franticness of our preparations.

"It was a good question, kid," Franky said, scruffing my hair as she walked by.

I preened, shooting Pippa a smug look. She seemed too stressed to bicker, hands shaking as she shoved a knife through her belt loop.

"Okay . . ." Stasia trailed off, ear to the sky. "Okay, I think it's in . . . Franky's office?"

There was a loud crash. Monitors ripped from the walls, wooden desks torn to shreds.

"I don't think insurance will cover that," Pippa joked, trying to hide her anxiety.

"Too bad I didn't get the monster attack coverage plan," Franky quipped, studying us carefully. "My office is on the opposite side of the exit."

"Okay?" Pippa's voice cracked.

"Which means now would be a perfect time to make a run for it."

The absurdity provided some much-needed levity, but it was time to be endangered, again. We listened to the silence above us, still as death.

"So, um, I'm having second thoughts," Pippa said, hands shaking. "This seems, um. It seems like a really underdeveloped plan, if I'm being honest. Maybe we should head back to the drawing board and think up a better way to—"

"Pip," Franky said, grabbing her hand, "it's now or never. We need to get out of here before the monster does, okay?"

"W-we just . . . run?" Pippa clarified, voice shaking with fear.

"What else?"

"Franky, you—you're going to get us killed."

"Not with that attitude." Her smile was sharp, on fire. "Are you with me?"

She didn't wait for a response. Turned on her heel and marched forward. Creatures of habit, we followed Franky into the labyrinth, quick pace picking up to a sprint, until we were running the entire way through. Like Cowboy Night, the games flickered to life around us, illuminated to light our path.

Footsteps echoed above us, startlingly human sounding. The door outside was within reach, an old wooden thing, decomposing under the weight of the building. Franky hastily unlocked the deadbolts, diving out into the warm summer air.

We didn't know what direction we should be running from, our jumbling haste almost comical. Franky sprinted towards her truck, cursing to herself as she instinctively unlocked it, loud beep echoing the air. No time to lose, we threw ourselves into the truck and locked the doors, finally finding time to glance around us.

"It's . . ." Pippa wheezed, out of breath. "Did it even chase us?"

"I don't think so." Stasia examined our surroundings, turning in her seat as Franky turned on the engine. "How do we know it'll come?"

There was a loud crash, somewhere at the back of the building. Shattered glass, objects thrown to the pavement. A loud howl echoed the air, almost mournful. A creature sad to realize it was left behind.

"It will," Franky said, jaw tight. She circled past the arcade, slowing to a near stop. The window out back was smashed, a trail of glass leading to the front. We followed it anxiously, eyes peeled for signs of movement.

Franky slowed to a crawl, tires crunching through gravel.

"I don't think it's—"

SLAM.

We all screamed, watching as the monster landed on the hood of Franky's truck. Nails digging deep into moss green paint, it panted, yellow eyes bleeding blood-red tears.

"DRIVE!" Pippa cried, desperately rolling up the window. "DRIVE, DRIVE, DRIVE—"

Franky's truck sputtered, old as the hills and twice as slow. Our windows froze, stuck in the humid air. The monster seemed to smile, jumping to the passenger side of the car, beaked face poking through the crack in my window.

I howled in fear, propelling backwards into Stasia. Franky cursed the engine, cursed the keys, truck sputtering to life and spinning out. We did two accidental doughnuts, monster hanging on tight, wriggling farther into my window.

Pippa reached back to fight with the handle, "C'mon, c'mon, c'mon," she muttered desperately.

The monster snarled, clawed hand slashing at the gap. Its nails caught on the glass, a horrific squeal of pain. The window finally gave way, rolling up. Howling in displeasure, the monster dropped to the ground before the window could decapitate it, running alongside Franky's truck as we sped across town. The sky stirred around us, an oncoming thunderstorm tracing the horizon. It crackled at the edges in preparation to break. We skidded into the ghost city; a desolate space, streets like set dressing. The monster howled in fury, falling behind to chase the back of Franky's truck. Something heaved, heavy and awkward. The horrific sound of nails scraping paint.

"It's trying to jump in the back!" Stasia yelled, spinning in her seat to track its movements. "Veer right, no, now left—"

BANG.

"What was—"

The truck caught the side of a curb, smashing into an abandoned car. We were thrown to the left, pirouetting through the air.

The truck flipped, and everything went black. Lost underwater, submerged in a sea of glass.

BLOOD

I came to a million years later, lying on my side, cheek pressed against broken glass.

"COME . . . HURRY!"

Stasia was screaming in my ear, shaking me with all her might. I desperately wondered if I might have a concussion, if the ringing in my ear would ever stop. I felt myself being dragged through a tunnel of knives, pulled to my feet by a million hands.

"Huh?"

My vision swam, finding Stasia and Pippa hovering over me, pinning my limp body against Franky's truck. It had landed right-side up, front bumper dented, windows smashed. Sweet smelling smoke filled the air, a birch fire nearby, I assumed, scrambling to regain use of my legs. I noticed a deep cut on my lower left thigh, wincing as I assessed the damage. It seemed to avoid any important arteries, but still ached whenever I moved.

"Are you okay?" Stasia whispered, assessing me at arm's length as Pippa frantically studied our surroundings.

I blinked, stumbling to the side. "I'm okay," I said, voice hoarse. My head ached, the smoke was giving me a migraine. "Franky—" I slurred, pinpricks of pain as I tried to move. "Where's—"

Sweet lucidity, my return to reality came slow. I scanned the area: burning fire, billows of dust, dented truck. No Franky.

"She ran ahead," Pippa said, pointing over her shoulder. "She bought us some time, distracting the monster, but we don't have much longer. We need to move."

I squinted, finding Franky waiting for us behind a concrete entranceway. The molding of a building never built. Old crime scene tape littered the scene. The infamous burial site, standing strong in a sea of debris.

"Are you okay to run?" Stasia asked.

I took a brave step forward, then another. I was stiff, achey, and my leg hurt like hell, but I knew I had to pull it together for my friends. I heard something scurrying behind us, a low growl echoing the air. The girls were terrified, I could tell, but they wouldn't leave me.

"I'm okay." I coughed, vision doubling. "I'm okay, just . . . just lead the way and I'll follow."

"We need to get to Franky." Pippa grabbed my hand. "I won't let go, okay? We might have to split up again, but you won't be on your own. I promise."

I wondered if I looked scared, or if her platitudes were projection. I grabbed Stasia's hand, connecting us in a chain. "Okay. I trust you guys."

There was a loud crash behind us, a clap of thunder as rain started slow at first, then thick like honey. Pippa squeezed my hand once, twice, then shot forward like a rocket. We moved in tandem. The ground twisted beneath us, dusty gravel slick like a slip-n-slide. Blood. I was running on blood. Blood falling from the sky, blood staining our clothes. I felt woozy, rust-red puddles soaking my Doc Martens. I closed my eyes and let Pippa pull us along, feeling nauseous with the effort of escaping.

Another crash. A sickly howl. It couldn't have been more than ten feet away, and I could smell the monster's warm, wet scent. Decaying girls. Rotten remains. I squeezed Pippa and Stasia's hand, pumping my legs harder.

Franky poked her head out from her hiding spot, blood draining from her face. "BEHIND YOU!" she screamed, jumping in place. "FASTER, FASTER, FASTER."

Sensing the futility of her space, she took off running, gesturing frantically for us to follow. Stasia and Pippa pressed tight to my side, screaming to follow Franky, keep following Franky. I obeyed, because it was the only thing on this green earth I had ever been any good at.

I crashed at her side like a meteor. I wanted to decompress, fall into her, but there wasn't time. Franky yelled something to Pippa as we ran, gesturing frantically back and forth, but I was too woozy to make sense of it. My head was buzzing, covered in cotton balls.

"SPLIT!" Franky yelled, grabbing my hand.

We took a sharp right, while Stasia and Pippa disappeared into a maze of abandoned machinery. There wasn't time to look back, no time to say goodbye. The monster let out a slow, sickly howl, heartbroken to have been outsmarted. Its aggression felt palpable, real as air. I was in pain, and I was scared, and all I could do was run.

Rain falling, fog thick like clothes. I chased Franky Delores through blood-soaked streets, desperate to make it out dead.

The pain wouldn't stop, and there was no time for Franky to explain it to me in a way that made sense. There had been a car crash. I banged my head up pretty badly. We made it out alive, but just barely. Franky's truck was okay, passable, but we couldn't risk it anymore. The monster was hot on our trail, and it had decided to become cruel.

"You were only out for a few seconds," Franky explained, ducking behind a pile of junk to catch her breath. "But the monster was getting aggressive. I led it away so the girls could wake you up enough to move."

I was touched by the act of faith, the kindness she performed.

"You saved my life," I said, kneeling on the ground beside her.

Franky tried waving me off, wouldn't meet my eye. Her kindness was strange, no bark, all bite. I couldn't focus long enough to figure it out.

"It's blood rain," she said, pointing at the sky. "I've read about it before. There's a natural explanation, but I forget it."

"Dust . . ." I said thoughtfully, sniffing the air. Smoke and decay.

"Right," Franky said, side-eyeing me. "Are you sure you're okay to keep moving?"

I didn't trust myself to speak, so nodded emphatically.

"Okay. We're meeting them by the junk pile," Franky pointed at the towering stack of trash and car parts waving in the wind. She pressed something into my hand, warm and dripping. "The flamethrower," she explained, forcing me to take it. "It's your weapon of choice. I didn't want to leave it in the car, figured you'd need it."

I was touched once again, then amused by the acts of love which made any dent in my sea of silence. Maybe none of my previous relationships had worked out because none of them had bothered saving my favorite weapon, then throwing themselves into danger to save me.

"Where's the monster?" I asked, watching Franky examine her knife, long as a forearm.

Franky pointed silently, watching my reaction. I followed her finger, lost for words when I saw it.

The monster, sitting on top of the junkyard. Patriarch of a kingdom of grief, inheriting what was once a utopia, and now a wasteland.

It might be the concussion, but it looked an awful lot like Franky's dad from this angle.

We traced spirals across the ghost town, trying to keep out of view, hidden from sight. The monster was a threat, obviously it was a threat, but it almost appeared to be waiting for us. Patiently sitting, watching for movement.

We caught sight of Pippa and Stasia at the midway point, reconvening by a pile of scrap metal.

"Any trouble?" Franky asked.

Stasia showed a gnash on her shoulder, a scrape of nails. "Nothing too bad."

"How's your head, Lawrence?" Pippa asked.

I blinked slowly to process the question, which seemed to be answer enough.

"I think it's handing our asses to us," I pointed out, vision still doubled.

"It seems so." Stasia smiled, skin gray. "This thing is too quick. Too ruthless. What are we gonna do?"

"We'll have to slow it down," Pippa said. "Hinder it enough so we can do some real damage with the fire."

"One among millions," Pippa joked.

"We'll need to move onto plan B." Franky started stretching, practicing moves with her knife. "Engage in hand-to-hand combat."

Delirious with pain and confusion, I burst out laughing, doubling over, nearly setting my flamethrower off as I thrashed about.

"How hard did she hit her head?" Franky asked, throwing her hands in the air when she noticed Pippa and Stasia imitating her moves. "Come on, fools," Franky ordered, grim mouth pushing down a smile.

"Yes, sir!" We mock saluted, army marching in a single file line behind her.

Dancing through a sea of debris, we made our way across a wasteland. Franky led us into battle, four friends walking into death row. I wondered if she felt like her father.

The edge of the clearing stood in front of us. Our last moments of shelter, of solace.

"Should we say a prayer?" Stasia asked. I wasn't sure if she was joking.

Franky looked at each of us, face grim. She had no gods, no guidance. Just her three disciples, following every step of the way.

"I hope we survive," she said, air of finality like a shadow.

"I hope we're okay," Pippa added, eyes trained on Franky.

Her concern was founded. Even if we survived it, without the monster hunt filling her edges, I worried she would deflate like a balloon. Empty and traumatized. At least with the monster hunt, she was alive.

There are worse fates than death. Franky knew that. She lived it every day, in the world her father left behind.

We marched straight into the barrel of a gun, standing in an empty patch of dirt, blood soaked and staring up at the sky.

The monster gazed down at us, curious, horrific. It underwent some drastic alterations in the time we had known it. Though its terror-struck, urine-yellow eyes stayed the same, each day it seemed to collect more limbs. Awkward and gangly in its attempt to play human.

This close, we could see the monster's artifacts. Its pile of trash, full of sentiment. I recognized the blue bikini I wore at age twelve, the one that made me lock myself in the bathroom because my aunt's boyfriend wouldn't stop staring. The push-up bra I wore in a photo I sent my seventh-grade boyfriend. My old cellphone, where all his friends harassed me for months after he shared the pictures.

Stasia and Pippa seemed equally transfixed by objects of their past.

"It has my lab notebook," Stasia murmured, reaching out before thinking better of it. "And the bible my youth pastor gave me. The creepy one, remember? He . . ." She swallowed. "And my lab coat from first year. The semester that prof tried to . . ." She trailed off, overwhelmed.

Pippa's were abstract, complicated, but I could make sense of small moments. The memories that made sorrow fall down her face like rain. A missing poster of Penelope, red handprint stamped across her face. A police notebook. A social workers report, an unmarked gravestone.

"Penelope. . ." she mumbled. "My history, my roots, everything I tried to ignore . . ."

The monster jumped to the ground in front of us, no less than ten feet away. I felt Stasia jump back, felt Pippa grab my arm in fear. I felt cold, but not unpleasant. Months of mania had led to this moment, it was almost poetic that I stood in front of Franky. The creature looked weary, greasy skin slick with blood. I thought of my millions of loose ends, dangling over my head like a noose. My old life, my attempt at a new one. Graduate school, rent, groceries in the fridge. My mother.

There was a strange comfort in our eternal estrangement. There would be no resolution, I know that now. I escaped the box she kept me in, and life just moves forward. I am warped and strange because of it, but I keep moving forward. What else can I do? Free from my mother's design, I've found a new alter to die at. I will be what Franky needs; I will protect her from the present, the past, from every ugly monster holding her pain.

I stepped forward, peaceful in my decision.

The monster pounced on Pippa before I could even offer myself as the sacrifice.

Pippa screamed as the monster jumped for her, slashing violently at the open sore from earlier. Its nails just missed, thrown to the side by Franky's blade.

We all stared in shock, watching Franky throw herself in front of Pippa, knife manically swiping through the air. Franky wasn't focused, anymore. Long gone were the moments of certainty, the mission to catch the monster. All that was left was blind fury, her paralyzing anger. The realest thing she had ever known.

"Franky," Pippa wheezed, trying to stop her. "Franky, be careful, you—"

"It hurt you!" she sobbed, surprising even the monster with the feral, unfocused slashes of her knife. "I—I've been so obsessed with the past, so preoccupied with proving the monster's existence, that I can't see what's happening right in front of me. I have blood on my hand, because I *wanted* blood on my hands. All I've ever cared about was validation, even if that came at the cost of other women."

The monster's head cocked to the side, considering this monologue. It watched Franky, watched the slow recollection of emotions and thoughts. The fear and hatred in its eyes mellowed to something else, something more confusing, and it backed away, leaving us alone for a moment.

We rushed towards Franky, each touching a gentle hand against her back, desperate to recharge her. The monster saw this opportunity and ran off, returning to its perch above the trash pile. It appeared to be digging for something, looking through its things.

"It's coming back." Pippa pointed, squinting through the dusk. "I think it has something."

We stood together, waiting. Franky took a tentative step forward, Frankenstein and her monster, the inherent horror of creation.

We stood, staring into its eyes. Two yellow moons staring back at us, reflecting pure terror across the field. This close, I could see it was holding something in its mouth, transferring it from cheek to cheek. Its eyes were bulging, horrified, skin sickly pale and covered in guts. It took two, three, five tentative steps towards us, expression peaceful. Mouth yawning open, it let what it hoarded fall at our feet.

Deirdre Valentine's left hand.

VEAL: PART II

It was a present for Franky.

"Jesus," she swore. Her voice was gravelly, scared. I glanced over at her. She looked shy in the starlight.

"Franky," I uttered, no plan. No reason. I just needed her attention on me, rather than the mess of bones and tendons that was once flesh.

"It's an offering," Franky said, stepping closer. "It's . . . it's being kind to me."

"Franky . . ."

"It's being kind," her voice broke, kneeling on the ground, looking up at the towering monster. Her bewildered softness was maternal.

Stasia, Pippa, and I stood on edge, scared. The monster's foaming mouth was inches from Franky's head. She reached up, fingers hovering above its greasy skin.

"It brought me that hand to replace my own," she murmured. "It . . ."

Franky looked down at the decomposing hand, curled in on itself, exposed muscles gooey like marshmallow. Her face crumpled, precarious hope crashing down around her.

"No," she uttered, shaking her head. "*No*. You will not win me over. You will not tempt me to freedom with a ladder made of women's bones."

The monster tilted its head to the side, as if confused. As Franky's mother denied Franky, Franky denied the monster. As Franky's father was the bearer of senseless violence, the monster knew nothing but its own world of pain.

"I understand what you are now," Franky said, hovering hand finally touching its skin. "I had to see you to make sense of the world. You're the only way I could understand what my father did to me."

The monster bowed its head, crumpling itself over until it was eye level with Franky.

"All you've ever been is a vessel," she whispered. "An empty vessel. That's all you are. I cut off the parts of the world that I hated, and I made you." Her voice caught. "I just made you. You're a hideous thing, made of anger and hate. And I won't let you live in this world, anymore, I won't. Because I'm not my father. I'm not the things he did to me, or the things he did to those girls." She lifted a knife above her head, gleaming under the cold moon. "I had to sever myself to survive, but I don't want you anymore. I don't—" She drove the knife deep into the monster's brain. "I don't want to keep you alive because I'm scared." Another stab. "Because I'm a coward who can't face the man my father really is." Another stab. "No, I know now." Stab. "I'm wide awake,"—stab—"and I"—stab—"will"—stab—"outlive"—stab—"you."

Buckling at her feet, the monster stared up at her, eyes soft with sadness. Horrifying as it was, it almost looked . . . understanding. Its yellow eyes bulged with fear, black blood bubbling.

"You're every ugly thing that man ever did to me." She touched its head. "And you're the grief I hold every single day, trying to live with that."

The monster's eyes slowly dimmed, yellow light flicking away. A lighthouse beam rolling out to sea. We watched blood ooze from its brain, watched Franky, scared and shaking, stare down at her handiwork.

Pippa pulled her away, knife slipping from blood-slick fingers. Taking this as my cue, I lit up the flamethrower, hot fire catching grimy white skin.

The monster was highly flammable. It was a creature of violence, after all.

Pippa and Stasia volunteered for clean-up duty, letting me flutter around Franky like a fruit fly. Since her assassination, she had gone dark. Occasionally muttered to herself about Frankenstein, occasionally twitched with tears, eyeliner smudging away.

"Talk to me," I implored. "You're too far away." I brought my hand up to knock gently on her heart. "Let me in."

She sniffed, head buried in her arms. She swayed side to side, motion sick in the mid-evening rust.

"Please," I begged. "What are you thinking?"

"I don't—" Franky stopped. Composed herself. Stared at a city of frayed wire, a thousand homes in the dark. "I don't know who I am, without this—this *myth* I've created to survive."

I watched Pippa and Stasia, watched them throw the monsters artifacts into the yawning fire. The rain had stopped, grass turning crisp, welcoming the fire with open arms. Franky sat on the ground beside me, knees crumpled into her chest, shaking hands pressed against herself.

"All I've been, all I've *ever* been, is a fairy tale I told myself so I could stomach being what my father left behind."

"You're so much more than that, Franky." I placed my hand on her head, cupped blood-sticky hair. "You're not veal. You're not trapped in this box, stuck from growth. I'm letting you out, I'm freeing you from this." I waved my hand around us. "This sack of shit hand you've been dealt. You're more than him, Franky. You've grown up in his shadow and you did whatever you could to survive that, but I need you to know that you're safe. You'll never have to make another monster."

Franky let out a shaky breath. I could tell she believed me.

"What are we going to do?" she asked. "What are we going to do about all of this?"

I eyed the fire, eating the monster and inching closer to the power lines.

"We leave."

I caught Pippa and Stasia from the corner of my eye, gave them a complicated look. They understood my request, my plan. They kept feeding the fire. Allowed it to crawl closer to the power lines, the city. I mourned a world before I found them; the four of us, tight as skin.

"Leave?" She laughed, bewilderment bubbling away as she caught wind of my plan. "Lawrence, no. No, you—you're insane."

I want to say I love you, but to say it is finite. To keep it locked inside my chest, it becomes a sentient, growing being. I harbor my own monster, growing it every day under Franky's careful smile.

She looked up at me, grim smile and spidery veins.

"I'll follow you anywhere," I lamented, mourning every second I spent searching for her. What wasted time.

"You're my prosthetic limb," Franky answered.

Franky, my sweet Franky. My museum. My mantra. My mosaic of monsters. I'll be your creature forever. I'll invent whatever folktale you need to keep you safe.

The fire caught hold of loose wires, power transformers melting like butter. We watched with sizzling sweet euphoria, alive like popping candy. Franky stood slowly, slipping her hand into mine, blood staining my skin. The fire, oh the fire. It was alive and dancing, reaching the trees now, ecstatic in its freedom. A new monster to unleash upon the town, one that only erases, never destroys. Franky wanted a clean start, a severance, and I gave it to her. We gave it to her. Stasia and Pippa walked back, standing on either side of us, joining hands.

"Fuck," Pippa announced succinctly.

We all nodded.

"Think anybody noticed?" she joked.

Stasia broke into laughter, as free and uninhibited as I've ever seen her. Franky followed soon after, dragging me along with her. We howled with laughter, leaning against each other, nearly falling to the ground. My injured side sliced with pain, slivers of lightning hot aches running up my ribcage.

Franky noticed my pain like a phantom itch, turning to face me, nose inches from my cheek. I instinctively leaned into her, feeling her teeth latch onto my skin. Playful. Tongue soothing broken skin, more fitting than a romantic first kiss under the stars.

I turned my face to meet hers, wanting both, wanting everything. Her violence, the tenderness that undercut her frail anger. My mosaic, my mystery. My gritty, gory, obscene lover. My Franky.

Her lips caught mine, blood-red and pulsing with pain. The collision was painful, I always knew it would be. Teeth knocking, lips swollen, nose smushed against mine. She was a feral thing, I'd never catch her. I'll spend my whole life trying to.

"I'll follow you anywhere," I promised.

"I'll never leave you behind," she answered. "I'll love you forever."

I once thought of Franky's devotion as an unpredictable, tenuous thing. I was always uncertain. But at her confession, her shaky promise, I realized that I was a fool to ever doubt her devotion. She loved me like an acolyte. More than her ghosts, her ghouls, her goblins. I was her monster all along.

"Thank you for believing," she whispered. "You're the first person who's ever believed me."

"I know all too well the violence men make. And what we have to do to live with that."

"Not anymore." Franky shook her head resolutely, eyes alive with the heat of the fire. "I'll spend the rest of my life walking away from it, but I won't hold it anymore. It's not my monster to keep. It's his."

We stared in silence.

"I need to move forward, but it's like time stays still, here. It sticks me in place. I keep seeing everyone move on without me, but I can't get past this. It's in everything I do."

"It's a glue trap of your own design, Franks," Pippa said. "You can leave. We can always leave."

Franky put her hand to the ground. It was September at last, temperature dropping as the sun set. Cool summer air, salt-tinged from the ocean wind. Franky looked out of place, suddenly; a creature too big for her former habitat. Our place in this ecosystem had expired. There was nothing left to do but go.

"So let's go," Franky said, simple as that.

The fire caught the grass, fickle and strange from the blood rain. Climbing weeds caught next, crawling to a peppering of trees which led to town. There was a pop from a nearby generator, louder than life as it fizzled. A loud explosion quickly followed, transmission towers lighting up the sky like fireworks. We stood, amazed at our catastrophe. Fire trucks and ambulances blazed away, police circling in.

"So let's go," Franky repeated, staring up at the colorless sky with an enchanted smile. It was hard to see her through the smoke, but I knew she looked beautiful.

Hand in hand in arm in hand, we walked to Franky's pickup truck, crowding into the small space. Heat blasting, synth rock playing, we peeled away, fire hot on our trail as we sped towards the bridge to civilization. The dawn was rising, fire insatiable. I glanced in the rearview mirror, mourning the lives I've left behind. Laying them to rest on the pavement behind us.

"Why did you agree to burn it?" I ask quietly, body pressed against her side. "The monster. I thought you wanted it for evidence?"

"No one would believe me." Franky smiled sadly. "They'll never believe me. I could show them video footage of every moment since I've been born: my father's violence, my mother's resentment, the years I've spent seeing a monster, and they still wouldn't believe me, and . . ." She stopped to think, aware that she had us at the edges of our seats, watching her. "And there's a lot of freedom in that. There's a lot of grief, but there's freedom, too. I'll never have to convince them, because it wouldn't work anyways. So it doesn't matter anymore. I know what has happened to me, to my loved ones. I've spent so long being bitter, angry, afraid. I've spent so long begging people to listen to me and see me, but it was all for nothing. They were never going to understand. And that's okay." It was at her shaky laugh that I believed her, my hands wrapped around her arm. "It's okay. So they don't see my monster, they've never seen my monster. I'm glad they haven't. I don't want people to suffer to justify my pain anymore. I don't need to be justified. I'd rather be loved."

"Well you're in luck, because we'll love you forever," I answered for all of us, because it was true. I could see the years ahead of us: the shared homes, the bright gardens. Dinner parties, homemade bread, nights spent laughing and crying and fighting and loving. Nights spent in Franky's arms, nights spent in mine. A small city, train rides, candle wax on thrifted coffee tables. A life honey warm by the luxury of our love.

"So I'm loved." Franky smiled, knee-driving towards nowhere with her hand high on my thigh. "What the hell do I do with that?"

42 YEARS LATER

The only technology left alive was the bowling alley security system. Years later, after we all skipped town, archaeologists examined the sinkhole city we left behind. Finding only one glitched video would play on loop.

Before the fireworks, the explosives, the rapture:

Four blood-soaked girls, fighting air.

Acknowledgments

This has been my dream as long as I can remember, which means every single person I've ever spoken to deserves thanks. To any friend, family, or loved one who has accepted random excerpts of a random story, thank you.

To my mother, who, upon learning I had a book deal, said, "I better not be the antagonist!"

To my father, who, upon learning I had a book deal, said, "I better be the antagonist!"

To my seventh grade English teacher, who gave me a book of Ginsberg poems and let me send countless manuscripts his way: thank you.

To my ninth grade English teacher, who said she'd be at my first book signing one day: this is your special invite!

To my beautiful editor Pia, who saw more for this book than I myself did and pushed me to take it to such a wonderful place. I am so proud of what we've created together and cherished every moment working with you. We're just like Sarah Paulson and Renée Zellweger in *Down With Love*.

To Jen and Kenna, who picked up on mistakes or inconsistencies I missed, even after a year of editing with a fine-toothed comb, thank you! My relationship with commas continues to improve.

To the entire ECW team, who were all so warm, supportive, and above all else, had so much faith in me and my book. Thank you for making me feel so at home, every email was such a treat.

And lastly, to Amber Heard. This book would not exist without the horrific spectacle of that trial, a time in which I watched those I believed to be smart, empathetic people, gleefully attack a victim of abuse. Heard's bravery was instrumental in building the world of *Veal* and shaped the emotional headspace I was in while writing this story. A story about a woman who is committed to her experience and will not atone for male violence.

So, this book is for Franky. For Amber Heard. For the women who cannot name this creature that haunts them, hurts them, but they feel its hatred every second they're alive.

For all women who are made to answer for the violence of men.

I will always be in your corner.

Give them hell.

MACKENZIE NOLAN was born and raised in rural Newfoundland. Working professionally as a social worker for several years, she found herself better suited to writing interpersonal dynamics, rather than solving them. *Veal* is her debut novel.

Entertainment. Writing. Culture.

ECW is a proudly independent, Canadian-owned book publisher. We know great writing can improve people's lives, and we're passionate about sharing original, exciting, and insightful writing across genres.

Thanks for reading along!

We want our books not just to sustain our imaginations, but to help construct a healthier, more just world, and so we've become a certified B Corporation, meaning we meet a high standard of social and environmental responsibility — and we're going to keep aiming higher. We believe books can drive change, but the way we make them can too.

Being a B Corp means that the act of publishing this book should be a force for good — for the planet, for our communities, and for the people that worked to make this book. For example, everyone who worked on this book was paid at least a living wage. You can learn more at the Ontario Living Wage Network.

This book is also available as a Global Certified Accessible™ (GCA) ebook. ECW Press's ebooks are screen reader friendly and are built to meet the needs of those who are unable to read standard print due to blindness, low vision, dyslexia, or a physical disability.

This book is printed on FSC®-certified paper. It contains recycled materials, and other controlled sources, is processed chlorine free, and is manufactured using biogas energy.

ECW's office is situated on land that was the traditional territory of many nations, including the Wendat, the Anishnaabeg, Haudenosaunee, Chippewa, Métis, and current treaty holders the Mississaugas of the Credit. In the 1880s, the land was developed as part of a growing community around St. Matthew's Anglican and other churches. Starting in the 1950s, our neighbourhood was transformed by immigrants fleeing the Vietnam War and Chinese Canadians dispossessed by the building of Nathan Phillips Square and the subsequent rise in real estate value in other Chinatowns. We are grateful to those who cared for the land before us and are proud to be working amidst this mix of cultures.

ecwpress.com